I0687528

MOONSTRUCK: SECRETS

SILVER JAMES

MOONSTRUCK: SECRETS is a work of fiction. Names, characters, places, and incidents are either the product of the author's imagination or are used fictitiously, and any resemblance to actual persons living or dead is entirely coincidental.

MOONSTRUCK: SECRETS

COPYRIGHT © 2015 by Silver James

All rights reserved. Without limiting the rights under the copyright reserved above, no part of this publication may be reproduced, stored in or introduced into a retrieval system, or transmitted, in any form, or by any means (electronic, mechanical, photocopying, recording or otherwise) without written permission of the author except in the case of brief quotations embodied in critical articles or reviews.

Contact: silverjames@swbell.net

Cover design © by *Clary Carey*, clarycarey@gmail.com

Cover Images: www.depositphotos.com
Woman embracing man ©sakkmesterke
Moon ©tankerblazer7

Edited by Gregory Alan

Print ISBN: 978-0989921756
ISBN-10: 0989921751

Published in the United States of America

9 8 7 6 5 4 3 2 1

DEDICATION

Sometimes, real life and fiction collide. Shortly after this book released in digital format, I was sharing lines from it for #1lineWed on Twitter. One of the lines had to do with the crash of a helicopter on a training mission and all souls on board were presumed killed. That afternoon, I heard the news about a military helicopter crash. Seven Marines and four soldiers were presumed dead when their UH-60 Black Hawk helicopter crashed during a routine night training exercise at Eglin Air Force Base in Florida. The Marines were part of a special operations group based at Camp Lejeune in Jacksonville, North Carolina, and the soldiers were from a Hammond, Louisiana-based National Guard unit. None survived.

This book is dedicated to the memories of those American heroes, and to all the brave men and women in uniform who have served and who continue to serve their country with honor and valor.

.

ACKNOWLEDGMENTS

Writing is the one profession where the voices in my head mean I'm only a little crazy when I talk back to them. I love my voices, even when they argue with me. Which they do. Way more than they should. Silly buggers.

As always, many thanks to my readers, the Wild Warriors on my street team, friends, and family. Y'all are the reason I keep writing the stories in my head.

I truly appreciate the help I receive from my critique partner Heidi, beta reader Siobhan, and cover artist Clary for the many "do-overs" until we get things right. I couldn't write anything remotely military without the help and guidance of my wonderful husband, Greg aka Lawyer Guy. Last but definitely not least, I want to recognize the fans of this series. Each email, Facebook comment, tweet, and visit to my website convinces me that the Wolves deserved to see the light of day.

One last caveat: Any and all mistakes are my own.

CHAPTER 1

"I NEED COFFEE."

"Damn. Listening to you, I'd think you were actually human."

"I *am* human, furball."

Sergeant Major Ian McIntire grinned. It was no secret to him that Major Hannah Jackson was human. The problem was the secrets she was hiding from him—not that he didn't have secrets of his own. The day his boss told him the unit was taking an officer into the field, he had not been a happy camper, and was even less so when he found out that officer belonged to the female persuasion. He did have to give credit where credit was due, though. Major Jackson was feisty and she had a mean mouth on her when she was caffeine deprived—which she had been for the past 48 hours. The instant crap that came with the MREs didn't count. Meals Ready to Eat, the military's version of Hell's Kitchen. He chuckled, a deep, rumbling sound that echoed in his massive chest. He watched as she stalked away into the trees. At least she was bush trained.

He chuckled again. The first time she disappeared into the woods, he'd followed surreptitiously—partly to make sure she didn't get lost and partly to see how she handled being in "the wild." She cleared out an area behind a bush, used her combat knife to dig a small hole, squatted to do her business, and then filled in the hole, packing the dirt with her combat boot, and scuffing leaves and grass back over the spot. Yeah, definitely bush trained. Of course, it had taken him an hour to tame the raging hard on he got from that one quick glimpse of her sweet ass. He stayed away from her after that.

While she used the woods as an impromptu latrine, Mac stowed his gear. Hers was already packed and ready. Yeah. Feisty, bush trained, and efficient. What more could a man want in a partner on a covert combat mission? Too bad she was female. He had nothing against female soldiers. He just found his attraction to this particular one a little too distracting and any lapse of concentration on this mission could get them killed.

The major slipped out of the woods, stooped to snag her pack, and shrugged it on. He looked away as she bent over. Not even the rough cloth and baggy cut of the woodland-patterned uniform could camouflage her curves when she put her ass in the air. A scene flashed into his mind—of her bent over a fallen log, her pants around her ankles, and him driving his dick deep into her sex.

"Fuck," he cursed under his breath. Yeah, that's the idea, stupid, his dick reminded him with absolutely no subtlety. As he hefted his own pack onto his back, he furtively repositioned his erection to a more comfortable location in his pants.

The two of them walked throughout the day only stopping every couple of hours to grab short rests and quick meals. They didn't talk. Mac led the way, which gave Hannah lots of opportunity to watch the big man. And, lots of opportunity to fantasize about what lay hidden beneath those baggy BDUs. Battle Dress Uniform. There was nothing dressy about the whipcord cotton material, the loose shape, or the multitude of pockets.

Long after nightfall and long after Hannah could no longer see clearly, the big soldier called a halt for the night. She let her pack slide to the ground and sank down beside it. Her legs felt numb to the hips. She was too tired to eat but knew she had to get calories into her body or she'd never be able to keep up. She blindly pulled out an MRE pack and tore into it. Leaning her back against the rough bark of a tree, she shoveled food into her mouth. She fell asleep between bites.

Mac took a little pity on the major when he realized she'd passed out where she sat. He'd pushed her hard. He knew men who wouldn't have managed the pace he'd set the last three days. He felt guilty—for about three seconds. He'd decided to punish her—for being a woman, partly, but mainly for being an IG. The fucking Inspector General's office did nothing but create havoc. He usually dropped in farther from the target than his team so he could thoroughly scout the terrain. This mission, he'd chosen to drop in even farther than usual. He'd set a demanding pace on a path climbing over mountains and wading through dense forests. She'd stayed with him every step of the way. Never a complaint. Well, except for whining about coffee. Then he remembered why she was there.

Fuckin' Congressionals. Someone with a stick up their butt had decided his unit needed investigating. He took her unfinished meal and wolfed it down. Then he took the evidence of their meal and buried it a little distance away to throw anyone off their trail. He returned, pulled her sleeping bag off her pack, and tossed it over her. He stretched out on his own bag. Once he was comfortable, he replayed the conversation he had back when Captain Harjo first told him Major Jackson was coming to Ft. Lyle Smith expressly to investigate the unit. He remembered the incident word for word.

🐾🐾🐾🐾

"WHAT THE HELL does the Inspector General want with us?" he'd asked.

Harjo had shrugged. "Who knows, Mac."

"So who is this Major Jackson the IG is sending?"

"The fourth assistant to the assistant director of the deputy director for the Office of Special Accounts and Operations, under the auspices of the Inspector General's office on special assignment to the office of the Chairman of the Joint Chiefs."

"Huh?" He tried to follow the chain of command and failed.

The captain looked up from the fax he'd just read from. "Rumor has it this guy came over from the BRAC Commission."

"Fucking Pentagon puke."

"Yeah," Harjo spat. The Base Realignment and Closure Commission left a bad taste in everybody's mouth. "Look, Mac, it's like this. Someone somewhere has decided all the money being channeled into special ops isn't being spent the way it was appropriated."

"Is this a Congressional investigation?"

"Maybe. None of my sources will confirm or deny. Doesn't matter who's called for the investigation. This IG guy is coming regardless. We open some of the files, let him get a look at our training, send him on his merry way, and keep our fingers crossed they don't mess with us."

"Training, Cap?" He stared at his commander then flicked his gaze toward the calendar hanging on the wall. "He'll be here during the full moon. What'll we do with him then? The boys aren't exactly quiet when they hunt."

"We're still covered by a need-to-know clearance, Mac. If he doesn't have top-level security clearance, then he doesn't need to know. Even if he does have the clearance, he doesn't need to know. No matter what Congress thinks." Captain Harjo looked fierce. "Hell, even if it's somebody within the Pentagon, the Wolves are safe. They need us whether they like it or not. They need what we are, what we do that no one else can... Or will," he added after a short pause.

"I hope you're right, Cap'n."

🐾🐾🐾🐾

MAC SNORTED AT the memory. Hannah stirred, seeking a more comfortable position. He briefly considered pulling her into his arms and letting her nestle her head on his shoulder. She might be more comfortable but he sure as hell wouldn't. He cupped his hard on, willing it to subside.

The major had been a complete surprise. The unit expected a staff puke—some skinny accountant type with big ears and thick glasses. Instead, they got Major Hannah Jackson—big, blue eyes, sandy blond hair, legs that went from here to there, and really fine curves.

She had combed through the mission files in Captain Harjo's office. All of them. She watched them train. And on the night of the full moon, she watched them change. The Wolves were just that. Werewolves, though the technical term was *Lupi versi pellis*. Loosely translated, it meant something like they turn the skin of wolves. Rumors about this unit had persisted since the Revolutionary War. Major Jackson knew what they were before she arrived.

Hannah also knew about the Atlantis Project, the Navy SEAL unit comprised solely of "mermen"— the result of some experiments at Area 51. The Air Force had wanted genetically engineered pilots who could breathe and function at high altitudes. The scientists ended up creating subjects with gills, men unaffected by the pressure by a deep sea dive and able to swim long distances underwater without aid of SCUBA gear.

The Navy jumped on board and spirited the initial batch of specimens off to an uncharted island in the Caribbean. Then she arrived deep in the Virginia countryside with the 69th Special Army Sci Ops Group, nicknamed the Wolves. The pack members were all volunteers, and they were all natural born werewolves— as if there was any other kind.

Team leader Sergeant Major Ian McIntyre was a mature alpha werewolf. He did not have to change. Standing there on the ridge next to the major, he'd fought the urge to shift and hunt with his pack mates under the huge harvest moon as it hung fat and golden on the horizon. Instead, he stayed in human form to watch the major's reaction. She had surprised him, not even blinking when the bodies of his men contorted and changed, growing fur and fangs. Hands morphed into paws, jaws elongated to accommodate sharp canine teeth. Bodies folded and shifted so arms became legs. Where moments before men stood on two legs, wolves now ran on four, howling at the moon as they sniffed the wind for some hint of prey.

He recognized the cool calculation in her eyes as she turned to him. "Feel free to hunt with your men, Sergeant Major. I've seen enough."

She dismissed him curtly, turned on her heel, and marched away. Some perverse sense of pride kept him in human form until she was out of sight. He finally stripped and changed, howling his frustration to echo in the night. If the look on her face was any indication, they were fucked.

The morning after she'd watched the team change, the major informed Captain Harjo she would accompany the unit on their next assignment and she handed over a copy of their orders—a rescue mission to retrieve one of their own. Her proclamation stuck in everyone's gullet. The mission could turn "wet" resulting in a political assassination at the conclusion of it, and they'd be parachuting into hostile territory—hostile in terms of enemies and environment both. Mac got the brilliant idea to keep the major out of it because of the parachute drop, which lasted just long enough for her to prove she was qualified.

She walked into the Quonset hut serving as the jumpmaster's office and paused at the door to look around. Long tables used to repack the parachutes stretched the length of the room. First Sergeant Carter took one look at her and when he quit laughing, he tossed a parachute to her.

"Who packed this chute?" the major asked.

"Me," Carter snarled around the stubby stogie shoved in the corner of his mouth. No one questioned him, especially about his parachutes. And First Sergeant Carter was known far and wide for eating officers alive— at least figuratively speaking. He was human, not pack, but his tongue could make even the bravest pack member wince.

The major immediately took the parachute bag over to a table, popped the cord, and stretched the canopy and lines across the table.

"Not that I don't trust you," she snarled back, "but I put my life in only one pair of hands. Mine."

She repacked her chute with cool precision. Impressed, Carter refused to let it show, still pissed about her questioning his safety record. Before climbing into the plane, she asked one thing.

"Where do you want me to land?"

"On my ass," Carter growled under his breath before replying louder, "The ground, Major, if you can find it."

Mac laughed out loud at the memory of that day and then smothered the sound, not wanting to wake up the major. She'd found the ground all right and Carter's ass. She'd popped her chute early and stayed airborne long after everyone, including Mac, touched down on the Landing Zone. Carter was bitching about women getting lost and being late when boots nailed him in the back. Major Jackson had silently swooped in behind them all and popped Carter. As he hit the ground face down, her boots touched down squarely on his ass.

"Is that close enough to the LZ for you, First Sergeant Carter?" she asked, sarcasm thick in her voice. She let the canopy collapse behind her.

"Yeah," Carter mumbled into the thick grass covering the field.

"I'm sorry, First Sergeant. I can't hear you."

"Yes, ma'am," Carter snapped louder. "You are on target, Major Jackson."

She delicately stepped off his butt as she shucked off the parachute pack. "Am I qualified to jump with the team, First Sergeant?"

"Yes, Major."

"Very good, First Sergeant."

She dropped the pack next to his head and strode away. Carter endured the team's ribbing though Mac managed to maintain a degree of composure even after the major was out of earshot. Since Carter was human, the major could sneak up on him fairly easily. But she'd taken the whole team by surprise. Of course, she'd come in downwind but even he'd been caught off guard. Unhappy with his team and himself, he kept a speculative eye on her.

Packing away thoughts and memories of the past, Mac returned to the present and the task at hand. He pulled a small GPS unit from a pocket and checked the map on it. They were well ahead of schedule—less than half a day from the rendezvous point. He glanced over at the sleeping woman. He was impressed even if he didn't want to be. He shifted on his sleeping bag in search of a more comfortable position. His dick was impressed, too. After three days in the field, her scent was everywhere. Instead of turning him off, the sweaty musk she exuded made him want to strip her down, spread her legs, and bury his aching erection so deep that his balls slapped against her ass.

"Jeez." The word hissed from his mouth. He had to quit thinking about her but Wolves liked to fuck. A lot. When a Wolf hit puberty and the change started, it didn't matter if the pup was alpha, beta, or omega. They had only one thing on their minds—sex. Girls and getting into their pants was the driving focus of every pubescent wolf. That urge didn't diminish with maturity.

Mac decided they would be in position for the rendezvous in plenty of time so he took the opportunity to scout the terrain around them before moving on. Intel had been a bit sketchy and he didn't like leaving things to chance. She'd hung tough enough he felt comfortable leaving her secured here at their camp while penetrating the deep forest. He'd shift into his wolf form to scout. If she handled the weapons she carried the same way she jumped out of an airplane, he had no doubt she could protect his flank.

He closed his eyes and concentrated on running through various scenarios. He was still alive because he always had a Plan B if things went to hell. He fell into a light combat sleep, his body resting even as his senses stayed alert for any possible danger. He'd go hunting right before dawn. The wolf inside would know if anything hunted *them*. The man inside dreamed of the woman sleeping less than four feet away.

CHAPTER 2

SHE WAS BEAUTIFUL in the moonlight, her skin glowing like pale silk. He licked her arm, which felt warm and smooth against the roughness of his tongue. Her blond hair caught moonbeams in its golden net and her eyes mirrored the color of the midnight sky. His long tongue swirled over one dusky pink areola. The nipple in its center puckered into a tight little bud. He bathed it and her breast before trailing his tongue down the slight rise of her belly to find the tight nest of blond curls at the top of her thighs. He sniffed, drawing the rich, female scent of her into his lungs. The smell of her made him want to howl. Instead, he dipped his head between her thighs to run his tongue down the length of the folds surrounding her sex. He lapped at her, flicking the tip of his tongue against her clit before sinking it into her tight entrance. God, she tasted like heaven. Sweet. Rich like the finest cream but with a sprinkling of salt that was irresistible.

He growled when her hands fisted in the fur of his ruff and he nipped at her clit. She gasped, writhing against him. His tongue once again found the swollen lips of her sex and sank into its creamy heat. She writhed harder, pressing against him, panting and crying for her release.

He urged her to roll over to her hands and knees. He mounted her, his hard, thick cock sliding into her wet core like it belonged there. His powerful haunches pumped, his cock gliding in and out of her slick channel. She was moaning now and pushing back against him to drive him deeper into her hot center. She shattered beneath him, her muscles contracting and milking him. He howled his release as his seed spurted into her. His. He claimed her for his own with a ringing howl.

🐾🐾🐾🐾

HANNAH WOKE UP, a choked-off cry dying in her throat. She fought the sleeping bag and sat up, bracing against the tree at her back. Ohmygod, her mind whimpered. She'd just been fucked by a wolf. She gagged at the thought even as she shook her head back and forth, trying to clear the fog. No. No. It didn't happen. Thank god, it was just a dream. She gulped in air to settle the nausea and then glanced over at Sergeant Major McIntire. His big chest rose and fell rhythmically as he slept. He wore a faint smile. She'd never seen him smile. Intrigued, she scrutinized him from head to toe. His dark auburn hair was close cropped, military style. Thick eyebrows punctuated his wide forehead with dark slashes. His eyes, she remembered, were a golden brown, like burnt honey, with amber lights glinting in their depths. His cheeks and jaw could have been sculpted by a Greek artisan and his mouth could give her grandmother a wet dream. She blinked. Those golden eyes were open, watching her.

"Problem, Major?"

"N-no," she stammered. She cleared her throat, embarrassed she'd been caught staring and mortified when her voice cracked as she lied about it.

He cocked an eyebrow and shifted to a more comfortable position. She glanced down the length of him, and there was a whole lot of length to glance down. He was at least 6'4", if not taller, and packed with hard muscle. Her gaze stopped about halfway and she cleared her throat again. That thick ridge stretching his pants couldn't be him. Could it? She licked suddenly dry lips.

The sergeant major choked off a groan as the tip of her tongue traced her lips. He looked like he wanted to eat her even as he raised one knee to block her view. Then he looked like he wanted to laugh when he caught her still staring at his now-hidden groin. She wouldn't mind eating him for dessert.

"Hey there, Little Red Riding Hood," he growled.

She blinked, cleared her throat a third time and then finally glared at him. "Get your mind out of the gutter, soldier." Embarrassed, she rasped out the order.

He grinned wider. "I don't think where my mind is currently residing is the problem, Major. Where's yours?"

Hannah turned away, guilty heat flooding her neck and face. The idea of making it with an animal was repulsive but where had that dream come from? She'd been turned on and excited by the wolf and that was just so sick she couldn't even examine her motives. She jumped when McIntire's hot breath tickled the back of her neck.

"I'll huff and I'll puff..."

A shiver skipped merrily down her spine like spidery fingers tripping over each vertebra. That was enough! She whirled around and faced the big man down, startled he was so close. They were all but nose-to-nose.

"Do I need to remind you that I'm the superior officer here?"

"You may outrank me, babe, but you ain't my superior."

The hard, feral look in the sergeant major's eyes frightened her but she didn't back down. "Down, boy," she barked, then added with a sneer, "What is it about you fuckin' alpha males?"

He growled and forced his hands to remain at his sides. Mac wanted nothing more than to wrap her in his arms and show her just what an alpha Wolf could do. Hot and bothered by his dream, he squashed the urge. He'd never fantasized about fucking a woman in his wolf form. Never. In his whole, long life. Ever. In fact, the idea sickened him. It was perverted but, if he was completely honest with himself, there was a part deep down inside the wolf that wanted to take this woman, and only this woman, precisely that way.

"We have a long day tomorrow, Major. I suggest you get some sleep."

"Yeah, that goes for you, too, Sergeant Major."

She retreated to her bedroll and pointedly turned her back to him. He grinned. God, but she fascinated him. Once this mission was over, he and the major were going to finish what that dream had started—only he'd do his loving as a man. He dropped back to sleep almost immediately.

🐾🐾🐾🐾

MAC PLANNED TO let Hannah sleep past dawn this morning. There was no need to push today, regardless of what he'd told her last night. He wanted to reconnoiter and had set his internal clock to "butt crack of dawn" so he'd have time to reconnoiter. He packed his gear and stowed it in the branches of a tree, then his uniform joined the stash. Naked, he reached for the inner wolf. In moments, a big black timber wolf sniffed at the major's hand.

She mumbled something and rolled over. The wolf sniffed her, liking what he smelled. The inner man reminded the wolf they had a job. With one last snuffle, the animal turned and trotted into the forest.

Without opening her eyes, Hannah rolled over onto her back and stretched. A couple of vertebrae popped as did an ankle and some toes. When she got home, she would deplete the whole tank of hot water while soaking in her whirlpool tub and then she planned to crawl into her space-age foam bed and sleep for a week.

God, but she hated the outdoors. Growing up on her parent's ranch in Wyoming, all she'd ever wanted to do was move to the city, live in an apartment, and curse rush hour traffic. Graduating from college at nineteen, she couldn't find a job. She stayed in school but even with an MBA, the job market was tight so she started her Ph.D. When an Army recruiter mentioned the military, she read the propaganda, did some research, and signed up. That was ten years and several tours ago. Along the way, she'd finished her doctoral degree at the Army's expense, been promoted regularly and often, and was now assigned to one of the most metropolitan areas in the nation— Washington, D.C.

But where did she spend all of her fucking time? Deep sea diving with the damn SEALS. Prowling through the bowels of deep bunkers with the spooks at Area 51. And now? Now she was in the gawddamn mountains with a fucking Wolf who gave her nightmares. She hadn't had a decent cup of coffee in over three days. Good and pissed now, she threw back her sleeping bag and sat up—only to discover she was alone.

"Sergeant Major?" Nothing. No reply. The grass was still flattened where his sleeping bag had been, but there was no sign of his gear or his big, muscular body. She pursed her lips and blew a tentative whistle, hoping he'd come if he were in wolf form. "Jeez." She rolled her eyes. "He's not a dog. He's a freaking werewolf. He's not going to come if I whistle."

The more she thought about it, the more she decided the sorry sonavabitch had gone off and left her. She was so going to have his butt up on charges when she got back to civilization. And that was definitely *when* not *if*.

A branch snapped in the underbrush and she froze. Civilization, hell. She was in the middle of enemy territory, and there was more than one body moving through the woods. She gathered her gear and looked for a place to stash it out of sight. That's when she saw McIntire's kit balanced in the tree branches above her head. Taking a page from his book, she shoved her stuff into another tree and climbed up after it. She settled on a branch midway up the tree, fairly certain she was hidden unless whoever was skulking around looked up. A patrol of six men filtered along the faint trail she and Mac had followed the day before.

She'd been to SERE school. Survival. Evasion. Resistance. Escape. As a female, she'd been subjected to lewd suggestions meant to sexually terrorize her, along with the more mundane threats of starvation, torture, and execution. Taught to cooperate just enough to stay alive until another option presented itself, she watched the rough-looking men tramp into the clearing. Her options had just expired.

Two men stopped right beneath her. Holding her breath, she focused on her madly beating heart, positive the men could hear its pounding rhythm. She prayed they wouldn't look up. She prayed that McIntire wouldn't pick this moment to come back. Then she prayed he would. *God, if they catch me,* she thought then squelched the scenario in her imagination. *Just please let Mac come rescue me.*

The clock in her head ticked slowly. In all probability, only five or ten minutes passed, but it felt like an hour. The men finally moved off. To her dismay, all six of the intruders stopped about twenty feet away and it sure looked like they were going to make camp. They gestured and talked, but not loud enough she could hear them, no matter how much she strained her ears to do so.

She couldn't believe her luck. They were going to cook freaking brunch. She wrapped her arms and legs tighter around the trunk of the tree and hoped her woodland camouflage would keep her hidden from sight.

🐾🐾🐾🐾

MAC ENJOYED RUNNING wild. Never permanently settled by humans, these woods provided many scents and textures to intrigue his wolf. He spent more time than he should have simply indulging the beast. Finally back in scout mode and nose to ground, he quartered the area. He was working back toward their camp when his nose picked up the first hint of trouble.

Men. Seven of them. Carrying guns. He trailed their scent. The wolf growled. The men were headed in the general direction of his camp. Hannah! He couldn't breathe. The wolf had one plan—go hunting. The man considered other options including getting Hannah out and away without being seen. The wolf was ready to kill the men if they'd harmed his mate.

Whoa. Mate? Where the hell had that thought come from? He wasn't moonstruck. No chance to think about it at the moment. For the first time in what seemed forever, he was well and truly afraid. He'd been stupid to go off and leave her alone.

Maybe, just maybe, the trail would break off and lead away from Hannah but he heard the men's voices up ahead. Damn. They were camped out in basically the same spot where he'd left the major. Mac tested the wind. He could smell Hannah but he couldn't see or hear her. Had she managed to hide? He worked his way closer, crawling belly down or flitting through the underbrush as he circled the clearing. He still couldn't find her so maybe she had managed to get under cover.

With infinite care, Hannah snapped open the flap on her holster. There was no way she could get to her M16 but she had her knife and the 9mm. The pistol had a full clip—fifteen bullets. The odds were six to one. She'd never fired at anything shooting back at her, but she wouldn't go down without a fight.

A charcoal shadow caught her eye. Was that a wolf? Had Mac come back? God she hoped so. Intent on watching the shadow to see if it was real or her imagination, she almost fell out of the tree when a quiet voice called up to her in heavily accented English.

"You will come down now."

She froze.

"Come see what I have caught," the man called to his companions.

Shit. He spoke Bosnian to the others. This was so not good.

"Come down now." His voice was hard, demanding. "Before I shoot you." Back to English again.

Well, that certainly provided incentive. She stared down at him. He had a rifle in his hands and while not pointed directly at her, it was aimed in her general direction. Nothing on her uniform indicated she was American. Her dog tags had been left at the air base in Germany. She carried no form of ID. Reaching blindly with her left foot for a toehold, she considered her options. She spoke German fluently. And French. Her Russian was okay, as was her Turkish. She understood Bosnian but her accent sucked. She'd never be able to pull off the native routine.

Before she could get all the way to the ground, one of the men snagged her around the waist and yanked her. Instinctively, she grabbed a limb, wrapping her fingers around it. Her action only stalled the inevitable. The rough bark scraped her palms raw but she landed on her feet. Even though her hair was cut short, once the guy had his hands on her, he had no doubts about her sex. He giggled as he felt her up. Giggled! Seriously? She bit her lip to keep from saying or doing something stupid.

The man who'd discovered her walked around her, a nasty smile on his face. "Looks like we have caught a little American spy," he told the others.

"How do you know she is American?" one of the men asked.

"The uniform," he explained. "The cloth is too good to be from any place else."

Shit. If she survived this, she would go a few rounds with the black ops planners. To be outed by the fucking quality of the material sucked.

Hannah was still stewing over that betrayal when one

of the men grabbed her crotch. Her hand shot out and flattened his nose—a purely reflexive action. The man with the rifle backhanded her across the cheek, and stars burst behind her eyes. The blow drove her to her knees.

"American whore," he sneered at her. "I will fuck you 'til you die." His hands went to his belt, and he unbuckled it.

Hannah caught him with a leg sweep that sent him crashing to the ground. At the same time, she pulled the Beretta and popped off three rounds. The first two shots went wide, but the third found its mark. One man went down with a moan, a crimson stain blooming on his chest. She rolled away from a kick aimed at her head but didn't get completely clear. The blow caught her in the ribs. Struggling to catch her breath, she continued to roll and aim the Beretta. Before she could acquire another target, a black blur streaked in front of her. The wolf attacked one of the men.

Pandemonium erupted. The man screamed but the sound abruptly ceased when the huge wolf ripped out his throat. She watched in morbid fascination for a moment then saw a man aim his rifle at the animal. She took him out with a tight pattern grouped around his heart. The wolf attacked two other men in quick succession, and neither moved. The only man left standing disappeared into the woods. The big animal followed, intent on chasing him down.

Hannah pushed up onto her knees and stared straight into the barrel of an old WWII German Luger. She'd miscounted—seven men in all, not six. In a vague, detached way, she was sorry her life didn't flash before her eyes. Maybe that meant she wasn't going to die. Or maybe it meant there was nothing in her life worth remembering at the point of death. That thought really depressed her. Jeez but her life sucked.

Her breath caught in her chest as the man's finger tightened on the trigger. Eyes wide, she watched his finger flex and pull, the whole thing blurring into slow motion. The pistol clicked on empty. Before she could recover, the wolf attacked. She crabbed backwards scurrying to get out of the way. After putting some distance between her body and the snarling wolf, she curled up in a tight little ball, her hands over her head and ears, trying to block out the man's screams as the wolf savaged him.

After a long moment of silence, the wolf nosed the back of her hand. Hannah lifted her head, not realizing she was crying until the wolf licked her face. The big animal growled at her and she giggled, on the verge of hysteria. Oh god. She swore the wolf was telling her that everything would be okay. She sat up, pulling her knees to her chest and wrapping her arms around them. She tucked her head against them, and started rocking. She'd just killed a man. Maybe two. She'd seen a wolf that was really a man tear men to shreds. Nothing would never be okay again.

Mac changed into human form as quickly as he could. He grabbed his uniform out of the tree but only pulled on the pants. Hannah curled around her knees, rocking, and sobbing. He knelt beside her and drew her into his arms.

"Shh, baby. Don't cry. It's okay."

"No, it's not okay." She shoved feebly at his chest. "You went away and left me, you bastard. And those men found me. They were going to…they wanted to…and then I shot one. Oh, god. I killed that second man." She balled up a fist and hit his bare chest. "You left me."

"I know, babe. I'm sorry. I'm so sorry. It's okay now. You're safe. I'll keep you safe."

When Hannah shoved against his chest again, he loosened his grip and let her lean away. He looked at her, glad to see her anger battled the fear.

"Fuck you, McIntire. I'll keep myself safe," she snarled.

He grinned. Yeah, she was impressive all right. "Yes, ma'am," he agreed. "I do believe you will."

"Where the hell were you?"

"Scouting, ma'am. We're about four hours from our rendezvous point and I wanted to get the lay of the land. Our intel didn't indicate any patrols in this region."

"Obviously our intel sucked."

"Yes, ma'am." Mac had decided agreeing with her was the safest course of action, especially when she was right. She'd stopped crying and he was eternally grateful. One more sob would have torn him in two.

"You're out of uniform."

"Yes, ma'am, I am."

Hannah pulled away from him and stood. She took about three steps then turned back to glare at him. "And that's Major Babe to you, Sergeant Major."

"Yes, ma'am, you most definitely are," he agreed with her retreating back.

He dressed quickly then hauled the rest of their gear out of the trees. He checked each of the men to make sure they were dead. They were. He nodded with satisfaction over Hannah's kills. One shot to the lung on the first and a tight three-shot grouping in the heart of the other. She was a hellava shooter. He'd been right. She could protect his flank.

All seven men were accounted for and he left them where they lay. There wasn't time to bury them. The major was squatting next to her backpack when Mac approached. He reached down, grabbed her hand, and hauled her to her feet without saying a word. He snagged her pack and draped it over his shoulder.

"I am quite capable of carrying my own gear," she snapped.

"Yes, ma'am, you are."

She stared at him, waiting for him to give the pack back to her. Instead, he walked off, ignoring her. Not knowing what else to do, Hannah stuck out her tongue at his retreating back then grudgingly followed.

CHAPTER 3

EVERY STEP MAC took was sheer torment. His balls ached. His gut ached. His damn dick felt like it was going to break it was so hard. He snarled. He knew why he had blue balls. The need to fuck the major reverberated with each stride. He did not want to examine the reason behind the tight knot of fear in his gut. He would see Hannah dead before he saw her stretched out beneath another man. And that scared the absolute crap out of him.

Hannah panted as she trotted to keep up with Mac's long-legged stride. Her ribs ached and it hurt to take a deep breath. She really wanted to sink to the ground, curl up in a ball, and have a good, old-fashioned crying jag. She figured she was entitled. She felt scared shitless, hurt, angry...and wanted the big soldier to stop, wrap her in his arms again, and tell her everything would be okay. She might even believe him.

Engrossed in her misery, she didn't pay attention to the footing. She tripped on a tree root and went down hard, face first with no time to get her hands in front of her to block the fall. Her breath exploded from her lungs as her bruised ribs met the ground.

Mac appeared beside her in an instant, cursing a blue streak. He'd been so angry at himself he hadn't once thought about what his brutal pace was doing to her. One look at her told him everything he needed to know. Her left cheek was bruised, she couldn't catch her breath, and her eyes looked glazed. Despite her fumbling attempts to slap at his hands, he jerked up her BDU blouse and tee shirt. A dark purple bruise the size of his hand covered her ribcage on the right side. She'd be lucky if the ribs were only bruised. Mac ran a gentle finger over the area. They weren't broken. He made the mistake of glancing at her face again. One lone tear trailed down her right cheek. Without thinking, he bent to kiss it away.

"I'm sorry." The catch in his voice matched the hitch in his chest.

"Don't." Her voice sounded utterly defeated.

"Sean Donaldson's a combat medic. He'll look at you as soon as we rendezvous." He bit back a snarl. Medic or not, the thought of another man's hands touching her made angry black dots swarm like a cloud of gnats before his eyes.

Hannah seemed hell bent on arguing. "I'm fine."

"Yeah, and I wear a tutu when I howl at the moon. There's a stream not far from here. We'll rest when we get there."

"I don't need a break."

Jeez but she was stubborn and the fact she didn't snark at his tutu comment was unusual. "Well, I do. C'mon."

Mac slung her pack over his shoulder again and gently hauled her to her feet. He kept an arm around her waist as he started off, setting a slower pace this time. He tried to ignore the sensations running through his body. God but she felt right beneath his arm. She fit. And that worried him.

No woman had ever fit before. Not even the ones who lasted longer than a one-night stand—though there'd been less than a handful of them. There was one good thing about being a Wolf. No STDs. A Wolf never got a female pregnant except on purpose—his nose was sensitive enough to know when she was in season, though there was no guarantee the woman would conceive and carry to term.

Mac considered the idea. His kind had called themselves *lupi versi pellis* since the early Roman Empire. Lupi. Wolves. Some scientists called the condition lycanthropy. Popular culture called them werewolves. Not much study had been done on actual Wolves. They tended to shy away from scientists, doctors, and researchers. He figured the condition had something to do with some weird gene linked to the Y chromosome. Wolves were always male. Even if a wolf mated with a female, there was only a one in a thousand chance a male child would carry the trait. A doctor familiar with the condition had tried to explain it once. Even if a Wolf mated with the same female a thousand times, the chances were still slim to none that she'd carry a Wolf pup. That's why the world wasn't overrun with his kind. Which was probably a good thing. Wolves gravitated to extreme careers—the military, law enforcement, crime. He knew one old, lone Wolf who'd been a mob hitman. They were tough, hard to kill, reckless, and had a tendency to fuck anyone with the right plumbing. They also liked to chase and kill things. Yeah, it was a good thing there weren't more than a several thousand of them in the world.

The going was rough and Hannah's injuries made it tougher. It took them almost an hour to cover the distance to the stream. He eased Hannah onto a boulder. As she collapsed, he stripped off the packs he carried, pulled out her sleeping bag, and unrolled it on a large flat rock. The edge of the rock hung over the edge of the rushing water.

"Lay down."

Her eyes narrowed and her chin jutted stubbornly.

"Lay down before I have to hurt you." He wouldn't intentionally hurt her but it might happen accidentally if he had to force her compliance.

Grumbling, she stretched out on the bedroll. She so didn't want to appear helpless in front of this man. It shouldn't matter, but it did. He was twice her size—had been in combat numerous times. She was a pencil pusher for chrissakes. She wasn't supposed to be tough and strong and sure of herself. But the perverse stubborn streak that demanded she be the very best at whatever she did wouldn't behave. She wanted this man to think well of her.

Mac took two bandannas from his pocket and soaked them in the cold water of the stream. Wringing them out, he pressed one gently against her cheek and the other under her tee shirt on her sore ribs. She hated to admit the cool cloths helped. Acknowledging how good those big hands felt on her skin just added insult to injury. She shivered.

"Cold?"

"No."

Mac reached out and cupped the back of her head. He angled her face up to the light filtering in through the tree branches above them, his hold a little rough. He gazed into her eyes. "Equal and reactive."

"Oh." Jeez. Her voice sounded small to her own ears. What must he be thinking? For that matter, what had she been thinking? That he would kiss her? Yeah, right.

"I was worried you had a concussion."

Did Wolves kill and eat their wounded? She shuddered. Lord but that was a nasty thought.

Like the water sliding past her perch, the emotions on Mac's face drained away leaving a stoic mask in their wake. The man scared the crap out of her but he also fascinated her. He was all beefy brawn and snarly sex appeal but when he'd pressed the cloth to her cheek, there'd been such tenderness in his touch her heart ached. God. She was an officer. He was a non-com. The Army had strict rules about fraternization. Hell, he was a freaking Wolf, a whole different species. But at that moment, all she wanted to do was sink into his embrace.

Mac let his hands fall to his sides. He'd felt her shudder all the way to his soul and he shut down. She couldn't stand his touch. Fuck. Why did he care anyway? She was an officer. She was *the* officer who was probably going to pull the plug on his unit. She was feisty. She was funny. She was brave. She was the only woman he'd ever wanted to impregnate. By the gods but she'd make a magnificent mother for his pups.

The hardest thing he'd ever done was walk away from her at that moment. They'd rest, and then follow the stream to the rendezvous point. Sean could check her. If Hannah was seriously injured, he'd abort the mission and call for an emergency extraction. His decision wouldn't sit well with the honchos at the Pentagon but he'd be damned if he'd risk her safety.

She sneaked looks in his direction, disappointed he'd moved as far away from her as he could get in the narrow area next the stream. She bit down on her bottom lip to keep it from trembling. She didn't want to be an Army officer at that moment. She just wanted to be a woman—a scared woman in need of some alpha male chest thumping. He probably hated her. How dare a female horn in on his precious mission! Then she had the audacity to go and get hurt and slow him down even more. She rolled over, giving him her back. Well, fuck him. Fuck him all the way to hell and back. She sighed. Yeah, that, too.

Mac watched her shoulders shake, knew she was crying. He forced himself to stay put. She was a complication he couldn't afford. If he touched her, took her into his arms, he'd be lost. He'd never be able to walk away from her. His head told him that was precisely what he needed to do but his gut clenched at the idea, and his heart absolutely rebelled against it. Eventually she stilled, asleep finally. He pulled out his radio and gave quiet instructions to the rest of his team.

The sun peaked at noon and slid toward the west. When he woke her, Hannah sat up gingerly and combed fingers through her short crop of tousled hair. He handed her a wet bandanna to wipe her face, then helped her to her feet. She didn't argue this time when he hefted both packs. Even if he'd been only human, he was more than capable of carrying them without breaking a sweat. Thank God he hadn't listened to her before. Had she carried the sixty-pound pack, she'd probably be down for the count.

He led the way along the trail leading upstream, setting a slow and careful pace without being obvious. He suspected Hannah's ego was a tad bruised and he wouldn't make matters worse by throwing her inadequacies in her face. The problem was he didn't think she had any. She was perfect. Well, except for the fact she wanted to shut down the unit and scatter the men who'd become his brothers. Plus, she couldn't stand his touch. Probably thought fucking a Wolf was a little too bestial for her tastes. He unconsciously hunched his shoulders. If they ever made love, it would be the first time his partner actually knew what he was. Hell, he wasn't sure he was ready for that. He reached back to help her over a rough patch. Her hand felt so fragile in his big paw.

Hannah appreciated the fact that the sergeant major traveled slowly. The nap had helped but she still felt beat up. Oh, wait. She had been beaten. She watched his rigid shoulders and his stiff neck. He must hate her. She knew they all thought she was there to shut them down. That wasn't true but she couldn't let them know the real reason. She was the biggest advocate the SciOps units had, regardless of branch. A civilian conglomerate was lobbying the Pentagon for control of certain SciOps teams. They'd all but taken over at Area 51. If the Atlantis Project didn't demand complete Navy specialization, they, too, would have been absorbed. Even so, they were still in a precarious position. Now the civilians were after the Wolves. She was determined not to let that happen. Dealing with the conglomerate left a bad taste in her mouth. She didn't trust them as far as she could throw them. And the cliché fit big time.

She finally put her mind on cruise control. Her head was splitting, her side hurt, and she ached deep inside where a man hadn't ever touched her before. God, she was such a loser. A fucking thirty-year-old virgin. It wasn't that she'd been determined to hang on to her virginity. It was just that no man had come along who seemed deserving—or one who could see past her brains. Then she'd laid eyes on Sergeant Major Ian McIntire. She sighed.

Mac heard the sharp exhale of her breath and glanced over his shoulder to check on her. The major wore her game face and was hanging in there, matching his shortened steps stride for stride. She was abso-fucking magnificent. Hannah was better than a Timex watch— she took a lickin' and kept on tickin'. He glanced at the sun then checked his watch to be sure. They weren't far now.

CHAPTER 4

HANNAH WAS ON her last legs when she stumbled into the small clearing a few steps behind Mac. Two men emerged from a crevice in the side of the rock fall covering the mountainside. One went to Mac to report. The other came directly to her. Without giving her a chance to protest, he picked her up and carried her inside the cave. She swore something growled but she was probably hallucinating.

The interior was dry but cool and she shivered despite the heat the guy holding her was radiating. He set her down on a sleeping bag knelt beside her. "Not sure you remember me, Major. I'm Sergeant Donaldson, the team's medic. I'm going to give you a quick examination now, okay?"

Hannah nodded, feeling light-headed. She watched his mouth and figured out what his words meant. She remained sitting up as he checked her ribs. Another man appeared and handed her a steaming cup of liquid. Hannah sniffed it suspiciously.

"Coffee?" Dared she hope? Or was her brain still making things up?

The man grinned at her. "Yeah."

"Real coffee?" She actually whimpered.

Now he laughed at her. "Yeah, Major. The real McCoy."

Hannah took a big gulp and yelped when it burned her mouth. She didn't care. Heaven was hiding in this cup. Heaven and salvation and despite the bruises and aches, she might actually survive this ordeal.

While the medic worked on her, the other team members met with Mac outside.

"They had her before you got there and she still took out two?" Michael Lightfoot, Mac's second in command, looked impressed.

"She ever kill before?" Jacob Nakai asked the question on everyone's mind.

Jacob was Navajo and the oldest member of the team. He'd been a Code Talker in World War II and was over a hundred even though he looked about sixty. Wolf genes were great in that regard. Most Wolves were either Indian or had blood ties to the ancient Celts—Irish, Scottish, Welsh. A rare few came from Eastern Europe. Mac considered Jacob's question for a moment. He blinked out of his reverie as Sean emerged from the cave. Mac was still bristling over Sean not only touching Hannah but picking her up. Holding her close to his body. He ground his teeth and forced himself to focus on what Sean was saying.

"No. Those were her first." The medic answered Nakai's question and then turned to him. "She's gonna have nightmares, boss."

"Maybe. She's tougher than she looks."

"That may be true but she's done now. I slipped her a tranq in the coffee. She'll sleep for a couple of hours at least, if not all night. I moved her to her bedroll."

Lightfoot glanced around the circle of men before returning his serious gaze back to his commander. "Where'd that patrol come from, Mac?"

He shook his head. "Damned if I know but I'd sure like to find out."

"You think they're on to us?" This question came from Danny Keegan, the newest member of the unit. The kid was so young he was still wet behind the ears.

Mac shrugged. He didn't know what to tell his team. This mission was more than top secret. No one was supposed to know their ultimate destination. Just the five of them and Joshua Harjo, their captain. Plus the man in the five-sided building who handed out their assignments. His gut heaved. Was there a leak somewhere? He glanced over his shoulder as if he could see through solid rock. He didn't like the place his thoughts went.

Suspicious, he strode back into the cave. He dug through Hannah's pack, then stripped her out of her BDUs and searched them. Nothing. No tracking device. No radio. No nothing. The knot in his stomach relaxed a little. It wasn't her. Relieved, he glanced at her. He'd stripped her down to her utilitarian cotton sports bra and panties but she could have been in Victoria's Secret for all he cared. The tranq had worked well. Hannah hadn't stirred at all as he mauled her. He stared down at her, blinking repeatedly when his vision shifted. He had a curious sense of seeing everything clearer. His heart skipped a beat or ten. His cock jumped to attention. This was it. She was the one. He could only stare at her, feeling like he'd been cold-cocked.

Jacob padded up behind him, watched him for a moment before bending to flip the edge of the sleeping bag over the sleeping woman. "You got it bad, boy," Jacob commiserated.

He growled and the older man laughed. "Yeah. Been there, done that. My mate got the tee shirt."

"Mate?" Mac was surprised. He knew Nakai was married but mated? Not many wolves maintained a permanent relationship. Finding a true mate seemed practically impossible but deep down, every Wolf craved the connection.

"Been together sixty-two years next September."

His jaw dropped. He couldn't imagine fucking the same woman for sixty-two years. Then he looked down at Hannah. Yeah, he could.

"Wolves mate for life, boy, and the Blood Moon is coming. Don't be doing anything stupid." He walked away, his footfalls silent, leaving Mac to stand and stare.

🐾🐾🐾🐾

HANNAH AWOKE JUST after dawn to the smell of lukewarm MREs and hot coffee. As soon as she rolled over, Sean brought her a cup of coffee. He checked her over while she sipped the magic elixir. She still felt a little shaky, and her joints ached like she had the flu. He handed her some ibuprofen.

"There's a spot in the back of the cave, around that corner," he said, indicating the direction with a tilt of his head. "You'll have some privacy."

He helped her stand and held a steadying hand under her elbow while she found her balance. Sean did his very best not to grin at the rumbling growl echoing through the cavern. He didn't have to look at his team leader to know who was responsible for the noise.

Hannah shuffled to the dark recess and did her business. Coming back around the corner, something tickled her throat and she scratched while tugging the neckline of her shirt. That's when she realized her drab olive tee shirt was on backwards. She'd immediately gotten drowsy after drinking the coffee last night and deduced the medic had sedated her. This morning, she was glad since she'd slept so soundly. Now? Somebody had taken liberties and she was pissed as hell. Any lethargy or residual fogginess was erased by a surge of adrenaline. She marched out into the cave and straight up to Mac. Standing toe to toe, she ordered him outside.

Mac's eyes flashed a deep, feral red and his men exchanged wary glances. Nobody challenged an alpha like that. Nakai just smiled.

"You got something to say to me, you can say it right here," Mac snarled.

"Fine," Hannah snarled back. "Who the fuck do you think you are, Sergeant Major?"

"The leader of this mission," he growled.

"And I'm a superior officer," she snapped.

"Not on my turf, baby."

"That's Major Baby to you, you fucking alpha bastard. Who the hell took my clothes off last night?"

He staggered back two steps. Red and black swirls clouded his vision. Someone took off her clothes? Someone touched her? Someone besides him? He forced a deep breath into his lungs. Oh, yeah. He'd stripped her down to bra and panties looking for a tracking device. Talk about a d'uh moment.

"Me." He didn't bother to feel sheepish. None of the men moved a muscle. If one had, he probably would have gone for the jugular even as part of his brain registered their amusement.

Hannah's mouth opened and closed a couple of times. She looked stunned, gasping for words like a fish trying to breathe out of water. "You?" She choked on the word.

"Yeah. The mission's been compromised. I was making sure you weren't a plant."

"A plant?" That set her off again. "You thought I was a gawddamed spy? Go to hell, Sergeant Major. I'm the best fucking friend you and this unit have. If it weren't for me, you'd already be in civilian hands and god knows what they'd be doing to you and your men."

Oops. Hannah clamped her mouth shut. Talk about letting the cat out of the bag.

Mac grabbed her around the both biceps, lifted her off the ground, and shook her. Her headache roared back to life as stars sparkled in front of her eyes.

"Put her down, Wolf." Jacob's quiet voice left no room for argument.

Mac glared at him then looked at Hannah. She was pale and shaking, her face twisted in pain.

"Oh, god, baby," he murmured. He didn't put her down. Instead he cradled her to his chest and whispered words into her hair as he kissed her cheek and temple.

The men all took a deep breath. Michael exchanged a long look with Sean. Jacob had been right when he talked to them last night. Whether Mac or the major liked it or not, their Alpha was in the process of claiming his mate and this was a hellava time for the complication of a moonstruck Wolf.

Hannah's teeth chattered and her skin felt hot to his touch. Mac wanted to kick himself. He carried her over to his bedroll and set her down. Squatting beside her, he glanced at his men. They all moved to the far side of the cave. Not that it mattered. Wolf hearing was acute and even if he spoke in whispers, they would hear what was said.

"I'm sorry, Hannah." She stared at him, big blue eyes glazed with shock and pain, making him even more uncomfortable than he already was. He rubbed the back of his neck, trying to work out some of the tension. He damn sure didn't need the complications of a mating ritual in the middle of a compromised mission. A moonstruck Wolf in mating heat didn't think very clearly. Had something to do with all the blood rushing from the brain to the balls. He reached out to touch her cheek, thankful she didn't flinch. Still, her eyes held fear that tore at his heart.

"There's more going on here than you realize." He gentled his voice despite the urgency he felt. "I need to know why you are here. Why here and why now?" He took a deep breath. He'd have to tell her sooner than later. Wolves mated for life. He'd never let her go. Couldn't let her go. "Once we get out of this mess, we have other things to discuss as well."

"Oh, like, I show you mine and you show me yours?"

Mac's cock flared to life. Oh, yeah, he definitely wanted to see hers and show her what his could do. He bit his tongue. "Hannah, that patrol wasn't supposed to be there. This mission is white ops."

She stared at him. Black ops meant all secret information was blacked out of reports and personnel files. Some redacted reports went up the chain and the only words left on the page were prepositions, pronouns and a few participles. White ops meant that the mission was a blank page. It wouldn't appear in any file. Anywhere. White ops was beyond secret. White ops really was a situation of "if I tell you, I'll have to kill you."

"Shit."

"You're tellin' me, darlin'."

"That's Major Darlin' to you."

He grinned at her, relaxing a little as her sass reasserted itself. "There is no way you could have contacted anyone before we took off." She cocked an eyebrow at him. "Okay, you might be good enough..." She arched both brows. "What? You're good but you ain't that good, babe."

"I think I liked darlin' better," she muttered.

Mac fought a grin at her spunk. "Why are you really here?"

Fully aware the rest of the team was hanging on every word, she told him. When a private think tank approached the Secretary of Defense, the Chairman of the Joint Chiefs dispatched her to Area 51 to investigate. She'd suspected there was some really scary stuff going on in Nevada but she couldn't get to the deepest sub-levels to find out exactly what was involved. So much of the R&D at 51 was medical or highly technical, civilian contractors outnumbered military personnel. With the exception of the seven SEALS who were even now being secreted away by the Navy, everything at 51 was now in civilian control.

Hannah hadn't trusted the civilian director in charge and had serious misgivings about his military liaison. She'd spoken briefly with some of the military personnel and they'd all confirmed her gut reactions. Two weeks after her return to Washington, all military personnel had been transferred from 51 and none had cycled in to replace them.

A suspicious soul by nature, Hannah started digging. Under her pain-staking scrutiny, the think tank morphed into a paper tiger. Every one of the addresses and phone numbers were blinds. None of the board members could be reached. And when she contacted the facility directly, all of the scientists were unavailable for interviews.

She'd gone to check on the Atlantis program and her suspicions were confirmed there as well. A Navy Commander took her warnings to heart. At his urging, the Navy declared Atlantis a failure and the members of the program were supposedly transferred to other units and then dismissed from the service—only they weren't. They were serving in a top secret unit that was more smoke and mirrors than fact. Not even Hannah knew where the SEALs had gone and that's the way she wanted to keep it.

The Chairman of the Joint Chiefs then dispatched her to check on the Wolves. The think tank engaged in some serious lobbying about taking the Wolves private. Phrases like mercenary force and plausible deniability floated around the Pentagon and Department of Defense.

The problem with the Wolves was that they had been around for over two hundred years. Francis Marion, the famed Swamp Fox, had used them during the Revolutionary War. They were part of Andrew Jackson's forces at the Battle of New Orleans the winter of 1814. During the Civil War, Wolves rode with J.E.B. Stuart, the Gray Ghost, while others marched with Sherman to the sea. The military finally got smart and created the 69th Special Operations team. The 69th filled a unique niche the Army was loath to lose. Since the Chairman was an Army general, he'd personally taken an interest in the situation.

Hannah's job was to gather enough information to prove the unit needed to stay not only an active Army component, but a highly secret one immune to any outside influence. Though their missions were already top secret, the 69th was a coveted assignment even by those soldiers without the qualifications to be a Whiskey Team member. There were armorers, quartermasters, and cooks. There were mechanics, drivers, and clerks. Though there were only three active Whiskey teams, over fifty soldiers provided support to each team. After two hundred years, it would be a little tough to declare the Wolves a failure and disband the unit.

The men gathered closer as Hannah confessed everything to Mac, but they made sure to keep him between them and the woman. A moonstruck alpha male was not an animal to trifle with. Sean watched Hannah for signs of shock or other problems. He sincerely hoped that Mac fucked her soon. If the big man didn't, none of them would be able to get within a hundred feet of her without a fight.

"So," she finished up. "What do we do now?"

"We'll stay here today and part of tonight," Mac declared. "If the mission is compromised, they'll expect us today as per the original timetable. Before midnight at the latest. If we don't show up, maybe they'll think their patrol got us. They didn't have any communications devices. The black hats won't know that patrol is carrion chow. We'll hit just before dawn tomorrow."

Hannah stared at him. She glanced around at the other men but they all seemed comfortable with his decision. "If the mission is compromised, it won't matter when you go in, they'll be expecting you."

Deciding discretion was the better part of valor, the men all skedaddled out of the cave, leaving Hannah alone to face Mac.

"You trying to pull rank again," he growled.

"No. I just don't want you or any of the others going home in a body bag."

He stared at her long and hard but she refused to look away. "We don't go home in body bags, Major. If one of us dies in the line of duty, the body is burned." His voice sounded so brittle she swore the temperature in the cave dropped ten degrees. "There can be no evidence of our true existence. Ever."

CHAPTER 5

THAT WAS HANNAH'S bottom line—no body bags. Especially not one with Sergeant Major Ian McIntire's name tag on it. She was hard pressed to explain why but her heart would surely break if something happened to him. Her body felt all hot and achy, and it had nothing to do with the low-grade fever plaguing her. Somehow, this man had crawled inside her skin. She snorted at the cliché, but he really was an itch she couldn't scratch. One part of her wanted to jump on him, rip his clothes off, and ride him until they were both exhausted. Another part wanted only to be held in his arms, finding comfort and shelter there. The last part wanted to throw things at him, and beat him until he understood what he did to her.

Mac watched her, but knew that if he didn't get up and leave right then he was going to take her. She was in heat, at the very prime of her cycle. She was his mate. He knew it in his gut...his brain...even his heart. That part scared him. He'd do anything to protect her, even die. And the way this mission was shaping up, dying was a real possibility.

Neither of them seemed to moved but Hannah was suddenly in his arms. His mouth devoured hers. His tongue forced its way between her lips and teeth, sweeping inside like the Mongol horde. His arms pinned her to his hard chest, and she squirmed against him. She fisted her hands in his tee shirt and pressed closer. Twisting around, she got her legs free and wrapped them around his waist. She rubbed her center against his hard cock and it swelled even more.

He smelled her arousal. Only supreme self-control kept him from ripping off her uniform. It was the only one she had. If he shredded it as he wanted to—needed to—she'd be naked afterward and then he'd have to kill his pack mates for looking at her.

Growling, he stripped her with a patience born of necessity. He pulled the olive green tee shirt over her head, severing the touch between his lips and hers for a heartbeat. A quick breath later, her bra followed the shirt. His fingers danced across the buttons on her pants and he broke contact only long enough to pull them and her panties off. His need was so fierce he could barely get his own boots and pants off. Part of him said unbutton his fly and take her. She was naked and open to him. That's all he needed. That was the wolf. The man cautioned him to slow down, to ensure her pleasure. This mating would set the tone for their whole life together. The ugly bruise on her ribs also served to remind him that she'd been battered and he had to be gentle. He would not hurt her. In fact, he could not—not intentionally.

With a rumbling growl, he lowered her to her sleeping bag and stretched out beside her. Her full breasts teased him with their proximity so he took one nipple into his mouth. The shadow beard on his chin rasped against the soft skin of her abdomen when she arched against him. Her dusky pink areolas were large for the size of her breasts and he loved the way they puckered from his ministrations. One hand trailed down to find the crisp curls between her legs. As his fingers combed through them, he discovered she was already wet. He groaned, grinding his erection into her hip even as his brain reminded him to slow down. He plunged one long, blunt finger into her moist heat.

"So tight, baby," he murmured against her breast. "You are so tight."

Hannah froze. What was she thinking? She could feel how large he was as his erection pulsed against her hipbone. Inquisitive, her fingers touched him. His cock jerked in reaction and she almost hyperventilated. She circled his shaft with her fingers and choked when her thumb and middle finger didn't quite meet. She pushed away from him, panicked, staring at his cock as it sprang from its pelt of thick auburn curls and pointed at his navel. If nothing else, she was good with numbers and she calculated the circumference, length, and mobility of him. Compared to her now seemingly inadequate equipment, there was no way Tab A would fit in Slot B.

A gloating smile spread across his face when he saw her eyes go wide at the size of him. That was one reason wolves normally didn't lack for bed partners. Even omegas were hung like porn stars. Mac stroked up the length of his shaft and ran his thumb over its swollen head. "This is what you do to me, darlin'." he drawled.

Hannah made a little noise that sounded like "Eep," and scrambled away from him, her eyes wide.

He made a grab for her and caught her ankle before she could crab completely away. A shadow of doubt flitted across his expression. "It's okay, honey," he murmured, pulling her closer. He buried his nose in her hair. "I want you like I've never wanted another woman, Hannah. I only want to make love to you. To give you pleasure." He kissed her again as he pushed two fingers into her wet core and swirled them around, pumping deeper into her. "You're tight, baby, but we'll take it slow. You can take me. It'll be okay." As he kissed her and she tensed even more, he finally got a clue. "Oh, God, baby, please tell me you aren't a fucking virgin." His voice was rougher than he intended.

The look on her face said it all. She pushed at his shoulders and little tremors shuddered through her. "I can't do this," she whimpered. "I—I—I've n— never...made..." The sentence was lost as she gulped. The word "sex" came out strangled as did something that sounded sort of like "man."

His big hands curled around her biceps and he set her back far enough that he could really look at her. The truth was there in her eyes. "You've never had sex?" Oh, Christ, what a grand cosmic joke this was. The wolf snarled with the need to mate even as the man puffed up, conceited and smug in the knowledge he'd be her first. When he recognized the tears glistening in her eyes, his manner gentled. "It's okay," he whispered. "We'll take it slow. It will hurt a little but..."

"You're the first man..." she started then had to clear the lump in her throat. "No one ever looked at me like you do. No one ever touched me."

He looked skeptical. "You want me to believe I'm the first to kiss you?"

Hannah shrugged. "Well, besides Jimmy Morton in the sixth grade when we played spin the bottle. But he told me that my lips felt like a raw mountain oyster, and tasted worse. He ran to the bathroom and threw up." Her breath hitched in her chest again. "Then I got glasses and braces and skipped some grades and...and..." The first tear silently rolled down her cheek. It was a hell of a confession to make to the naked man lying beside her.

God but she remembered it all so clearly. Around her peers, she was uncoordinated and gangly. Between her knobby knees and stringy, dishwater blond hair, she was the uber geek—so nerdy not even the geeks could stand to be around her. She didn't even have to wear a bra until she was a junior in college. Of course, she'd only been sixteen at the time. Finally, in grad school, she'd made a few friends though she suspected they kept her around because she was smart and would tutor them for free.

Mac watched the emotions roll across her face and was stunned. Hannah had no clue how beautiful she was, how desirable. He leaned in and his tongue licked up her cheek, tasting the salty trail of her tear. His lips sought hers and his tongue traced the seam between them. He leaned back and made a smacking noise. "Nope," he declared. "You definitely do not taste like cow nuts to me."

A choked giggle burbled from deep inside her and he captured the sound in his mouth. He nuzzled his way along her jaw to her ear. "That was then, Hannah, and not to sound trite, but this is now. You are the sexiest, most beautiful woman I have ever seen in my life. You are smart and funny and brave and I want you so much I can barely talk." He took a deep breath and looked into her eyes. "I want to bury my dick so deep inside you that we feel like one body. I want to wake up to find your blue eyes looking at me and your lips ready for my kisses. Before we are done, I will have kissed and tasted every inch of your body. And you'll enjoy every moment, Hannah, because your body is made for mine. When we come together, we will fit hand in glove."

He kissed her again as he eased her back on his sleeping bag. "It would have been nice if your first time was in a feather bed with silk and satin but I won't be able to walk if we wait until we get back to civilization." He rolled one of her nipples between his thumb and forefinger as his other hand captured one of hers and pulled it down to his groin. "Touch me, Hannah. Get used to what I feel like."

Hannah did. She had no choice. His cock felt like satin stretched over steel. The head, as large as a ripe plum, was smooth as silk and drops of pre-cum already pooled in the slit. Her forefinger traced the throbbing vein running its length. Mac's breath caught in his lungs and his shaft danced against her palm.

"See what you do to me, baby?" He slid one finger slid between the moist folds of her sex as his thumb found her clit and flicked across it. Her breath caught in her lungs.

Mac chuckled, a self-satisfied, rumbling growl. "And that's what I do to you, darlin'."

His fingers dipped inside her again, stroking, probing, stretching. He slid down her body until his shoulders pushed between her thighs. He nuzzled the soft skin where her thigh met her groin and drew in a deep breath. Her scent almost overwhelmed him. This was his woman, his mate. He'd be able to find her anywhere by scent alone. She smelled faintly spicy, like cloves, and sweet like jasmine after a summer rain. His tongue tasted her and her essence was flavored just like her scent—spicy, sweet, a touch of saltiness.

Hannah couldn't catch her breath. Something wound tighter and tighter deep in her core. As Mac continued to lick and nuzzle her, she wanted to laugh, to cry, to do...something she didn't even have a name for. His tongue and teeth teased her clit as he pushed two fingers and then three into her. She arched against him, wanting, needing more. As the first spasms of her orgasm grabbed her, Mac moved back up her body. His thumb now worked her clit as his mouth found hers. Her whole body tensed and stars sparkled behind her eyes.

"Yeah, baby, oh, yeah," Mac murmured against her mouth. "Now, Hannah, now. Let go, baby, I'll catch you."

Mac positioned his cock and as Hannah rocked with the waves of her very first orgasm, he plunged inside, pushing through the tight muscles that proved her virginity. As the walls of her vagina clutched around him, he pushed deeper and deeper until his sac nestled against the sweet curve of her ass.

He took a deep, shuddering breath, on the absolute edge of control. He lay still, letting the spasms from her orgasm sweep over him. Her body stilled, finally, and her wide blue eyes looked luminous.

"Ready for another one?" A wicked grin stretched his cheeks. He was back in control.

"Oh, yes. Please?" She remembered to breathe. "But I thought it was supposed to hurt?"

His grin turned wolfish as he slowly pulled out of her. "I told you we'd fit, babe." Her eyes grew even wider when he reversed direction and pushed deep within her. Slowly, he repeated the action. Out. In. Satin rubbed against silk. In. Out. Deeper. Faster.

She learned Mac's rhythm, arching to meet each of his thrusts. That odd sensation built within her again, like there was a tight spring stretching between her heart and womb. With each thrust, it wound tighter and tighter until she thought she'd snap in two. His heart pounded against her breast, and his muscles tightened and clenched beneath her hands just before she shattered once again. She felt him come, jetting once, twice, three times, and again. The hot spray of his seed doused the fire deep inside her.

Sucking in a long shuddering breath, she looked up at him and saw herself reflected in the amber gold of his eyes. Her eyes were heavy-lidded, her lips swollen from his kisses. She looked like a woman well loved and realized she was exactly that. She recognized possession in his gaze, but tenderness as well. In that moment, she understood. She would never be able to walk away from him.

"Mine," he whispered to her. "Now and forever mine."

And just as clearly, Hannah realized that Mac would never walk away from her. She swallowed hard and nodded. As she looked into his eyes, the whole world shifted—earth, air, time. Their lives felt irrevocably entwined now.

Her fingers trailed across his skin, tracing his high, sculptured cheekbones, his strong square jaw, his lips just as swollen from her kisses as hers were from his. She wanted the words—said and received on both sides—but knew instinctively love had nothing to do with this. What had occurred between them was more primal, more instinctive, more...well, just more.

Still inside her, Mac rolled over and pulled her on top of him. "You okay?" His voice sounded gruff to her ears.

She wanted to shout, to scream, *NO! My whole fucking life has changed. I'm not me anymore. I don't understand what just happened and I'm scared shitless.* Instead, she replied coolly, "Yeah. Fine. You?"

His hand stroked down her spine and she fought the urge to arch and curl against him. He knew exactly what he did to her and his roguish smile just rubbed it in. She snarled at him.

"Fuck you, Sergeant Major."

"You just did, Major."

She braced her palms against his chest and tried to push off of him. His arms tightened around her back as his hips surged into her again. She gasped.

Good grief. He was hard again. "No," she told him through gritted teeth. He arched an eyebrow and she wanted to slap him. "We have a mission and I can't be too sore to walk." Yeah, she decided. That was a good argument. The mission. This...this whatever had just happened couldn't happen again. His maleness simply overwhelmed her and she couldn't risk losing control. She didn't understand what had happened between them and she wasn't sure she wanted to examine it too closely. In self-defense, she got aggressive.

She was right, but Mac didn't like it. He would have to figure out what to do with her. Later, he decided. He needed to talk to Michael and the others before he made any decisions regarding the mission. Reluctantly, he pulled out of her and let her push away from him. He reached for his pack, grabbed a canteen and a bandanna from it, and handed them to her as she stood.

"Sorry. A spit bath is all I can offer."

Semen dripped down her inner thighs. With horror, she remembered she wasn't on the pill. What thirty year-old virgin with no prospects needed the pill? And he hadn't used a condom. Her eyes widened and she gulped air, a breath away from hyperventilating. So much for controlling the situation.

Mac took one look at her panicked face and knew what she was thinking. He stood up in one graceful move and wrapped her in his arms. While he'd like nothing more than to have gotten her pregnant, and suspected he probably had, he was smart enough to realize now was not the time to tell her. Later, when they were all safe and back in the States, he'd explain things to her. Instead of the truth, he murmured sweet nothings into her hair and soothed her with his touch, stalling the inevitable.

"Oh, crap. Crap-crap

"We didn't…no birth control."

"The odds are against you getting pregnant your first time."

"That's an old wives' tale," she spat.

"You seem to know a lot about it for a virgin," he teased.

"Fuck you," she snarled.

"Yes." He smiled. "You will."

Hannah balled up her fist and smacked him on the chest. Her blow didn't faze him a bit and made her hand hurt like hell. She squeezed her eyes shut right before she heard the discreet cough at the mouth of the cave.

"Oh, shit." Mortified, she snagged her clothes and made a beeline for the back of the cave where the little alcove provided some semblance of privacy.

Mac watched her long-legged stride with pride and admiration. God but she had a sweet ass. The next time he took her, he'd be cradling its softness to his groin. His dick was still semi-hard and he wiped at it with his dirty tee shirt before rummaging in his pack for a clean pair of boxers. He pulled them on and was buttoning up his pants as Michael Lightfoot came around the corner.

CHAPTER 6

LIGHTFOOT'S NOSTRILS FLARED. "Got the dirty deed done, then." He sniffed again. Mixed in with the scent of sex was something sweeter, tangier. Blood. He glanced around the cave. "Is she okay?" His question sounded blunt.

Mac ducked his head. Wolves in mating lust had been known to rip their partners. Hannah would be pissed when she found out that every man in the unit knew what they'd done. But, hell, they were all Wolves. All they had to do was sniff the air. "Virgin," he admitted, both pride and remorse evident in his cocky grin.

The other Wolf's mouth hung open. "Well, shit. Is she still speaking to you?"

"Barely. I suspect the loss of her virginity pales in comparison to the fact that we didn't use a condom and she's not on the pill."

Lightfoot stared. "Please tell me she wasn't in heat..." His voice trailed off as he interpreted Mac's expression. "Oh double damn shit. Of course she was in heat. That's why you couldn't keep your paws off her."

Hannah's voice rang through the cave. "Why don't we just make an announcement to the whole gawddamn Army."

Mac pressed his lips together and bit them, trying vainly to keep from smiling. Lightfoot called on every bit of wisdom from his ancestors to keep his face stoic. Hannah marched up to the two men, her fists planted on her hips, her lips a tight slash across her chin, her eyes a blazing blue.

Mac flashed an easy-going smile. "Honey, we're a bunch of Wolves. Our sense of smell is…well, a little more developed than humans."

She'd done some thinking while dressing. She'd planned on talking to Mac in private but his cavalier attitude succeeded in royally pissing her off.

"Fine. And I bet their sense of hearing is just as good, so hear this all of you." Her voice turned louder at the end of the sentence. She whirled on Mac and got right up in his face. "If we get home and I find out I'm pregnant, I'll just get an abortion. No harm. No foul. You can go your merry way, Sergeant Major, and you can be double damn sure this will never happen again."

Too late, she recognized the narrowing of Mac's eyes and the flaring of his nostrils accented by the twist of his mouth. And if that hadn't been enough of a clue, the growl rumbling deep in his chest heralded bad things about to happen. If he'd had hair on the back of his neck, it would be standing up like the ruff on an angry dog. Or in this case, one seriously pissed-off wolf. She took a frightened step backwards and then another. Stiff-legged, Mac stalked her until her back hit the cave wall. He was so livid his entire body vibrated.

"You. Are. Mine," he gritted out. His hands, braced on either side, pinned her against the rough rock. "When I get you pregnant…not if, Hannah, when, I will take care of you and the pup."

Her eyes grew round and her skin blanched. Pup? Oh, god, was she going to have puppies with this man?

Lightfoot glimpsed expression of horrified panic on Hannah's face and realized what Mac had said. "Oh, crap," he muttered. Turning on his heel, he jogged outside. Jacob Nakai, as the oldest and therefore least threatening member of the pack, needed to talk to Hannah quickly.

Her knees shook and then gave out completely. She rode the rough stone at her back down to the floor of the cave. Wrapping her arms around her bent knees, she huddled in on herself. She swore she wouldn't cry; bit her lip until it bled to keep from it, but still the tears streamed down her cheeks. She couldn't look at Mac. She'd never been so scared in her life. In fact, she almost wished the Bosnian patrol still had her. Pup? She'd forgotten he was a different species—human but not. God, if she were pregnant, would the baby come out with fangs and a tail?

Mac was so furious he was shaking. Abort his pup? No way in hell. He had spilled his seed in her intentionally. They were mated. That she would consider killing his child was—. He choked on his anger. At that moment, he hated Hannah Jackson with all his heart. Not even her tears or the waves of fear rolling off her could calm him down. "I will kill you first," he told her coldly. Turning on his heel, he marched out of the cave and left her in a pitiful heap.

Hannah sobbed so hard she couldn't catch her breath. Jacob Nakai found her huddled against the back wall of the cave fighting to breathe. He reached out with one finger and touched her arm. He grimaced when the woman jumped and jerked away from his touch. Shaking his head sadly, he tried to figure out what to do. They were in the month of the Blood Moon and from her scent, Jacob could tell she'd been both a virgin and in heat. She was neither now.

He sighed. Matings like this were always so hard. He and Tala, his mate, had known each other from childhood. She had always known what he was. In the sixty-two years of their marriage, they'd been lucky to have three children, all female. Jacob loved his daughters. And he loved his wife.

His heart went out to the major. He squatted on his heels in front of her and laid a gentle hand on the top of her head. Her tears stopped but dry sobs now wracked her frame. Whether the tiny spark of life she carried inside her would be Wolf or not, he could not tell.

"Hush, daughter," he crooned. "You must listen to what I say to you. Listen and understand."

She shuddered beneath his touch but worked to get her breathing under control. "I'm sorry," she panted out. "Hysterics is not one of my strong suits. I don't...I don't lose control."

Jacob smiled. This one had grit. She would be one to ride the river with. "He will not hurt you physically," he soothed. "He is angry at your words but that heat will cool. He will remember what he said in anger, and regret that he has hurt your heart. Children are very precious to us, daughter. Can you understand that?"

She raised her head to look at him and his heart wrenched at her sorrow-ravaged face.

"To sire a son who is a Wolf is the hope and dream of us all. To sire any child is a cherished wish. Wolves do not spill their seed in unfertile ground and any woman who is not a potential mate is unfertile. Do you understand?"

Hannah tried hard but her brain just wouldn't wrap itself around what Jacob was telling her. She shook her head.

"Wolves like to fuck." His tone and words were both blunt. "But we never leave our seed in a female at a time when she could conceive. Unless she is our mate."

Hannah nodded slowly, beginning to understand.

"Some of us marry for love, but still children come few and far between. I have been with my mate for sixty-two years, and she has blessed me with three daughters. Some Wolves go their whole lives with no offspring." He let those words sink in before adding, "Tala is both the mate of my heart and the mate of my soul." He watched, waiting for her to comprehend his words. "Some of us are blessed, or cursed depending on the Wolf, to have mates of the soul. Wolves mate for life as a rule though it is easier to walk away from a heart mate. What has happened here, to you, to the Sergeant Major, we call this moonstruck." He recognized the curiosity in her expression. "It happens fast, when least expected and the Wolf who is moonstruck is..."

"Crazy?"

He chuckled before his expression settled back into sober lines. "Yes. That is a way to explain them. But this is a very serious time, daughter. To leave a soul mate could kill a Wolf."

She stared at him, aghast. "Are you saying that the Sergeant Major...that I..." A whimper swallowed her words.

Jacob shrugged, a wry smile crinkling his mouth. "Sometimes the gods get cranky or bored and they play a practical joke on us. Sometimes they are just pissed. Who knows why the gods have picked you, but you are his soul mate just as he is yours. The two of you are matched in every way, two halves of the same whole but not fitted together yet." He dropped his hand so that it lay gently against her abdomen. "That which will bind you sleeps here now."

"How can I marry—" She hiccuped and tried again. "How can I marry a man who doesn't love me? God, is marriage even an option?" She hated that her voice squeaked.

"How can he not love you, daughter? You are the sweetness in his life. He would die to protect you and what you carry. If you turned your back and walked away from him, he would follow. He has no choice."

She gave a sad little snort. "And that's what it all boils down to, isn't it? We have no choice."

CHAPTER 7

JACOB FELT SORRY for this young woman. Mac had reacted in typical alpha Wolf fashion yet he hoped she would understand in time. He touched her cheek. "I will send Tala to you when we return home. She will answer your questions, even those you are uncomfortable with."

Hannah stared at the older man. "Will I really give birth to a puppy?" She almost choked on the words.

"Ah." Enlightenment. Mac had spoken without thinking. A Wolf referred to all children as pups. That this woman, who had no experience with their world, believed she would birth an animal should not have surprised him. He shook his head. "He spoke in haste, daughter, and then in anger without thought. The child you carry will be normal in every way. If it is a son and he carries the Wolf trait, your mate will know and will train him, though the first change will not come until much later. Do you understand?"

She hiccuped. "It won't be furry?" She hated the whimper hiding beneath her question.

Jacob smiled reassuringly. "I promise, daughter. Your child will not be furry when it comes into this world. And I make another promise. Your Wolf will love and cherish both you and your child. Your life will be much easier if you can find a small piece of your heart to give him, even if you cannot fully love him in return."

She hiccuped again as she shook her head. This was too much to think about right now. The growl from the front of the cave sent a shiver of fear up her spine.

Jacob jerked his hand away and eased back from her. "Wolves are possessive, daughter. It would be wise to keep your distance from the rest of us, as we will you. Nature has conspired against the Alpha. He has much on his mind—the mission, your mating, and the Blood Moon approaches. We are all on edge because of that. Please do not judge him or us too harshly until you come to an understanding of your place in our world. Can you do that, daughter? Will you?"

Could she? Hannah had always thought she was open-minded. That was one reason she'd been tagged by the General for this assignment. Mac hadn't hurt her physically. Oh, his words had sliced her heart into pieces and he'd scared the shit out of her, but she had to admit he'd mostly been gentle with her, had eased her through the taking of her virginity. She put away the thought of losing her virginity. She'd think about it later, when things weren't so...moonstruck. Her right palm curled over her abdomen. Was a baby truly there? Had she conceived? Did the old Indian know for sure? God, this was all too much. She'd resigned herself to being alone for the rest of her life. She'd refused to own a pet, afraid she'd become that caricature of an old lady with seven cats her only family. And now this? Could she live with an overwhelming alpha male?

She looked at Jacob, her eyes begging for understanding. "I don't know," she whispered. Her voice grew a little stronger. "Once we get home... Once everyone is safe... Then I'll think about it and decide what I'm going to do."

Jacob watched her, listening with his heart for the true meaning of her words. Mac was a very lucky wolf indeed if this woman consented to be his mate. Her consent and acceptance would go a very long way toward making their lives happier. She was strong, intelligent and resilient—all traits necessary to survive in the world of the pack, especially as the mate of the Alpha.

He stood up and smiled down at her. "I will send Sean in to check your injuries though I warn you, the Sergeant Major will not be far behind." His smile became a smug grin. "Wolves are not known for their tolerance of other men getting close to their mates."

Hannah snorted. That had to be the classic understatement of the year.

Jacob had a few choice words to deliver to his team leader. As predicted, he found Mac standing just inside the mouth of the cave. He roughly shoved the bigger man outside and bared his teeth when Mac growled at him.

"You may be Alpha but I am Elder and you will hear me, Wolf."

Mac rubbed his forehead with his right hand. "This is turning out to be a royal cluster fuck."

"You are an ass, Ian McIntire." He glared the bigger man into silence then continued. "You left that child thinking she is going to have a litter of puppies."

Mac groaned and ducked his head. Christ. Hannah was only human. For all her intelligence, she actually knew nothing of his world. He'd reacted like an unchanged juvenile to her words. He realized, in retrospect, that she'd also spoken without thinking. He hadn't offered her words of love or commitment. For all she knew, he'd take off, leave her high and dry. No wonder she'd reacted with threats. He stared at Jacob, his own suspicions confirmed by the look in the older man's eyes. Hannah carried his child. And, he'd probably screwed up any chance at having a decent relationship with her.

While Jacob put Mac in his place, Sean slipped into the cave. He found Hannah, arms curled around her knees with her back pressed against the rough stone of the cave wall. He could tell she'd been crying and his nose told him most of the rest of the story. Known as one of the mellowest member of the squad, even he was uptight. The Blood Moon was only a week away. They needed to be well away from this place and each other before the moon hung full and ripe in the night sky.

The Blood Moon was the traditional time of pack challenge. The Wolves had a very definite pecking order based on their military ranks. During the time of the Blood Moon, every alpha felt the urge to assert himself, and even betas and omegas were restless. Wolves in the military were all alphas at heart so they took leave and just stayed far away from one another. As long as there wasn't another Wolf around, there was no need to thump chests, get furry, and bleed an opponent to establish dominance. The Blood Moon coupled with the new mating of the Alpha and the screwed-up mission really complicated things.

"Hey." He squatted next to her. "How're the ribs?"

Hannah refused to look at him. "Fine," she mumbled.

"Want to pull up your tee shirt so I can take a look?" He grinned as she flicked her eyes up at him. "No offense, but I don't want the Alpha to chew off my hand for touching you." She snorted but did as he asked. "Looks better this morning. I think they're just bruised. Having any trouble breathing?"

"Only when I get hysterical."

He chuckled. Yeah, the Alpha was definitely going to have his hands full with this one.

"Why do you call him the alpha? He's a sergeant major."

He rocked back on his heels putting a little more distance between them. "All of us are alphas," he explained, "or we wouldn't have made it into the 69th. Wolves in the wild..." he chuckled again as he interrupted her bewildered look and amended his explanation. "When we're in the civilian world, we have a tendency to follow a pack structure. Each pack has a leader, *the* Alpha, with a capital A. Mac is our Alpha. In the military, the man who'd normally be the Alpha in the real world always seems to have the rank to be in charge."

Hannah nodded, her brow furrowed in thought. "Will you answer another question for me?"

"Depends," he replied honestly.

"What's the significance of a blood moon?"

"Ah. Once again, semantics. It isn't *a* blood moon; it's the Blood Moon, again capitalized. That's the full moon when all the alphas can challenge each other for pack dominance."

She gulped. "You mean you guys will all turn furry and try to eat each other?"

He shook his head. "No. We don't challenge in the squad. Counterproductive. Normally, we're all on leave and far, far away from each other. But, in the week or so leading up to the full, we get a little cantankerous and cranky."

"Uh huh. A little cantankerous and cranky? That's not exactly what I'd call it." While her sarcasm was obvious, she also unconsciously rubbed the goose bumps on her arms.

For the first time, he saw the bruising on her arms and recognized the shapes as fingers. His eyes flicked from the bruises to her face. "Did he hurt you anywhere else?" He didn't realize he was growling.

Her eyes narrowed as she stared back, trying to figure out why he'd gone all snarly. "Who? The Bosnian?" Then she noticed he was looking at her arms. She could see the marks Mac's fingers had left on the inside of her biceps. "Oh." Until that moment, she was unaware Mac had marked her in his anger. Her cheeks flamed and she ducked her head. "No," she answered quickly. "And I don't think he meant to do this. I bruise easily." God, she hated herself right then. She was making excuses for him even if her response was the truth. She didn't care if he hunted her to the ends of the earth, but if he ever touched her in anger again, if he ever abused her, she was gone. She blinked. She was already considering staying with him.

Good lord, what was wrong with her? She'd lost her virginity to the man and now she was going all goo-goo and dopey and....shit. This wasn't like her at all. She took a deep breath, gratified it only hitched in her chest at the very end.

Sean nodded, as if he'd read every thought flitting through her head. In a way, he had. The major's face was most expressive, her emotions rolling across it like a movie. He relaxed. Some Wolves went bad, or were born that way. Abusing others became second nature to them. He'd never thought the Sergeant Major would become one of those. He wasn't sure he could take the Alpha in a fight but he'd have to challenge the other man if he ever hurt this woman again. He stood up and smiled down at her. "Come on outside when you feel up to it."

She watched him walk away, his stride long and lanky, much like the man himself. The last thing she wanted to do was face the unit, but she also refused to cower alone in the cave. She found one of Mac's bandannas and his canteen. Wetting the cloth, she wiped her face. Resigned to the inevitable, she pulled her BDU blouse on over her tee shirt but didn't button it up.

She was just turning the corner to the entrance when Mac turned the same corner and they smacked into each other. Instinctively, Mac grabbed her upper arms to steady her. She grimaced in pain and he swore, the words hissing out between his clinched teeth. Before Hannah could react, he'd peeled her blouse down from her shoulders. He growled at the bruises on her arms.

"Down, boy," she snarled. "Before you do something else stupid."

Stung by her words, he dropped his hands. He'd been the one to mark her and was shamed by his loss of control. Before he could stop himself, he reached out and brushed her cheek with one finger. "I'm sorry. I've screwed this up from the get go. Can we start over?"

Mac waited while she gave him a cool once over. He deserved her disdain, and probably more. He was afraid the little cry that escaped her lips was one of fear until he saw the gleam in her eyes.

She stared up into his burnt amber eyes. She saw regret there—regret for the way he'd treated her, and sorrow as well. Other emotions lurked beneath the golden depths—tenderness, possessiveness, admiration, and just maybe, there was respect there, too. She took a step back so she could look him up and down. She fought the grin struggling to stretch her cheeks. If she had to be tied to a man for the rest of her life, she could have done a lot worse. Lord but he was some serious eye candy. Before she could stop it, a slightly hysterical giggle escaped. Embarrassed, she pressed a hand to her mouth. She could do this. She would do this. Oh, hell. Who was she kidding? She had to do this. And he did make her go weak in the knees every time she looked at him.

"Fine," she replied, her tone tart. "But you ever lay a hand on me like that again, I will cut off your balls and eat them with hot sauce."

CHAPTER 8

MAC ROARED WITH LAUGHTER and as the members of his team spilled into the mouth of the cave, he grabbed her. Lifting her completely off her feet, he kissed her long and hard. Savoring her taste, he finally pulled his mouth from her lips. He chuckled. "And you would, too, wouldn't you?" This woman who had come so unexpectedly into his life absolutely captivated him. His life would never be dull with her in it. Now all he had to do was complete the mission, get all of them home safely, and away from each other before the Blood Moon rose, all while desperately needing to fuck this woman blind. Life was just fucking grand.

Embarrassed, Hannah balled up her fists and hit him in the chest. Hard. It still didn't faze him. "You could at least pretend that hurt," she groused. He continued grinning at her. "Put me down." She huffed out the words so hard, her bangs ruffled.

He did, letting her slide slowly down the length of his body. When her boots touched the soft mulch cushioning the floor of the cave, her body would have continued heading south if he hadn't held her upright. His touch...hell, just the proximity of so much male testosterone set off all her nerve endings and made her weak in the knees. Wet heat pooled low in her body.

Polite coughs reminded them of their audience. She figured every man in the cave knew what her body craved. Scarlet, she buried her face in Mac's chest. He smirked at his men over the top of her head even as he wrapped her in his arms.

"Cut that macho shit out." Her voice was muffled by his shirt but everyone heard her.

The men just grinned back at their Alpha. Mac laid a soft kiss on the top of her head. "You need to eat something and then you can rest here."

She pushed away from him. "What do you mean *rest here?*" She gave him a hard look. "I am so not staying in this cave while you guys go gallivanting about the countryside."

Young Danny glanced at Sean. "Gallivanting? Do people really talk like that?"

She turned around to glare at the younger man. He gulped and ducked his head as Sean chuckled.

"I guess *she* does, Danny boy." He looked at the couple. "She does need rest, Mac." His eyebrows waggled. "And I do mean rest."

Hannah flushed crimson as Jacob spoke up. "There is no shame, daughter. It is good that you desire your mate so much. These others, they are just envious. Even after sixty some years, when I have been away from Tala?" A slow grin emphasized the twinkle in his knowing eyes. "Even the grandchildren know not to call for several days."

She forced her mouth to stay closed. That was way too much information. Sex was just not something discussed in public, especially not sex so up close and personal.

Jacob's face returned to its normal stoic expression. "You have much to learn, daughter, and not much time within which to do so. Even now your body is adapting and changing to our ways. The desire will not go away. It will only get stronger the further you get with your pregnancy."

Hannah sputtered. "Oh, great. Let's just tell the whole fricking world. I screwed the gawddamned capital A Alpha and he's so fucking puffed up because, according to you, I'm having a puppy. And now because of raging hormones or whatever, I'm turning into Slutty Sex Girl. Fine." Mac tried to touch her. She whirled and her fist caught him on the point of his chin. The blow actually staggered him back half a step. "Just call me uber-bitch because you are so not touching me ever again. I am a grown adult woman. I control my body. Period. End of discussion."

She stalked back into the main body of the cave, sat down on Mac's bedroll, and promptly burst into tears. Her body ached for Mac's touch—actually, physically ached. She was so wet with wanting him that she might have to change clothes. Without warning, what little food left in her stomach rebelled. She managed to make it to the alcove before she puked up her guts.

Moments later, Mac knelt next to her pressing a cool, wet cloth to her forehead. "I'm sorry, baby," he crooned as dry heaves racked her body. Wolf pregnancies were never easy and if Hannah carried a male child with the wolf gene, it would only get worse. He didn't want to think about the odds of Hannah carrying their child to full term. When she could finally lean up against him with no further ill effects, he wiped her mouth and kissed her forehead. "You really do need to lie down and rest, Hannah."

"This isn't me," she whispered, a tear squeezing out of the corner of her eye to trickle down her cheek. She brushed it away, the flick of her fingers angry yet vulnerable.

"I know, baby."

"I'm an adult. A fully competent woman. I don't fall apart in a crisis. I don't cry and get hysterical." She drew in a ragged breath. "What the hell have you done to me?"

He kissed the damp corner of her eye. "I've fallen in love with you." She thumped his chest with her fist. He grinned down at her. "Is this where I'm supposed to say 'ow'?" She hit him again, as hard as she could. He continued to grin. "Hannah, you are the most amazing woman I've ever met. You are smart, brave, and ballsy as all get out. I couldn't have picked a better mate and mother for my children if I'd gone looking." He pulled her into his lap and cradled her head against his shoulder. "Only a few women would have made it this far. Most would have fallen apart yesterday when you were captured and beaten. You didn't. Any other woman would still be huddled in a corner having the screaming-meemies after what occurred this morning. You aren't. Sean and Jacob assure me that your emotional reaction to all this is extraordinarily calm, all things considered. They want you to know that your physical reaction is completely ordinary. I'm sorry you're embarrassed, baby. No one here is doing it intentionally. It's just the way we are. Our senses are—"

"Yeah, your senses are," she cut him off. "I'm just..." She swallowed hard and then a dry chuckle grated out. "I guess overwhelmed would be too mild a term."

Mac let out the breath he'd been holding. "The men don't mean to make you uncomfortable, Hannah. Believe it or not, they are almost as excited about this turn of events as I am. I can promise you that any one of them would lay down his life to protect you."

She rubbed her chin against his chest, unconsciously seeking to touch his skin, though his tee shirt remained stubbornly in her way. God, but she craved the feel of him. She sighed and his arms tightened around her automatically.

"You need to lay down for a bit." Not waiting for her acquiescence, he stood up in one graceful movement, still cradling her in his arms. He strode out into the cave and set her down gently on his bedroll. "If I'd had a choice, I would have done this completely different."

Hannah bristled. Choice. Yeah, there was that word again. They didn't have a choice. He'd told her he had fallen in love with her but she didn't believe him for a New York minute. It was too quick. He didn't know anything about her, or she him. Love had nothing to do with their situation. Lust. Lust and hormones. That's all it was for him. She rolled away from him, giving him her back. And that's all it was for her, too, if she was completely honest with herself.

Mac forced down the hurt that knotted in his chest. He had to give her time. He touched her on the shoulder, his hand barely brushing the cloth of her blouse. "I've got to meet with the men to brief them about tonight. Come on out when you feel up to it. I know food is the last thing on your mind but you'll need some sooner than later." He stood up and strode toward the mouth of the cave. Without turning around, he added, "I *am* sorry, Hannah."

The Wolves waited in the small clearing outside the cave. They'd been field-stripping their weapons and checking ammunition packs. He studied each man in his unit, reading the body language. Only Sean looked up.

"Morning sickness?" The medic paused his inventory of the medical supplies in his pack.

"Yeah."

Sean returned to his task, ignoring a sharp click near his ear as Lightfoot shoved a clip home in the M25 sniper rifle he carried. The weapon used two types of clips. Had he been going in strictly as a sniper, he would have loaded the five-round clip. One shot, one kill. The clip held four more than he'd actually need. However, he was providing high cover for this mission. That meant the twenty-round clip and several more loaded on an ammo belt for backup. They expected a hot firefight.

Nakai honed a combat knife on a whetstone. The edges were already sharp enough to shave with in cold water, but the rhythmic motion steadied him. Danny hunkered on his heels drawing designs in the dirt. This wasn't his first mission with the wolves but he was nervous. Mac knew the feeling. This one could turn to shit in a heartbeat.

He squatted next to Lightfoot and pulled the GPS unit from one of his cargo pockets. The other men watched, waiting expectantly. "We hit the compound at oh four hundred. With luck, they'll think we're here to hit Zekerija so he and his guards will have already vacated the premises."

"What happens if Tornjak is already dead?" Lightfoot's voice reverberated with deadly intent.

Mac stared at his second-in-command for several heartbeats. "Depends on how he died," he replied cryptically. Tornjak was one of theirs. Their mission was to free him or erase his remains. He nodded to Lightfoot. "High cover." His second blinked in agreement. "Nakai, you and Danny have our back trail, and will cover Sean and I when we come out."

Sean grinned. There were things besides medical supplies in his packs—explosives and shaped charges just some of the surprises. In addition to being the team medic, he was also the demolitions expert.

"What about me?"

Five startled gazes turned to stare at Hannah. Four of them turned wary and waited for Mac to say something.

"You'll wait here. We'll pick you up on the way to the extraction point."

"No."

That one word hung frozen in the air between them.

Mac choked on his first response, took a deep breath and tried to reason with her. "Hannah," he began.

"No," she barked. "I will not be left behind to twiddle my thumbs."

"Yes, you will." His voice remained deadly calm. "I will not risk my men or this mission because you feel the need to prove yourself." He glared at her, fury etched like on his face. "I will not risk you...or our child."

"Prove myself?" Hannah was spitting mad. "Oh, no you don't, fur face. You are the only macho creepo around here. I don't have to prove a damn thing to anybody. I am going, just as was originally planned. And that's an order, Sergeant Major."

His eyes blazed with golden fire. "You. Are. Not. In. Charge. Major." He bit out each word, his hands opening and closing into fists at his sides.

He spat out her rank with so much bitter irony in his voice she actually took a step backwards. Subtle movement on each side caught her attention. Lightfoot and Sean had shifted almost imperceptibly. They were now in position to insert their bodies between her and Mac should something occur.

Hannah jutted her chin at him. "I will not be left hiding in this godforsaken place." She swallowed hard remembering how she'd felt waking up the day before to find Mac gone. A small shiver skittered through her at the memory of her beating. Closing her eyes, the faces of the men she'd killed swam before her and her stomach roiled. Choking down the bile, she asked, "What happens if you don't come back?" She waved her hand in the general direction of the other men. "If they don't come back?" Her voice quivered and she hated that the sound revealed her fear. She planted her fists on her hips and glared not only at Mac but all the men, hoping to cover her terror with bravado.

"She can come with me." A noncommittal shrug accompanied Lightfoot's calm statement. "That was the original plan. If need be, I can send her ahead to the pickup zone while I cover you."

Mac started to tear his second a new one but hesitated long enough to take a deep breath to calm down before he did something completely stupid. "We need to eat and get some rest before we do anything," he finally said. "We move out at oh two hundred." He glared at Hannah before turning on his heel and stalking away from the group.

She took two steps after him before Lightfoot grabbed her arm. They both heard the growl from the edge of the woods and he immediately let go. "It would be better for all of us if you stayed here tonight," he said, both his words and his voice blunt. "He needs to focus on the mission and he will not be able to do so if you are in danger." He left unspoken the thought, *Or if you are near one of us.*

Hannah stared at the spot where Mac disappeared into the woods, so angry she wanted to stamp her foot in frustration. Did it occur to any of them that she might be in more danger if she stayed here alone? The thought of being abandoned in this wild place was almost enough to make her hyperventilate. Good grief. She was a soldier; she *could* find her way back to civilization. But what would happen when she did? Even if there was an American Embassy in whatever city she made her way to, she had no identification, nothing to prove she was American but her word. This was a white ops mission. Even her boss would deny her existence.

The men drifted back into the cave, leaving Hannah alone. She found a boulder and sank down beside it, using it as a backrest. If she stayed right there, they wouldn't be able to sneak away and go without her. She wouldn't put it past Mac to do just that. As the sun filtered through the trees to dapple her face, she relaxed. Her eyes drifted closed as the emotions and physical exertions took their toll. She dozed off within minutes.

Mac found her sitting against the boulder. Her eyes were shut and she looked sad, even in sleep. A cold lump lodged in his chest. He didn't want her anywhere near the upcoming operation, but the thought of leaving her behind, unprotected, almost paralyzed him. He couldn't detail a man to stay with her for two reasons. One, his team was small and each man had a specialized job to do. Second, the thought of another man alone with her would eat him alive. Jealousy was an ugly emotion. He was still trying to decide what to do with her when she stirred in her sleep.

"No," she mumbled. "Won't come back."

He settled beside her and touched her cheek. "Yes, I will," he promised.

"No," she argued, shaking her head. Still asleep, she mumbled, "No. Alone. Can't be alone." Her hands clutched at her belly. "Can't."

A single tear trickled down her cheek and he caught it on his fingertip. He held it to the light and marveled at the prism effect, as brilliant as a diamond. He smiled. That was Hannah. *His* Hannah—a diamond in the rough. He really was falling in love with her and suspected that he'd started the plunge the moment he'd laid eyes on her in Captain Harjo's office. Lord, was that only three weeks ago? No wonder she didn't trust him, or this thing that bound them so tightly. If he'd been strictly human, he wouldn't trust it either. Her pregnancy further complicated matters. Wolf pregnancies were never easy and the chance of miscarriage was ever-present. He couldn't risk Hannah and the baby. He wouldn't. The cold lump in his chest turned to an icy fist. He had no choice. He'd have to.

CHAPTER 9

MAC SETTLED HIS back against the rock and drew her into the curve of his arm. He cradled her against his side and laid his cheek on the top of her head. She cuddled against him with a contented sigh. "I promise," he whispered into her hair. "I won't leave you." He sighed. "Fuckin' rock and a hard spot," he snarled softly.

"Tell me about it," Hannah snarled back.

"I thought you were asleep."

"I was. Sort of. What do you call it? Combat sleep. I..." She pushed away and looked up at him. "I can't stay behind." Hannah gulped. Considering she worked an ultra top-secret job at the Pentagon, she was basically an honest person. It chafed to lie. That didn't mean she wasn't good at poker, but this wasn't Texas Hold 'Em. "I'm a fake..." She stopped and blinked, unsure just what name to call him. "Uhm...Ian. I talk a good game but when I woke up and you were gone yesterday? I panicked. Then I got pissed. And when I got caught, I was scared to death." She tensed to keep from shivering. "Please? Don't leave me here. I don't understand this whole alpha male claiming thing. But I'm damn sure not interested in any of the men in the unit." He cut her words off with a kiss.

She squirmed. His arms tightened. She resisted the urge to bite his tongue.

"Mac." His name was swallowed in the kiss. "Only my mother called me Ian."

She pushed back from him and scrunched up her nose. "Ewww. Way to kill the moment, stud."

He let out a slow breath and she recognized his resolute look. "I'm sorry, Hannah. If I'd known about the patrol, I would never have left you alone." His thumb touched her bruised cheek, a light feathering of rough callous over silky skin, and he winced.

She searched his face, saw both tenderness and regret etched there. Did he regret she was the one he'd be stuck with for the rest of his life? Was it true that they were trapped in this relationship? She knew nothing about Wolf life. And if getting pregnant was such a big deal, how had she popped so quickly? She had so many questions but there was no time to get the truth from him. Her nostrils flared as she breathed in slowly and deeply. He watched her intently, like a hunter homing in on his prey. She didn't like that image much but it was truthful. Truth. It all boiled down to truth.

"I have a lot of questions to ask." She shook her head, stopping his reply. "They'll have to wait until this is over. I understand that. But we need to clear some things up. I'm not a soldier, Mac. What happened before? That was sheer dumb luck and terror despite the basic training. I know this mission has gone to straight to hell and this...thing...between the two of us is happening at the worst possible time." A wry grin tugged the corner of her mouth. "My sense of timing has always sucked." Mac stared at her mouth, groaned and shifted his legs. She swallowed a nervous giggle. "Look. The thing is, you can't go all macho right now. I can't stay behind. That means I have to be around one of the guys or stick with you. Since you plan on penetrating the target, sticking with you isn't exactly high on my list of priorities. Let me stay with Michael. You guys do what you have to do, we all get our butts on the chopper, and get the hell back to civilization. I'll take leave with you and you can explain this mess to me."

He growled and his eyes narrowed as he stared at her. "Mess?"

She rolled her eyes. "Are you going to tell me this thing..." She gestured with her hand, pointing first at his chest, then at her own. "Whatever it is between you and me isn't a mess? Don't take it so damn personally. It *is* a mess. One we'll figure out with time." She stared up at him, her gaze locked on his face. "I'm not going anywhere. Okay?"

His breath slid from his lungs in a slow hiss. "This is a first for me, too," he admitted. "Just so you know, I'm not going anywhere either. We'll get through it together. Deal?"

She nodded. She felt the same relief showing on his face.

Mac stood and lifted her to her feet. "You should get some sleep. We have an early start and it'll be a long day."

🐾🐾🐾🐾

DARKNESS FILTERED SOUNDS as she laid there trying to both see and listen. Hannah knew what "inky black" meant now. Even with her eyes wide open and adjusted to the dark, she still couldn't see a thing. A faint rustle across the cave had her straining to hear. Cloth rubbing against itself, the brush of whipcord fabric as one of the men shifted position. The arm holding her close tightened, a reminder that the soft thump beating beneath her cheek was an echo of Mac's heart.

"I'm not ready to let you go."

Her eardrum felt the words as puffs of air yet she heard them as clearly as if he'd shouted them from the nearby mountains. Her heart, heretofore marching along steadily, danced a stutter step. Her cheek brushed the comfortable cotton knit of his standard-issue tee shirt as her lips quirked into a one-sided smile. His heart had stuttered, too, as he mouthed those words against her ear.

A discreet cough, muffled by the dark, shattered the moment. Firm lips brushed her temple before the arm holding her fell away. Mac sat up beside her.

"Cover your eyes."

Peeking from behind her fingers, she still squinted against the flare of light from his flashlight. Other lights flashed on, their beams cutting through the thick gloom with laser precision.

Mac pressed a canteen into her hands. "Go do what you need to do, but hurry." His gruff voice, so used to command, left no room for argument. She found her own flashlight atop her pack and scurried around the corner to the alcove. When she returned a few minutes later, the cave was bare. Mac waited for her near where they'd slept and he pointed her toward the mouth of the cave. He followed, erasing their footprints with a branch.

In the clearing, the Wolf pack waited patiently in the chilly night, all of them chowing down MREs. The thought of food made her mouth water, but not in a good way. Out here, there was a bit more light. The moon, waxing gibbous as it rode the far horizon, illuminated just enough of the forest their flashlights were unnecessary. She couldn't distinguish faces but their breath manifested as ghostly tendrils whenever they exhaled. She reached for her pack, her hand colliding with Mac's. She shook her head, he backed off. She still had something to prove—at least to herself. Jacob Nakai soundlessly disappeared into the woods. Strong hands helped settle her pack on her back as Danny Keegan drifted out of sight. The reassuring grip of Mac's hand on her shoulder urged her forward. His touch directed her, luckily, because the forest had swallowed Jacob and Danny. Sean Donaldson fell in behind Mac and she guessed Michael Lightfoot guarded their rear, though she could hear neither man as they blended into the shadows.

After almost an hour of steady walking, the group stopped just over the crest of a high ridge. In the valley below them, a river meandered like a silver ribbon beneath the pearly light of the moon. At a wide bend of the river, a dark blob left a dirty thumb print before it coalesced into a jumble of buildings as her eyes adjusted. Deep in the bowls of that medieval block of stone, another Wolf awaited release—by rescue or death.

Before she knew what was happening, Mac pulled her to his chest, his arms imprisoning her as his lips mashed hers. Need, and something more, something primeval, surged inside her. She met his harsh kiss with a demand of her own, her arms circling his neck as she clung to him. "You damn sure better come back to me," she hissed against his mouth.

"You damn sure better be here when I do."

Just as quickly as he'd grabbed her, he released her and was gone. Wraiths drifting through the ground fog followed him. One. Two. Three. She was alone with Michael. She didn't ask if there was anything she could do. There wasn't. She watched him set up his sniper nest with calculated efficiency. Wait. That's all she had to do. Her stomach rumbled. *Now* she was hungry. She shed her pack, found an MRE by touch, tore into it, and wolfed it down. Partially sated, her gut relaxed and she did, too.

🐾🐾🐾🐾

MAC DIDN'T NEED the tiny electronic device fastened to his ear to tell him his team was ready. The two guards at the front gate simultaneously sank to their knees. This was a deadly dance he and Sean had choreographed often. Sean found the keys on his victim and with an economy of motion, the medic had the portal unlocked and open scant inches while he moved the guards out of the way. They slipped through the gate and filtered through the inner yard. A few lights braved the darkness, the illumination they shed not near enough to banish the shadows. Mac didn't bother with the main doors, heading instead toward the side of the building to a little used entry. If their intel was correct, this door led directly to the dungeons below the castle. With sure fingers, Sean pressed a small charge into the lock. A moment later, after a faint sizzle and pop, the door opened as he pressed his shoulder against it.

Like water rolling downhill, they plunged down the moss-encrusted steps. Stepping onto a solid, stone floor, they prowled down a wide hallway. Up ahead, a sliver of dingy light oozed from beneath a wooden door. From behind the door, the wet slap of leather against bloody meat echoed with rhythmic thuds. Mac's nostrils flared. Blood and pain crouched behind that ancient barrier.

With well-rehearsed precision, they crashed through the door. Mac went low, his silenced Beretta hissing and spitting like a deadly cat. The man holding the broad leather strap above his head looked surprised even as life faded from his eyes. A second man, lounging in a comfortable chair pushed against the far wall, had no time for his shock to register as a red dot blossomed in the middle of his forehead. He died between one blink and the next.

Mac winced as he glanced at the man strapped naked to a table. The prisoner's groin, laced with cuts, resembled raw meat. Sean was already bending over him, syringe in hand.

"It's okay, Tornjak. We're here to take you home." With sure hands, Sean administered painkillers and then set to work with field dressings. They had scant minutes to get the captive packaged and away.

Mac stripped the uniform from the man in the chair. Tornjak's eyes stared vacantly as they pulled the uniform pants up his legs and carefully fastened the fly. They fit his limp arms into the sleeves of the shirt but didn't bother to button it up. With more care than his speed indicated, Mac hoisted the man onto his shoulders and headed toward the fresh air beckoning from above them. One part of his brain registered the fact that Sean was laying a few booby traps to discourage anyone who might come along.

They made it back to the outside gate in the wall with no complications. Two figures materialized from the shadows as they stepped through the portal. Jacob flashed a signal. Mac nodded and moved on, following the wall to the steep hill rising to the ridge above the castle. Michael lay in wait up there, even now sighting in his sniper rifle. Up there, Hannah waited for him. He smiled despite the muffled groan from the man over his shoulder. They were going to pull this off without a hitch.

Then all hell broke loose.

CHAPTER 10

HANNAH BIT DOWN on the fleshy part of her thumb to keep from screaming. With the aid of night-vision glasses, she had watched the stealthy assault. When the four men of the Whiskey Team reappeared with the fifth and headed for the rendezvous point, she exhaled and removed the goggles. She closed her eyes so they could adjust to the darkness, but when she opened them, the blinding incandescence of parachute flares filled the sky. The barking chatter of automatic weapons added a sharp staccato to the booming detonations of hand grenades.

She almost wet her pants when a hand clamped onto her thigh.

"Help me." Lightfoot's voice barely registered above the cacophony filling the once-silent night. He still wore his night-vision goggles.

"Oh, God." She whimpered, guessing he'd been blinded by that first flare. She ripped the goggles off and tucked them inside her jacket. She discovered one of Mac's bandannas in her pocket. "Close your eyes." She bound his eyes with the cloth, praying his retinas weren't permanently damaged.

"You have to cover their back trail."

His quiet voice sounded so matter-of-fact, she almost believed she could. "I'm not a sniper," she protested.

"You don't have to hit anything. In fact, make sure you don't hit one of us."

Just like that. Simple and in a nutshell. *Don't hit one of us.* She whimpered again but shifted over to line up with the sniper rifle. The goggles gouged her abdomen. She pulled them out and fitted them into a pocket. "I can do this."

"Yes. You can."

Had she actually said that out loud? Since Lightfoot answered her, evidently she had. She took a deep breath and then another. She put her goggles back on and her hand only shook a little as she wrapped it around the grip and touched the trigger with her finger. Sighting through the scope, she searched the slope for movement. Green specters darted from one phantom tree to another. One. Two. Three. Four. The first looked misshapen, like a caricature of the Hunchback of Notre Dame. Mac. She was sure of it. He still had a man slung across his shoulders. A flicker in the corner of her vision caught her attention. More apparitions darted up the slope in the wake of the Wolves. She aimed at one well wide of the four and squeezed the trigger. The rifle bucked in her hands and bullets zipped through the trees.

"Remember your firing discipline." Lightfoot's voice carried a cutting edge. She'd probably fired off at least ten rounds—half of the ammunition in this clip. She fumbled, looking for more clips. Two magically appeared next to her hand. "Squeeze gently," he reminded.

At least her wild burst had sent the hounds to ground. She found the Wolves again and focused along their flanks and back trail. A wary head popped up. She squeezed gently. Leaves rained down and the head disappeared. Lightfoot didn't say anything but she could almost feel his smile. Moments later, her ears picked up a thin whisper. He was saying something into the radio headset he wore. A figure darted between two trees. She fired off another round and grinned madly at the grunt of pain. *Ha! Take that you miserable piece of shit.* Her elation was short-lived as four more apparitions scurried across her field of vision. She emptied her clip. Before her fingers closed on a second clip, Lightfoot's hands brushed hers out of the way. In seconds, the fresh clip slid home and he released the rifle back to her.

"Get ready. I want you to fire three short bursts at whatever you see moving. Wait thirty seconds, fire off one more quick burst to empty the clip and close your eyes. When I say go, leave the rifle and we're getting the hell out of here. Do you understand?"

She shrugged into her pack as her inner accountant cringed. "I am not leaving our packs or the rifle behind." She was adamant. She heard the rustle of whipcord and figured he was shrugging. "Ready?" She wasn't sure if she was asking him or herself. At his touch, she squeezed off the bursts and then counted, "One, one thousand. Two, one thousand." At thirty, she emptied the clip, her eyes already closed. Thunder boomed and light flared beyond her closed eyelids as the castle keep lit up like the Fourth of July. Blindly, she groped the sniper rig and managed to break it down. On her knees, she slung the M25 over her shoulder, pushed to her feet, and reached for Lightfoot's hand. "Which direction?"

"North, back toward the cave."

With as much stealth as they could muster, the two of them stumbled through the forest. She tried not to get pissed that even blinded and carrying a pack, Michael was more sure-footed. "How far to the LZ?" she panted.

He stopped and cocked his head, listening. "Not far. We need to hurry."

Off to the right, she caught the tell-tale whumpf of a mortar round firing. Instinctively, she fell forward, taking Lightfoot with her. She buried her head as the sky lit up. "Bastards." She ripped the goggles off, the forest bright enough now for her naked eyes to pick out their path. "Let's go." She struggled to her feet and pushed on.

Approximately half a mile further, even her ears could pick up the throaty grumble of the Blackhawk's engine. They were almost home free.

Even as the last flare died, another lofted skyward. Small arms fire chattered like incensed squirrels. An angry wasp whizzed past her cheek.

"Run!"

She didn't need his urging. Her legs were already pumping. They burst into a large clearing side-by-side, though Lightfoot's hand rested on her shoulder for guidance. Like a sleek and deadly bug, the helicopter squatted in the center. Another wasp buzzed by much too close for comfort.

"RUN!" Mac's voice reverberated in her chest, filling her lungs and heart with a final burst of speed as she put her head down and charged toward the chopper. She faltered when Lightfoot's hand dropped away. "Run, baby." Mac's voice whispered in her ear and she realized Danny was leading Michael as Mac ran beside her even as he stripped the rifle from her shoulder. Each breath seared her lungs and her legs turned to lead but she kept running. Without warning, she was boosted off her feet and tossed. She skidded across the metal floor of the chopper as it lifted off.

"MAC!" She screamed his name.

"Right here, baby." His arms pulled her back across the deck of the Blackhawk and held her close. "I've got you."

Her fingers clawed through the material of his jacket and fisted in his tee shirt. She clung to him, fighting to swallow the sobs lining up like cars on a freight train. Despite the fact her cheeks were slick with tears, she choked out, "I'm not crying."

Mac stripped off her backpack and shifted them both up onto the hard bench seat, leaving more room on the floor for Sean to work on the unconscious Tornjak, now secured in a Stokes rescue basket. He settled her in his lap. "Of course you aren't." He rubbed his cheek across the top of her head, his whiskers snagging in her hair. He simply held her like that for a long time, the whupwhupwhup of the rotors matching the beat of their hearts.

Eventually, almost all of them slept, vibrations from the twin engines quietly throbbing through the cabin soothing everyone's frayed nerves. Mac watched the scenery scroll by as the pilot skillfully skimmed the treetops. Thank god the Blood Moon leave was almost here. They'd transfer to a C-130 at Tuzla Air Base in Turkey and fly directly to Virginia. After a quick debrief with Captain Harjo, the unit would go their separate ways for a month of R and R. Hannah stirred in his arms. He kissed her awake, hungry for her company. When she pushed back to look up at him, his dick throbbed in time with the engines. She squirmed in his lap and he grinned wolfishly. "Have I told you lately that I love you?"

"No."

"Well, I do, darlin'."

"That's Major Darlin', to you."

CHAPTER 11

HANNAH OPENED BLEARY eyes and gazed around the bay of the C-130. The men with her were all sleeping. How the hell they could get comfortable on these godforsaken web benches was beyond her. She punched at the hard lump beneath her cheek and got a grunt in reply. Oh, yeah. Mac had padded the bench with a couple of sleeping bags for her and offered his leg as a pillow. Only his freaking thigh was hard as damn rock. Fucking alpha male.

She glanced over at the wolf stretched out on another sleeping bag. Tornjak. Their mission. He'd been brought aboard in human form strapped into a Stokes basket. Soon after takeoff, Mac had hunkered beside him, whispering to the critically injured man. Hannah didn't believe he'd live to see their destination. Then he changed. Agonizingly. Or so it seemed to her, with the popping of bones, the keening whine erupting from his throat. But afterward, she understood why. As a wolf, he had fur. His human skin had been all but flayed from his body. The fur covered him, would help keep infection out, help speed healing. He'd have scars. But he'd most likely live now.

Rolling onto her back, Hannah tried to get comfortable

with her knees bent up. The plane's engines droned, sending vibrations through her whole body. Her stomach felt concave and while it growled its hunger at her, she also knew there was no way she could eat. She'd already "visited" the facilities—a metal box with a round lid not-so-fondly referred to as the crapper. It hung on the bulkhead of the plane, out there in front of God and everyone. The damn thing had a high platform she'd had to step up on, and needed Mac's assistance—all to her embarrassment as she was choking back her latest round of nausea.

Mac shifted positions and his broad palm rested on her stomach, at once loving and possessive. After the debrief at Ft. Lyle Smith, the 69th's base of operations, she'd return to her apartment in Washington and make an appointment with her OB-GYN. Luckily, she used a private doctor instead of a military MD. What the hell was she going to do about her career? "Mixed" marriages were frowned upon only slightly less than officer and enlisted relationships. At least Mac would be off somewhere on what they called Blood Moon leave so she would have some time to think and plan.

"Forget it." Her head bounced on his thigh as he moved beneath her when she looked up at him. He was wide awake and staring at her. "I'm going with you."

"W-what? Going with me where?"

"Back to DC. And to your doctor. Then we'll figure out where we'll live.'

"Where *we'll* live? You mean, together?"

She couldn't decide if he was amused, pissed, or more likely, a combination of the two. "Yes, Hannah. Together. I'm not leaving you."

"I have a job, Mac. So do you. Mine's in DC. Yours is in Bumfuck, Virginia."

"One of us will commute."

"It doesn't work that way."

Mac clenched his teeth to choke back his next

comment. Everything that made him an alpha Wolf demanded Hannah quit. To come to him to live. Where he could take care of her. Where he could fuck her whenever they felt the urge. Where he could ensure her safety and that of their child. He instinctively knew it was the wrong thing to say to her. He had to give her time and his fucking wolf would just have to be patient.

He shifted again to ease his erection. His damn dick had a mind of it's own and right now, it wanted to be buried in his mate's cunt. Then his mouth watered. She had the sweetest pussy he'd ever tasted. She stiffened beneath him and he reined in his desire.

"How did you know what I was thinking?"

Raising his chin so she couldn't see his proprietary grin, he cleared his throat. "Remind me to play strip poker with you."

She pushed his hand away and swung her legs over the web bench so she could sit up. "What's that supposed to mean?"

"Let's just say your face is very expressive."

"Bullshit." She watched him, her eyes narrowing into a fierce glower. "You're laughing at me."

"No. Not at all." *Much.*

"What do you mean, *much?*"

Now it was his turn to be surprised. He offered a thought in his mind. *I love you.*

"Yeah, right. I don't think love has anything to do with it."

Well, crap. They really were mated, not that he'd seriously doubted it, given his reaction to Hannah. True mates shared unique abilities, though at various levels of skill. Considering the strength of their connection, he shouldn't be surprised they'd be able to communicate in what was basically complete sentences, rather than just the ideas he could share with his team when they were all in wolf form. His wolf reveled that they were so close while the human part of him worried about giving too much away.

"Look, darlin', we have a whole crap load of stuff to work through. Let's get home. Get your pregnancy confirmed since you won't take my word for it. And then we'll figure shit out."

The plane hit some rough air and Hannah grimaced, looking more than a little green. Sean had scrounged up a bucket for any further in-flight emergencies and Mac hooked it with the toe of his combat boot just in case. Eyes closed, head back, feet planted on the vibrating deck, Hannah gulped convulsively. Her hand instinctively reached for his, seeking his strength.

He smoothed his thumb over the back of her hand in slow circles and pictured doing the same to her nipples. His dick liked that idea. A lot. They couldn't get back to HQ fast enough. Ft. Lyle Smith had been named for some hero in the War of 1812 and to avoid getting it confused with the place in Arkansas, the locals fondly called it simply Ft. Lyle. As Command Sergeant Major, he had his own quarters. As soon as they debriefed with Captain Harjo and the team leaders for Charlie and Delta teams, he was taking Hannah to bed. When he was thoroughly and completely sated, and so was she, then they'd drive to DC. He had a month's leave coming and he planned on taking every second of it to spend convincing Hannah she was his and they belonged together.

Her fingers tightened convulsively on his and Mac glanced over at her face. A light sheen of sweat coated her skin. She'd pressed her head back against the bulkhead and was breathing in short, panting gulps. "Babe? What's wrong?"

She swallowed and he swore her color paled even more. The sprinkling of freckles across her nose and cheeks stood out like a bunch of crazy connect-the-dots. She swallowed again and a tiny trickle of drool escaped the corner of her mouth. Anger flashed through him. His mate was suffering and there wasn't a damn thing he could do about it. His wolf's power swelled until every man on board came awake.

Sean glanced over and immediately went digging in his medical pack while Nakai dug into his pack for MREs. The older man ripped through several packages until he found what he was looking for. Holding up a package of crackers like it was gold, he looked at the others. "We'll need more."

Lightfoot and Danny joined the treasure hunt. In a few minutes, they had six packages of crackers, a packet of Dramamine, and a bottle of cold water. Nakai approached Mac and offered up the gifts. "Some crackers first. Then a sip of water. Medicine. Sip of water. Rest of crackers if she holds them down." He patted Mac on the shoulder. "When we get home, get the girl a steak. She'll both need and want it."

The two of them exchanged a look and Mac broke eye contact first, staring at Hannah with new wonder. Was it possible she carried a Wolf? All children were a blessing but a pup that carried the Wolf gene was truly a gift granted to very few. After Nakai returned to his seat, Mac ripped the plastic around the first package of crackers.

"No."

"Hannah..."

She burped and covered her mouth with her hand. Mac desperately hoped it was the quality of the light turning her skin green.

"Honey, I promise, this will help. Eat some crackers." He held one up in front of her but she refused to open her eyes. "Open up. Please?"

Hannah grimaced but said, "Only because you said please." She left her mouth open and Mac slipped a cracker inside. She dutifully chewed and swallowed. After a long minute, she opened her mouth again and he slid another cracker in. When she'd finished the package, he offered her the bottle of water. After a few sips, she leaned her head back, eyes still closed.

Her color returned to something approximating normal and she no longer gasped for air. Mac offered her the Dramamine and more water. She opened her eyes and held out her hand, palm up, to take the pills. Mac ripped the packet with this teeth and dumped the two tablets into her hand. It looked so small next to his. He liked Hannah's hands. She had long, slender fingers but there was strength in them. She didn't wear jewelry. No rings or signs that she wore one. He liked that too. It meant his ring would be her first and only. As she lifted the pills to her mouth, he realized he could see all the veins on the back of her hand. Her skin appeared paper thin. His gaze fixed on her face. The delicate skin around her eyes looked bruised—beyond the injuries she'd sustained—and he could see the lacy tracings of the veins just beneath her skin.

His thumb and forefinger found a stray lock of her short hair and rubbed it's silky softness between them. She was such a complicated mixture of hard and soft, feminine and gruff, sexy and innocent. And he would die for her and their baby. He would do whatever it took to see her safely through the pregnancy. He would leave the Army. He would walk away from his men. His entire world had narrowed down to this woman and the child she carried. Then she threw up all over him.

CHAPTER 12

THE RECEPTIONIST CALLED Hannah's name. Mac stood with her but as they reached the door marked "Private," a nurse cut him off.

"Patients only." She pointed toward the chair where he'd been sitting. "Wait there." She ushered Hannah through and then closed the door in his face. He tried the knob. It didn't turn. He pivoted and headed to a corner of the reception area where he could see the entry door, the reception desk, and every other person there. More precisely, every other woman there. There were no men. Just him.

Some of the women ogled him openly. His wolf preened and he would have been happy for the attention a month ago. Now he couldn't care less. He had a mate and she was behind a locked door with people he didn't know and didn't trust. His *pregnant* mate. Every protective bone in his body was ready to snap.

The entry door opened and Mac snapped to attention. The male delivery driver faltered three steps into the room. Mac barely contained the growl rumbling in his chest. The guy dropped his eyes in submission, handed over the packages to the receptionist, got her signature and skedaddled back out the door. The wolf settled a little. That was one less male in the vicinity of their mate.

Ten minutes passed and Mac, pacing from one side of the room to the other, was ready to start ripping chairs apart. An older woman eyed him with sympathy and patted the chair beside her. "Sit down, young man." He started to ignore her but she patted the seat again and with an arched brow, uttered one word in an imperious command. "Sit."

Startled, he did.

"That's better. This must be your first."

He could only nod, struck mute by her demeanor.

"Not to worry. Dr. Brennan is an excellent doctor. He was there for the births of all four of mine, plus two of my grandchildren."

Her admission helped Mac settle, even if his wolf remained restless. This woman was a grandmother. That meant the doctor had to be older. Not that he was worried about any man wooing Hannah away. But men were men and the thought of another's hands—he leashed the snarl.

The woman laughed and placed her warm palm on his forearm. "At ease, son." She leaned closer to his ear and in a conspiratorial whisper, admitted, "I should think being an OB-GYN is rather like being a bartender at a strip club. After staring at pussy all day, the last thing you want is more of it up close and personal."

Mac snorted, choking back laughter instead of growls this time. A warm glow spread through his chest. In forty or fifty years, Hannah could be this woman. He enjoyed the idea of watching her mellow with age.

The door to the back opened and a nurse stood with it open, a file in her hand. "Mrs. Lyon?"

The woman patted his arm. "Help an old lady, son." She flashed him a wink.

Mac scrambled to his feet and with great care, helped Mrs. Lyon stand and offered her his arm to lean on as she shuffled to the door. The nurse stepped back and let them pass in front of her, as she pointed out the exam room.

After guiding the woman inside and helping her up on the table, Mac started to back away. Mrs. Lyon crooked her finger and he leaned toward her. She planted a kiss on his lips, her eyes twinkling with devilish lights. "You're a good boy. Now get out of here and go find your lady."

He did, slipping down the hall in search of Hannah. He found her scent coming from a room near the end of the hall and heard two voices—Hannah's and the first nurse. No doctor yet. Or had he already come and gone? Mac inhaled deeply, separating the scents. Two males but neither of them fresh in this room. Good. He was in time. He heard the nurse walking toward the door and he faded back, ducking into the empty room across the hall.

She left with a brusque, "The doctor will be in shortly."

As soon as her footsteps faded down the hall, Mac was out, across, and in. As he opened the door, Hannah glanced up, an expectant look on her face. She paled when she realized it was him. As much as he wanted to crowd her, to gather her into his arms, he didn't. He also hid his smile. Hannah wearing an exam gown covered in purple tigers and lime green elephants was a sight he wouldn't soon forget.

"I need to be here," he said, and dropped into a chair. Hannah's clothes were tossed on the chair next to it and he folded them out of habit. He'd just finished when a precise knock on the door heralded the doctor's arrival, along with the prune-faced nurse. The doctor seemed surprised to see Mac but after a scowl, he simply ignored him. The nurse glowered. Mac glowered back. Then both the medicos ignored him until Mac growled when the doctor asked Hannah to lay down and put her feet in the stirrups.

"You. Out. Now." The doctor, a man pushing almost seventy, scowled at him.

Mac wanted to argue but Hannah's expression made him reconsider. "Fine. I'll be right outside."

Mac paced the hallway outside the exam room. He

couldn't believe he'd been ordered out by the doctor and Hannah. Their mating was still fresh enough his wolf prowled just beneath the surface of his skin. His human half understood why another man was touching Hannah. His wolf damn sure wanted that shit to stop.

They'd remained a day and a night at Fort Lyle, with Hannah sleeping most of the time. She'd stayed awake long enough for the debriefing in Captain Harjo's office and then she'd collapsed. Literally. Mac had carried her to his bed and joined her, but only to hold her while she slept. He was worried sick despite reassurances from Nakai that this was normal for a Wolf pregnancy. She'd awakened the morning after, showered and dressed in her BDUs, and they'd stopped for breakfast on the way to Washington, DC. Hannah had inhaled the steak she ordered, then hate half of his. Wolf pups wanted protein.

Now they were at the clinic where Hannah's doctor worked. She'd called and gotten an emergency appointment. He passed the door and growled, prowling to the far end. An older woman stepped out of the nearest exam room and glared.

"You are scaring the other patients. Go out to the waiting room and wait."

"No." The word was little more than a snarl. He pivoted and headed back the way he'd just come. His wolf was so not a happy camper. There was a man in there. Touching their mate. Touching her intimately. Mac swore that once they were out of this place, he was never letting Hannah out of his sight. Ever. The man admitted the idea was not only imbecilic but impossible. The wolf didn't care. He liked that idea, liked it a lot.

The door cracked open and the nurse slipped out. She shivered as his glare pinned her. "I'm going in now." He didn't give her a choice, grabbing the door from her hands before she could close it. He strode in, all but thumping his chest. Hannah was sitting up on the side of the exam table, her bare feet swinging nervously. She glanced at him before dropping her eyes. His heart seized.

"What's wrong?" He sounded gruffer than he'd meant to but he'd gone numb and he felt lucky his voice worked at all.

The doctor shook his head. "Nothing at all. Mother and baby are doing fine, though she's a little anemic." He patted Hannah's shoulder and Mac bit back the urge to gnaw the man's hand off. "The receptionist will have your prescriptions ready when you check out. Get dressed and I'll see you next month." He stepped away and disappeared through the door.

Hannah scrambled off the exam table and scurried into a corner. Her clothes were folded neatly on a chair. She grabbed her shirt and held it up on front of her. "Get away from me!" Her voice rose in pitch and the whites were showing around her eyes.

His wolf liked this game. He stalked her. She kept her shirt in front of her exam gown and backed away until she hit the exam table. She scrambled over it and he got a glimpse of her thighs and ass. He and the wolf both appreciated the view. "You can't run away screaming like a little girl."

"The hell I can't." Hannah gulped, and then realized he'd boxed her in. She had no place to go.

Mac gentled his voice and before she could react, he snagged her hand, clasping it in his massive paw. The difference in size and texture always blew him away. He tugged gently, drawing her closer. "I love you."

She swallowed. Hard. His gaze fastened on her throat before lifting to her eyes. "I'm not going anywhere, babe. We're in this together."

Hannah radiated stubbornness from the lift of her chin to her glinting eyes. "How can you be so calm?" She swiped the tears on her cheeks. "How can you just...accept this? Accept us? And how can you love me? We...we don't even know each other."

"I can because I've waited all my life for you, for this

moment." A proud smirk crinkled his cheeks. "I'm gonna be a dad."

Her face molded into a panicked mask and she started to hyperventilate.

"We can do this, darlin'." He folded her into his embrace and held her with utmost care. "Just breathe, Hannah."

"Do I have a choice?"

"Nope."

She sighed against his chest. "Well, okay then."

🐾🐾🐾🐾

HANNAH PUSHED BACK from the comforting wall of muscles surrounding her. "So this is it. It's all real."

Mac nodded but didn't step back to give her air. He still hadn't quite recovered from their ordeal at the doctor's office. The wolf needed reassurance and Hannah's touch was the only thing that worked. The man needed her close just as much. She'd ridden home in silence—an uncomfortable void stretching between them. He wanted to give her room to adjust but he was needy enough at the moment to have trouble giving it to her.

As soon as they walked into her apartment, he'd pulled her into his arms and just held her. That had been ten minutes ago. She hadn't moved until now.

Raising her chin so she could see his face, she studied him as if she could find some clue to the Universe in his expression. He wished he knew what she saw.

"I mean...we're like joined at the fucking hip or something now? You don't need to sugar coat it. I want the truth."

"The truth? That's simple. You're my mate, Hannah. You wouldn't be carrying my child otherwise. We aren't joined at the hip as you so graphically put it. But I won't ever be far away."

"That's a lie. If you get deployed—"

"Yeah, about that."

"Look, life is complicated enough with me being an

officer and you a non-com." She pushed against his chest and with reluctance, he loosened his arms and let her step away. She dropped her shoulder bag on a table near the door, along with her keys. And simply stood there, her shoulders hunched. He could smell the sharp ammonia scent of defeat wafting from her.

"Hannah? Look at me, babe." He kept his voice soft, crooning, as if he was approaching a wounded animal. In a way, that's just what Hannah had become. Not only wounded, but cornered too. None of this was her fault, beyond being born the one woman he was meant to spend his life with, to love and cherish with every breath he took.

He closed the distance between them, touched her shoulder to ease her around. Mac watched as panic devolved into resignation. He bit back anger and despair both. Hannah was his mate. And she was having his baby. Whether she liked it or not. And she needed to understand that he came with the package deal. Something flickered behind the hard glint of her eyes. Was that hope? Or was he just a sap for thinking so?

CHAPTER 13

"JUST LEAVE ME the hell alone." Hannah ripped the strap of her messenger bag over her head and tossed the thing onto the table.

Mac watched her, his expression wary. She'd been fine two hours ago when he last spoke to her at her office. Something had happened between then and now. Granted, it could just be pregnancy mood swings but he got the feeling it was something deeper. "Babe?"

"Why are you here? Don't you have someplace to be? Have someplace to go? Besides here?"

"Ah..." He continued watching her, keeping his hands shoved in his pockets despite the deep-seated need to go to her and pull her into his arms.

She stomped into the kitchen, opened the refrigerator, stared at the contents. Her shoulders were so stiff she looked starched and pressed. Mac leaned his hip against the breakfast bar, arms folded across his chest, and remained silent. He was beginning to know her, to understand her moods. Someone had put a bug up her ass.

Hannah closed the fridge, turned to the pantry and opened it. Again she stared at the jars and boxes stacked inside. Mac wanted to feed her. Which was a weird reaction but the need was almost visceral. Her lips were pinched and her eyes bruised. She didn't sleep, not the way she should. She'd sleep for an hour or two—or pretend—and as soon as she thought he'd dropped off she'd get up and wander through the apartment. Her apartment. He'd thought being surrounded by the familiar would help the situation. It didn't. He had enough time in he could separate from the service with a minimum amount of fuss. Problem was, what the hell would he do?

Money wasn't a problem. He banked everything, made investments. He'd never mentioned his net worth to her. All the Wolves were pretty much set for life. He *liked* army life. He was alpha enough to want the command of his team, to enjoy the structure of their life. Fuck, he was the unit's Alpha. No one disputed that. Captain Harjo might run the admin side, but Harjo was human. Among the Wolves, even those on the other teams, Mac held the ultimate power.

"Stop. Just...fucking stop." Hannah's words whipped out, caught him by surprise.

"Stop what, babe?"

She threw her arms up and growled out sounds of frustration. "Stop being. Being you. Standing there staring at me. All smug and shit."

Okay, there had to be some hormones mixed in there somewhere and that was a whole 'nother mine field. "Not feeling particularly smug at the moment. What's up, Hannah?"

"Stuff. Just stuff, okay?"

"No. Not okay. What kind of stuff?"

She slammed the pantry door and marched toward the hall leading to their bedroom. If she got inside and locked the door on him, he'd be pissed and would take the door apart to get to her. Mac caught up in three strides and gently circled one of her biceps with his fingers. "Hannah?"

Jerking against his grip, she finally gave up and leaned against the wall, head back so her face was angled toward the ceiling. Hannah closed her eyes and breathed deeply. "Go away, Mac. I can't deal with you right now."

"Not happenin', babe."

"Gawdammit. Will you just leave me the fuck alone? Get out. I don't want you here. I don't want you touching me. I don't want you breathing my air." Her muscles tensed as she brought her fisted hands up like a prize fighter. She took a swipe at him, one he easily ducked.

"Don't you get it?" She was all but screaming at him. "I don't love you. I don't want you in my life. And I don't want this damned baby!"

Anger surged through him, as cold as liquid nitrogen and just as deadly. Buried deep inside, his intellect battered at the fury. *Breathe*, he reminded himself. He'd marked her skin once before in a rage, forgetting how delicate her skin was, how fragile she was beneath the tough exterior. His fingers locked around her arm but didn't squeeze.

"You want to tell me who the hell put this bug up your ass?" He gritted the words out and something in his expression finally registered with her. For a heart-shattering moment, fear flashed in her eyes and nausea roiled in his gut. He dropped his hand, backed away, shoved his fists into his pockets. "Gawddammit, Hannah. Do you really believe I'd fucking hurt you? You're carrying my pup. I'd cut off my hand before I hurt you."

"And that's the gawddamnmutherfuckin' bottom line for you, isn't it? The baby. You don't give a flying Philadelphia fuck about me. I'm just a baby machine for you."

The vehemence of her words and the wounded look on her face mauled his heart. He was missing something, something important. Dammit, he didn't do feelings. He was an alpha wolf and his old man had been a complete and total sonavabitch with a big ol' helping of asshole heaped on top. Until Hannah, women had been for screwing. Yeah, he made sure they left with a smile on their face but Hannah...she was his fucking life. And she didn't know that. Which was the problem. His intellect kicked that flickering light bulb into life.

Mac had to inhale more than a few deep breaths to settle his wolf. The damned animal was riled up—panicked over Hannah's threat, the need to protect and soothe its mate, and the man's inability to fix things. He let his anger simmer for another few minutes then forced it to cool. Once it was gone, he was swamped by Hannah's feelings—fear, exhaustion, and something he didn't recognize, some emotion he couldn't put a name to.

Hannah pushed her hair off her forehead and closed her eyes. "Please, Mac. Just...go away for awhile. You're...you...sometimes I can't breathe. You're so...big. You fill up all the space. Take all the air."

It took every ounce of strength in him to walk away from her, to do as she asked when everything down to his very core wanted to wrap her up and hold her. "Okay."

She didn't open her eyes at his growl. If she looked at him, she'd fall apart, start blubbering, and let him walk all over her. She'd lost control of her life the moment she insisted she accompany the Wolves on that damned mission.

Things were happening. Rumors at the Pentagon. Bad shit was coming and she needed to—hell she *had* to stop it before it rolled right over Mac and the others. She was tired all the time, couldn't eat unless it was freaking rare meat. She was teetering on the edge and there were sharpened stakes on both sides if she fell.

Hannah felt Mac's withdrawal, actually physically felt when he left. Just one more bar on her cage. But she could breathe. Almost. Why couldn't he understand? No one had ever loved her and what he claimed to be love was more like obsession—a smothering blanket of crazy desire, jealousy, and dammit, she was not the heroine in some twisted movie of the week. Was she?

Werewolves were real. Okay, technically not werewolves. Wolf shifters. With DNA that wasn't strictly human. And Navy SEALs with gills. This wasn't a movie of the week, this was a B movie version of "Aliens."

Mating for life? How could she trust that? And not hurting her? She rubbed absently at the spot on her arm that still throbbed from his grip. Violence lived in that alien DNA of Mac's and now it lived in her baby's. She'd never had a lover, never believed there'd ever be a man willing to hitch his life to hers. That happened to other women. Not her. She was all about the brains. Hell, she didn't even have friends. Acquaintances, but not friends. There was no one she could call up, suggest beer and pizza and let's dis men. Her stomach revolted at the thought of both beer *and* pizza.

Giving up, she padded into her bedroom, stripped, and climbed into the shower. Water as hot as she could stand it poured down on her head and shoulders, sluicing down her body. She looked down. She'd never been model thin but she'd always had a flat stomach and now there was a pooch. A pregnancy pooch. Her hand curved over it protectively.

"Fuck. I'm having a baby."

She turned off the water and shivered in the sudden loss of heat. She wrapped up in a bath sheet while avoiding the mirror. Since the damn thing took up most of one wall, that was a feat but she knew she looked like shit. She didn't need her reflection to remind her. What the hell did a man like Ian McIntire see in her anyway? He was freaking gorgeous, all chest-thumping alpha male, muscles, and a face carved from granite. She *knew* when he was near. Felt it in her bones, and her first glimpse of him weakened her knees while her breath caught in her chest.

She wanted him. Wanted him with every atom of her being. But she didn't trust him. Didn't trust the insta-lust-love-bullshit feelings between them. At the same time, how could a man like Mac want a baby? And the baby mama that came with the package? Therein lay her problem.

A dull ache formed high on the left side of her chest, right behind her heart. How could she feel his absence so viscerally? "Screw this."

Pulling on ratty sweatpants and a long-sleeved teeshirt that had seen more than its fair share of washings, Hannah stared at the bed she'd shared with Mac for the past month. Something twisted inside and she couldn't force herself to climb into it to sleep. She wasn't missing him—much. And it was her damned bed. But he'd taken it over, like he'd taken over her life. The fuckin' sheets smelled of him, of them. She wasn't a Wolf but his musk was so strong, it filled her nose.

Tired. She was so fucking tired of everything. She just wanted to sleep. Five hours. Five hours wasn't asking too much, was it? Hell, she'd settle for three, so long as those three were uninterrupted, straight-through real sleep. With robotic motions, she turned away from the bed that was no longer hers and stumbled into the guest room.

🐾🐾🐾🐾

MAC WATCHED HER sleep, fingers curling against his palm to keep from touching Hannah's hair. That tousled cap of wispy blond would feel like silk sliding through his hands. Shadows haunted the tender skin beneath her eyes, deeper than the dark sweep of her lashes. The pregnancy was taking its toll on her. Her legs kicked in restless motion as she tossed from her side to her back. She wasn't truly showing yet, this early in the pregnancy, but he could sense the slightly rounded fullness of her stomach despite the obscurity provided by the layers of blankets and down comforter.

He wanted to wake her, to gather her into his arms, kissing and showering her with words of love. That wasn't his way. He was a soldier. A hard man living an even harder life. But she made him want to be soft, to be tender. For her. For their baby. His son. And wasn't that a swift kick in the ass. He didn't have much time—his orders for a new mission that superseded his leave had just come in—and due to their earlier argument, she'd sought solitude in the guest room. She was so angry she wouldn't even sleep in their bed—with or without him.

Well fuck that. She was his mate. He had need of her, and whether she believed it or not, she needed him. He stripped down to his boxers—the only concession he'd give her—and then slipped into bed next to her, spooning to her side, his hand resting possessively on her tummy.

Her thick lashes fluttered, deepening the bruised coloring beneath them. She rolled away from him and muttered, "Fuck off, Mac."

"No."

"Why are you here?"

"I sleep much better this way." And so would she, if she'd only admit it. "I love you, Hannah. Go back to sleep."

And she did, with him pressed against her back, holding close the two most precious things in his life. This woman had become his everything. She was the first thing he thought of in the morning and the last memory in his head as he slid into the light combat sleep that passed for his rest period.

He had no idea mating could be this powerful, this all-consuming. What he shared with Hannah? It was so opposite from what his mother and father had. Nakai knew, had tried to tell him. Nakai and Tala had been together for what seemed like a couple of lifetimes. The old Navajo was in his nineties, though he looked fifty and remained on active duty with the 69th. Wolves could live to ripe old ages, though they seldom did. They were a reckless breed, born to fuck and fight, according to the old bastard who sired him.

Yeah, Mac had been totally unprepared for the slap in the face Hannah Jackson gave him. He'd almost lost her and the hot blood in his veins still turned to ice water at the memory of her being held prisoner by those Bosnian terrorists. He'd fought the attraction, kicking and screaming each step of the way. Until he realized she was fertile, that she was his, that he'd never leave her.

She stirred in his arms, still restless and he wondered if his thoughts were spilling over. They did sometimes, just as he picked up hers when their emotions ran high. Between that melding of minds and the overwhelming need for her—to fuck her, keep her safe from the gawdamned world, to love her—he was well and truly screwed. Mated. True mates. Moonstruck. It didn't happen often but when it did? Oh yeah. It was like getting hit by a Mack truck.

Mac wanted Hannah to trust him, to trust what was between them. The angry words they'd hurled at each other echoed in his memory. She still believed he was only here because of biology. Hormones. True, that had led him to her, but it didn't keep him craving her touch, or explain the all-consuming need to be with her. That was all her fault. She was the most messed up, stubborn, idiotic, frustrating... She whimpered in her sleep and he slammed those thoughts down.

Nosing the spot right behind her ear, he followed up with a light feathering of his lips there. "Don't you see, baby? Don't you understand that you are my everything?"

CHAPTER 14

THE SOUNDS OF people wrapping up their work day whispered beyond the half-open door of Hannah's office. Four days. Mac and the team had been gone four days. She couldn't sleep. Could barely eat. Her skin felt stretched tight over her bones, and itchy.

No one in her chain of command had tripped to the fact that Mac had forced himself into her life, that she was pregnant with his child. How the fuck did she get into these things? Despite being pissed as hell at him, the last good night's sleep she'd had was after their fight. When he'd crawled into bed and just held her. What was it about the damn man that put her dander up? If she wasn't wanting to jump his bones, she was wanting to beat him bloody.

And the absofucking cherry on top of her sundae? She couldn't even drink coffee. The alien monster in her belly rebelled if she even thought of swallowing a drop of life-sustaining caffeine. A wave of nausea rolled through her and she gagged.

A sharp rap on her door straightened her to attention and smoothed her expression into poker ready. "Colonel Bradshaw? Come in, sir."

Her mentor, who was only a year or two away from his

first star, pushed the door open and stepped across the threshold. His brows scrunched together as he raked her with his gaze. "Damn, Major. What the hell's wrong with you?"

Her heart tripped in her chest but she kept her expression unruffled. "Sir?"

"You look like shit."

Great. She'd never been one for wearing makeup and she'd obviously botched the job of hiding her sleepless nights. "A touch of flu, sir. I'm fine."

"You don't look fine to me. Take some sick leave. Lord knows you have plenty stored up. Contrary to your belief, this office is capable of running smoothly when you aren't here. Go home. Get well." He glanced at the diver's watch on his wrist. "I don't want to see you until Monday morning. And that's an order."

Panic surged and she bit her tongue to keep from blurting out the words on its tip. Four more days. Alone. Staring at the walls of her apartment. Her empty apartment. At least coming to the office offered the sound and clutter of normality.

"Major?"

"Yes, sir. Understood, sir." The words tasted like sour milk in her mouth. She shoved up out of her chair and began shuffling the papers on her desk back into their files. "I'm headed out as soon as I shut down here, sir."

"No dawdling, Major."

She nodded, not trusting her voice. Her throat ached from swallowing the urge to cry but she managed to choke out, "Roger that, sir. No dawdling."

He pivoted and left and it wasn't until Hannah was on the platform waiting for the Metro that she wondered why he'd come to her office. She shifted the messenger bag to the opposite shoulder. She'd dragged all those files home. If she didn't work, she'd go even crazier than she already was.

Hair prickled on the back of her neck and she fought

the urge to turn around. Someone watched her. As people gathered around her, Hannah shifted to her left and backwards until she had a pillar to lean against. Checking out the people around her and those standing further back in the station, she homed in on a man about thirty. Fit. Dressed in a black turtleneck and wearing a dark navy pea coat and a knit watch cap pulled low on his forehead.

The train rumbled into the station and passengers surged forward. Hannah let them pull her along. Watching the man from the corner of her eye, she waited until he stepped on the next car before she ducked behind a large woman. Staying low, she braced against the flow, working backwards to the pillar, where she slipped behind it. The train pulled away and Hannah joined the flow of passengers exiting the station. She'd take a cab home, even if it cost an arm and a leg.

Torn between real worry and the idea she might just be paranoid, Hannah had the cab drive past her apartment building twice, from different directions. She couldn't tell if anyone was watching her or not. She'd purposely rented in the heart of DC, thriving on the noise and crowds but the things she loved about urban living now worked against her. She paid and dashed through the front door. Unwilling to deal with the elevator, she hiked up three floors, slipped into her apartment, locked and dead-bolted the door behind her. Leaning back against the solid metal door, Hannah drew in deep sucks of air.

She'd just gotten her nerves under control when her Blackberry phone chirped and she almost screamed. Her hand was shaking as she withdrew it from her bag. She answered it with a breathy, "Hello?"

"Hey, babe—"

"Mac? Mac!" Her tears could no longer be contained and she was sobbing his name.

"Hannah? Baby, what's wrong? Is everything all right? Hannah?" Mac's gut clenched and he had to force air into his lungs so he could talk. Something was wrong—really wrong. "Honey, is it the baby?" He caught her shuddering breath and his heart broke, fearing the worst.

"Oh." Her voice sounded small. "Yeah. The baby. Always about it. It's fine. What do you want?"

Fuck. He rubbed his palm over the bristly hair on his head. What had he done now to screw up? "What's wrong, Hannah?"

"Nothing."

"You're lying." His muscles locked up. Had she done something stupid? Had she terminated the pregnancy as she'd so often threatened? "I'll be there late tonight. We'll talk."

"Stay away from me, Sergeant Major."

Dead air echoed through the speaker as he stared at the satellite phone in his hand. Fury flared, sending heat winging through his bloodstream. He felt the eyes of his entire team focused on him and he raised his head to glare.

"You fucked up." Sean's cocky grin begged to be wiped off at the point of Mac's fist.

"He's right, Mac." Lightfoot met Mac's gaze squarely. "You need to listen to him."

"Fine, Donaldson. Enlighten me."

"What's Hannah's biggest fear?"

Mac opened his mouth, started to say "Losing the baby" then clamped his jaw shut. That was *his* biggest fear. What was Hannah's? He didn't have a clue and that pissed him off. The woman was his mate. He should know what frightened her, what she felt, why she felt that way. "Okay, smart ass. You tell me."

"That you don't care about her. That all you care about is your son."

"That's a fuckin' lie. Of course, I care about her. She's my fucking mate, dammit."

Nakai stared at him, expression stoic though slightly condescending.

"What?" Mac glared at the older man, then at each of us teammates.

"Ah...Mac?" Sean took his life in his hands. "Thirty-year-old virgin. The woman has issues."

Mac scrubbed his temples with the heels of his palms. "What the hell are you saying, Sean?"

"Commitment issues. Self-confidence issues. Look, dude. The woman is a brainiac, right? That's what she's known for. Boys don't make passes at girls who wear glasses. Yeah, she comes across all tough and shit but that girl is a marshmallow inside and at the moment, she's holding onto her life by her fingernails. You take her virginity in a cave, impregnate her, move into her life thumping your chest, and it's all about the baby." Sean held up his hand when Mac started to interrupt. "Yeah, yeah. We're Wolves. That's what we do. But she's not. Mac, she thinks the only reason you want her is because she's pregnant."

"That's not true."

"Isn't it?"

Sean didn't move fast enough. Mac was on him in half a heartbeat, taking Sean to the ground. Mac's hands fisted but rather than throwing a punch, he wrapped his fingers around the other man's throat with every intention of strangling him. When Sean remained relaxed and submissive, Mac loosened his grip but didn't get off.

"I tell her I love her."

"Shit, dude. Words are easy. Guys say that crap all the time to get what they want. Have you ever asked Hannah what she wants? Think about it. She doesn't know anything about us, about our society. You're Alpha. You roll in and take over because that's who you are. Yes, the baby is important, but so is she."

Mac sat back on his heels and Sean pushed up to sit, arms draped over his bent knees. "My point is, you need to romance her. You need to treat her like a woman not a baby incubator."

Nakai placed a hand on Mac's shoulder. "The child will thrive or not. Losing a pup hurts our hearts, Wolf. Tala and I have three daughters. They are healthy. They are stars to light my night. But there were others. Two more daughters. And two sons. One was a Wolf. Each loss left a hole in our hearts and our tears were enough to fill a river. But Tala is my mate. She is the best of me. We fit, like two pieces of a broken pot. Do you understand?"

Considering the old Wolf's words, Mac closed his eyes and searched deep inside. He'd mishandled Hannah from the beginning. As Sean pointed out, she relied on logic, numbers, routine. While he was overjoyed at the pregnancy, she was terrified. Terrified on levels he was just now beginning to comprehend.

Terror was a good word for the waves of emotion he'd heard in her voice. He stiffened and sat straighter, the sense of wrongness washing over him again. Behind the hurt, which he now recognized, there was real fear. Something had scared her, something that had nothing to do with their child. And he was hours away from her.

🐾🐾🐾🐾

MAC PARKED HIS crew-cab pickup two blocks away from Hannah's apartment. He glanced at Sean and Lightfoot, read their expressions. They felt it too. Something hunted in the dark. Sean was already stripping. Moments later, the door opened and a golden-brindle wolf leaped to the sidewalk and padded off. Lightfoot followed, a long, slim padded bag strung over his shoulder.

"Give me ten minutes to get to the roof." The Indian sniper faded into the shadows and was gone. He would provide high cover.

He had to stay inside the truck. Mac knew this. Sean needed time to scout, Lightfoot time to get into position. That didn't make his wolf happy. Mac and his animal both wanted to rush to Hannah's apartment. To touch her. Smell her. See for themselves she was safe and unhurt. At seven minutes, he exited and locked the truck. He, too, faded into the dark. Three minutes later, he was close enough to hear the conversation of the two men parked across the street from Hannah's building.

"I'm starved."

"We can't leave until the next shift gets here."

"Man, the bitch isn't going anywhere. This is stupid. She doesn't know anything."

"Yeah? Then why did she give Johansen the slip?"

The man chuckled. "My old granny could give Johansen the slip. He was probably too busy trying to pick up some skirt to see the bitch get off the train at her stop. Doesn't matter. We know she's up there now, all locked in for the night. And for the next four days. She was ordered to stay out of the office until Monday."

"Will that give our guy enough time?"

"Above my pay grade, man."

What the fuck? The insinuations baffled Mac. What was Hannah involved in? Why had she been ordered home? And who gave that order? Who were these guys? He glanced up, picked out Lightfoot's silhouette on the roof above the car—a brief glimpse just to show him where the sniper had set up his nest. A moment later, Sean trotted down the sidewalk, stopping to sniff along the way. He paused at the front wheel of the car, lifted his leg, and marked the tire.

"Fuck!" The passenger opened the door and yelled. "Get the hell away from here, you stupid dog!"

Sean growled but ducked back like a startled—and submissive—dog. He darted across the street and blended back into the landscaping around the building's door. A few minutes later, a couple arrived and Sean followed them in. Mac wanted to stay and listen to the men but his wolf was frantic to get to Hannah. He spent another few minutes circling around and approaching the building from the back. He discerned no threat from that direction and within a few breaths, he'd picked the lock on the back service door and was headed up the stairs to Hannah's floor. Sean was waiting for him.

She's there. Alone.

Mac allowed air to fill his lungs for the first time in hours and his muscles unlocked. He pressed the doorbell and listened for movement inside. When none came, he started work on the locks.

Call.

Distracted, he stared into Sean's eyes. That made sense. He pulled out his cell phone and keyed in Hannah's number. He heard the landline ring inside, then the answering machine pick up. "Hannah, answer." When she didn't, he dialed her cell phone. Then he texted her, though his fingers fumbled over the keys as his anxiety mounted.

He was about to kick in the door when his phone rang. "Hannah?"

"What do you want?" Her voice quivered.

"I'm outside the door. Let me in."

"Go away."

"Hannah? Baby? Please. Let me in." He sucked in a breath to settle both himself and his wolf. "I'm about five seconds away from kicking in the door. I don't want to do that, but baby? Somethings wrong. Why are two guys watching your place?"

Her gasp shredded his last thread of self-control. If Sean hadn't darted in front of him, he would have kicked the door. Instead, he caught the sound of locks and deadbolts turning. As soon as she opened the door, he swept Hannah into his arms.

"God, baby. Are you okay? Please tell me you aren't hurt. If anything happened to you... Fuck. I don't know what I'd do." His hands stroked and soothed and touched her everywhere as he made sure she was fine.

When he could breathe normally, he gestured Sean into the apartment and kicked the door shut. Mac cupped Hannah's cheeks in his palms and gazed down at her.

"You may not believe me, darlin', but trust me. If anything ever happens to you, I'll hunt down every sonvabitch that ever hurt you and rip out their throats."

As relief washed through him, his muscles unlocked more and he started to tremble from the adrenaline drain. Unable to help himself, he swung Hannah into his arms and sank onto the couch with her cradled in his lap. "Okay, baby. Tell me. What's going on?"

Words spilled out of her. The orders from Colonel Bradshaw. The files she'd brought home. The tail at the metro station. She hadn't known about the shadows across the street. With little argument, she packed a bag and within fifteen minutes of their arrival, Hannah followed Mac and Sean, still in wolf form, down the stairs and out the back way. Fifteen minutes after that, they were headed away from DC, toward Ft. Lyle. Three teams of Wolves would damn sure keep her safe. Or they'd die trying.

CHAPTER 15

IF IT HADN'T been for her doctor's appointment, Mac would have kept her in the wilds of freaking Virgina. Hannah had all but convinced herself she was imagining threats behind every bush, despite evidence to the contrary. Thing was, once she got back to DC, things seemed to have smoothed out. No tails. No shadows. No hair raising on the back of her neck.

Maybe life would start to bear some resemblance to normal. The last time she'd felt in control was the moment she'd nailed First Sergeant Carter in the ass during her trial parachute jump. How did she get into these situations? The paper under her bare butt crinkled as she shifted positions. Thank God Mac had dropped her off. He'd mentioned some stuff he had to do at the Pentagon and that one of the Wolves would be waiting for her if he didn't get back by the time her appointment was over. Not having him there to growl at the doctor would help the exam go faster, but she had to admit she was getting used to his presence.

The guy was sexy as hell, if a girl went for that whole chest-thumping alpha male deal. Sadly, she was turning into one of those women. The man had ways of worming through her defenses. He brought her coffee. In bed. Made just the way she liked it. And with him there, she could drink it. Go figure. He remembered her favorite foods, watched her favorite TV shows even if he hated them—just so he could sit next to her and cuddle. Hell, he'd even held her hair more than once during morning sickness. The man was insidious. And she missed him when he wasn't there. Still, her heart remained frosty in that block of ice she'd erected around it. She had no choice. She was falling for the big jerk and she didn't trust him with her emotions as far as she could throw him—which was all of about two feet. Maybe. On a good day.

A light tap on the door signaled the arrival of doctor and his nurse. Hannah could put away her dark thoughts for the moment. She had this other thing to worry about and wasn't about to admit to the doctor she referred to the alien in her belly as Ripley. She'd already been weighed and measured. Now she got poked and prodded and lectured.

"You've lost weight," the doctor complained.

"That's a bad thing?"

"When you're pregnant, yes. Eat more."

"Uhm...morning sickness."

He grabbed a pad and scribbled out a prescription. "Take this. It will help with the nausea. If you crave something, eat it. Unless it's dirt. Or paint." He shoved the slip at her. "See me next month."

Hannah had just slipped on her boots when the door opened again. She wasn't expecting to see Mac and the grim expression on his face had her straightening.

"We have a situation." He pulled a sheaf of papers from a pocket of his combat pants.

All officer now, Hannah skimmed the info. "Oh. Fuckityfuckfuckfuckity. Shitandpissitalltohell. I have to get back to the office. Figure out what's going on."

"Captain Harjo is already working on it."

Her knees suddenly weak, Hannah sagged, only to be caught up in Mac's arms. He reluctantly deposited her back on the exam table.

"I don't know what's up but I will get to the bottom of things. I'll make sure you and the others are safe."

"In case you haven't noticed, babe, we can take care of ourselves. And those who belong to us." He cupped her cheek. "And you belong to me, Hannah."

A bit of the ice around her heart melted. "Do I? Belong to you?"

"Yeah. You belong with me, too, darlin'."

More ice cracked. If she wasn't careful, it would turn into the freaking spring thaw. She studied him, her gaze tracking over every inch of his face. He'd buzz cut his hair so it was just a dark shadow against his scalp. The slight dent in his strong chin was obscured by the dark scruff covering the lower half of his face. His was the face of a warrior, sculpted from granite with wide, deep-set eyes, an aquiline nose and a full mouth. She fixated on that mouth, remembering how it felt assaulting hers, his quick, clever tongue. The parallel lines between his brows knitted as he tried to figure out what she was thinking. He wasn't beautiful. He wasn't even handsome though he turned female heads from the sheer...force of his presence. He was good-looking, yes, in a rugged way. She thought *warrior* again.

He'd surprised her. Every fucking step of the way. She expected him to cut and run. He stuck like glue. She ran. He chased. She put up barriers. He tore them down. He was relentless. Implacable. Steady. She saw single-mindedness in his expression. And honor. Duty. And when she got lost in the honeyed warmth of his brown eyes, she saw love. For their baby, yes, but for her. Her. For the very first time, she recognized her importance and all his words played back.

"Hannah? Babe? What is it?"

She circled his wrist with her fingers. "You." She leaned toward him, brushed her lips across his. His soft exhalation teased her skin and she leaned her forehead against his. "Let's go fix this mess, soldier."

She understood now. Mac got her. Life wouldn't be easy, but they'd get through it. Or kill each other trying.

🐾🐾🐾🐾

HANNAH SHOVED FINGERS through her messy hair. A month. She'd been searching for answers for a fucking month and had nothing to show for it. Of course, she was combing through files all by herself. She didn't know who she could trust. She'd spoken to the Secretary of the Army, quietly, in the garden of his home where she'd been invited to afternoon tea by his wife. Who wanted to throw her a baby shower. She trusted him. And she trusted the system. She had to. The Wolves had been safe for...two hundred damn years. Their secret held close by a handful of military officers and the commander in chief.

She felt like a hamster on a damn wheel and she was fucking tired of the squeaking. Her door swung open and the "What the fuck" on the tip of her tongue died as she recognized the intruder.

"Don't you know how to knock?"

"I don't have to knock to come in here."

"Oh? Really? And what would you have done if the Secretary had been sitting here."

"He wasn't."

"But you didn't know that."

"You just don't get it, do you? I *always* know when a man is near you. Besides, the Secretary wouldn't come to you. You'd be in his office." He smirked a little, which only served to piss her off more."

"Get out, Mac. I have work to do."

"So do I."

He stalked around the desk and Hannah gulped. "I don't have time for cat and mouse games."

"I'm not a cat." The wolfish grin stretching his lips was proof of that.

"Dammit, Sergeant Major McIntire, get the fuck out of my office."

"Pulling rank doesn't work, Major Darlin'. You should know that by now."

She thumped his chest as he pinned her against the back of her desk chair. He didn't bother saying "ow." They both knew she couldn't hurt him with her fists. She'd tried—often—just to make a point. He always backed off, only to return with an icepack for her injured hand and a kiss for her bruised ego.

"You need to rest."

"I can't."

"An hour or two isn't going to make a difference."

"It might. I'm still tracking leaks, Mac. And getting transfers set up for all the support personnel. I've got work to do."

"Not at the expense of our child. These months are crucial, Hannah."

Mac gentled his voice and his manner. Hannah had adapted to her strange new life with better graces than he would have, if the combat boot had been on the other foot. His mate was a stubborn, infuriating woman. And he loved her.

🐾🐾🐾🐾

HANNAH READ THE information in the file for what was probably the tenth time. None of it made sense. She'd acted on instinct, getting the sailors undergoing the experiments in Nevada out, their location deeply buried. And now the Wolves were in the crosshairs, evidently targeted for what they were. She didn't know what to do, who to talk to, wasn't positive if the information she had was correct. That *if* was a big one. She'd been combing records for five months now and frustration bubbled just beneath the surface of her calm. Whenever she thought she had a thread to tug, the damn thing would break. Or disappear. Numbers. She had to follow the numbers and those slimy little bastards were worse than a pond full of just-hatched tadpoles. There were thousands of them all swimming in different directions.

The hairs on her arms prickled and she glanced up. Mac lounged in the doorway of her office, brawny shoulder braced against the jamb.

"What are you doing here?" She didn't mean to sound bitchy but her emotions shifted over into that territory when he flashed that superior I-know-everything look she hated.

"You need to eat."

Glancing at her watch, she blinked in surprise. Almost two. Where had the morning gone? She was supposed to eat something every couple of hours. She hadn't since six that morning when she'd inhaled a protein drink on her way out the door. Life was less complicated when Mac was back at Ft. Lyle. In self-defense, she snarled, "I'm fine."

"Don't be stubborn, babe."

"I don't have time for this."

"Then make it."

"Command Sergeant Major—"

"Don't pull rank, Major. It just pisses both of us off." He pushed off the wall, his gaze lasering in on her expression. He read her, his nostrils flaring at her scent—the ammonia stench of fear overlaid with the dusty odor of her exhaustion. "Hannah? What's wrong?"

She pushed fingers through her short cap of blond hair as she looked away. "Nothing."

He checked where the people outside her office were located. Several milled around though most were at their desks. Mac closed the door but didn't go to her. He wanted to. Wanted to take her in his arms, but he remained where he stood, feet planted shoulder-width apart, leaning against the door. "You're worried. What is it?"

Scrubbing at her forehead with the heels of her hands, she continue to avoid looking directly at him. "Someone is hunting the Wolves." She hesitated a long moment before dropping her hands on her desk and glaring up at him. "There's a leak."

"How do you figure?" Mac's expression didn't change though his heart tripped double time.

"You thought the same on that last mission to Bosnia. And..." She shoved the file toward him. "Here." She waited while he read, doing her best not to fidget, despite the fingers of her left hand drumming on her thigh under the desk.

His stony gaze met hers. "There's someone inside. Well placed."

"Yeah. You, the teams. I have to get all of you out of their reach."

"You as well."

"No. I need to work this. Find out who's behind it all."

The color of Mac's eyes morphed to frozen coffee and feral red glinted in their depths. "Have you considered the fact that you're a target too?"

Her head tilted to the left as she lifted that shoulder in a negligent shrug. "I'm smarter."

"No."

"No, I'm not smarter?"

He growled his frustration at her flippant question. "No, I won't let you endanger your life, or the baby's."

"If I don't figure out what's going on and who's targeting Wolves, the baby will never be safe."

She was right, and he fucking hated it. If he had hair, he would have been yanking it out by the handful. So far, only Captain Harjo and the Whiskey teams knew Hannah was carrying *his* child. She was showing now, had put in for maternity leave beginning with her eighth month. Her superiors had adopted a don't ask-don't tell attitude. She had six months accumulated and he'd been working to convince her to take all of it. He was getting ready to insist—but he had to wait. He'd come to tell her he had a mission. Short term. The team would be gone no more than a week. But she'd be on her own, here in Washington, in the fucking middle of the snake pit.

Hannah closed her eyes, exhaled, and rolled her head

on her neck. He could hear the snap, crackle and pop. "Why are you here, Mac?"

He had to be blunt, especially since she was in a pissy mood. She wouldn't appreciate him trying to roll her in bubble wrap. "We have a mission."

Her eyelids jerked open and she blanched as she looked at him. The pungent scent of ammonia filled the room. "When? Where? Why?"

Mac tossed her a cocky grin. "You left out who and how."

"Gawddammit, Mac."

"It's okay, babe. This is just routine. It's been on the roster for awhile. Even before the Bosnian operation came up. Escort duty. No more than a week, and not a hot zone."

"I don't like it." She laid it off on the fact that she hadn't tracked down the threat, not to her own nerves jumping at the thought of him being gone. They didn't see each other every day. She was still in DC, he was in western Virginia. He could get there fast if she needed him. On a mission? She'd be on her own while he was out of country.

He wrapped her up in his arms despite her desultory attempt to get free. "You have Captain Harjo's number. Call him if there's a problem. I'll get to you ASAP. And he'll get you covered until I can get here. Okay?"

"Fine. Just...fine."

Mac laughed and kissed her forehead. "No, it's not fine. I'll be back as quick as I can. Try to stay out of trouble, Major."

"Yeah, like that's gonna happen."

CHAPTER 16

HANNAH DUCKED THROUGH the door leaving behind bright sunshine. She paused as her eyes adjusted to the dimmer light inside the restaurant and to scan the room for Mac's imposing bulk. He wasn't there. She glanced at the phone still clutched in her hand to make sure she'd read his text message correctly. This was the place.

A hostess walked up, a smile spreading across her face. "Meeting your husband here?" Hannah blinked in confusion as the woman continued. "I'll show you to your table. He had to step out for a moment."

Still on autopilot, Hannah followed and dropped down on the chair that faced the room. Had Mac been there, he would have occupied that spot. She'd relinquish it when he returned. Her phone dinged and she read his next message.

GO TO LADIES ROOM.

She heaved out of her chair and glanced around. As a waitress approached she asked for directions and followed them. The hallway was brightly lit and she could easily read the signs on the doors as she traversed its length, though another text came through before she reached the restroom.

ALARM ON DOOR DISABLED IM IN ALLEY

More than a little nervous and slightly pissed over the cloak and dagger routine, Hannah pushed through the door and stepped out. Mac was waiting, looking anxious. Of even more concern, Lightfoot guarded one end of the alley while Sean waited at the other.

"What's going on?"

"We've got to go, baby. C'mon." He stuck a hat on her head and tugged on the brim. "Keep your head down"

She wanted to dig in her heels but instinct spurred her to follow Mac. By the time they reached Sean, Lightfoot had caught up to them. In moments, the four of them joined the flow on the crowded sidewalk, separate but together. Mac steered her into a parking garage but held her back from the elevators while the other two Wolves sprinted up the stairs. A few minutes later, an elevator arrived, with Sean inside.

No one said anything until they reached the 6th level. Mac guided her out of the elevator just as Lightfoot pulled up in a Ford Expedition. She climbed into the back seat, followed by Mac while Sean jumped into the front. More than a little freaked out by all their secretive behavior, she faced Mac.

"What the hell, Mac?"

"We need to talk, baby."

Something about the timbre of his voice had her studying his face. "Fuck, Mac. What's happened?"

"We lost Whiskey Team Charlie."

"Wait. What? Lost them? Lost them how?" Currently, there were only three active Whiskey teams in the 69th — Bravo, which was Mac's team, Charlie, and Delta. "They weren't on a mission."

"No, they weren't." Mac's expression hardened. "It was reported as a training accident. Chopper crash. Allegedly."

Hannah's eyebrows tried to hold hands as she furrowed her brow. "Are you saying there wasn't a chopper crash?" She was having a hard time keeping up with the conversation, especially since no word of any accident had come across her desk.

"No, it was allegedly a training accident. The chopper crashed and burned, with the men of Charlie Team on board."

"I'm..." She breathed and rubbed at her temples with her fingertips. "I'm not following, Mac."

"Charlie team was sent on a training mission. Their chopper allegedly crashed, killing all on board."

"Okay?"

"Except not everyone died." Mac's gaze flicked to Sean.

"I saw the pilot of that chopper, Major. Two days after the alleged accident. Alive and breathing."

Her brain finally caught up. "Wait. What are you saying, Mac? They were killed? Intentionally?"

"Yeah."

"Fuckityfuckfuckfuckitallthewaytohellandbackagain." She forced air into her lungs. "Captain Harjo?"

"Doing his best to uncover the cover up."

"Start at the beginning. No, first. What about you guys?"

"We're good. No missions, training or otherwise. Same with Delta."

While Mac filled her in, Lightfoot drove aimlessly around Washington, often doubling back or making last minute turns. Hannah's brain once again caught up. "Are we being followed?"

Lightfoot caught her gaze in the rear view mirror. "Not anymore."

"I want you to take early maternity leave, Hannah." Mac's voice was very soft but each word was underlined with steel.

She held her tongue until they were behind the doors of a hotel room on the outskirts of DC, where Nakai and Danny awaited them. None of the Wolves said anything, their attention focused on Mac. He stood at the window, watching the snarl of traffic crawl by outside. Two queen-sized beds, a long dresser with the TV bolted to it and a round table with two chairs filled the room. Danny had been sprawled on one bed, watching TV, but he'd shut it off and now sat on the edge of the bed. Nakai sat in one of the chairs, but the other had been pushed back from the table.

Sean shoved that chair so hard the table wobbled when the two pieces of furniture collided. "We need a planning session with Captain Harjo and Delta team."

Mac didn't turn around. "No. Just us. We don't know who to trust." He glanced toward Hannah. "C'mon, babe. I'll take you to our room so you can rest."

"Excuse me?"

Leaving the window, he faced the room. "We need to make contingency plans."

"We do, yes."

"Not you. Us." Mac indicated the other Wolves with a sweep of his eyes.

"Oh? Really?" Her tone had everyone but Mac edging toward the door.

"Hon, you're pregnant. You need to rest."

"Did you just fucking go there? Seriously? The hell with you, Sergeant Major. I outrank you."

"Dammit. We aren't having this fight again."

"No. We aren't." She blanched as the full implications of Mac's statement hit. "You don't trust me." Each word burst out covered in bitterness.

"Now, Hannah—"

"Don't you fucking dare, Ian McIntire. Don't you dare. You can't placate me. You don't trust me. Fine. Well, here's the deal, slick. You can't do a damn thing about this situation. I can. Because I'm the fucking major and you're just a pissant Command Sergeant Major."

Mac reached for her but she backed away, putting the entire room between them. "Don't you fucking touch me. You don't have that right. Not now, not ever." She flicked her right hand. "If they stay, I stay." She muttered a string of curse words of which only "fuckwit" was recognizable. "You don't fucking get it, Sergeant Major. I've been working to get the Sixty-ninth disbanded, personnel reassigned. I've been working my gawddamned ass off to get everyone away. I'm this fucking close."

He opened his mouth to say something but she was across the room in a flash. Nailing him in the chest with both hands, she hit hard enough he stumbled back half a step. "But I wasn't fast enough and Charlie team is dead because of it." Tears glistened on her cheeks and she dashed them away with the back of her hand. "Fucking hormones. It's my job to keep you safe. All of you. Let me do my job. Even if you don't trust me."

"Trust has nothing to do with it."

"Seriously? You don't trust your commanding officer. You don't trust the other Whiskey team. Why the flying monkey shit would you trust me, you fuckwit?" She balled her hands into fists, keeping her arms stiff at her sides and breathed through her nose.

Mac scrubbed at his scalp with curved fingers. "Dammit, babe."

"I am not your *babe*. Just your baby mama."

"I've asked you to marry me." His eyes glinted feral red as he took a step toward her, his own fists held stiffly at his sides. "And this is completely different. You being involved is...It's too dangerous."

"And being married to a Wolf isn't?" Laughter tinged with hysteria burst out and Hannah clapped a hand over her mouth to stifle it. "You just don't get it, *Command* Sergeant Major. Someone—someone with real power and way up the chain of command—is hunting Wolves. Let me do my fucking job. I'll cover your asses, get you far away, make you untouchable."

"How?"

Hannah seemed to wilt and was surprised when Sean guided her to the empty chair. She was tired, so damn tired. Tired of being scared, of being alone, of Mac. She couldn't breathe, couldn't sort out her feelings for him or for the baby growing inside her. The kid decided to say hi, kicking so hard her tummy rippled. She pushed hair off her forehead before propping her chin up on one hand, with her elbow braced on the table. "It's what I do, Mac. Numbers. Analysis. Moving things around. Hiding them in plain sight. It's what I've been trying to do since Bosnia." Her shoulders lifted with a deep breath and she exhaled sigh. "I failed Charlie team. I won't fail Bravo or Delta."

"Fine. Just…fine."

"Good. Now get out of my way. I need to call a cab and get back to work."

🐾🐾🐾🐾

HANNAH FLIPPED THROUGH the file on her desk, anger swelling in her chest until she couldn't breathe. There was no way to sugar coat it. She marched—or more precisely, waddled, being almost eight months pregnant—to Colonel Bradshaw's office. She chugged past his aide like the Little Engine That Could.

"You can't—"

She shut the door in his face and pivoted toward the man who'd been her mentor for years.

"Major?"

"Colonel."

"You seem a mite perturbed."

"Ya think?" She slammed the file on his desk. "What the hell's going on?"

He pursed his lips and inhaled, giving her a moment to calm down. She arched an eyebrow instead.

"Precisely what we feared, Major."

She dropped onto a chair. "Then we need to disband the Wolves. Now."

"We can't."

"Why the fuck not? Do you want the rest of these men to die?"

"These things take time."

"I can transfer or separate everyone from service by the end of the week. And make it look like business as usual."

"Hannah, I know you think you're helping them, but this situation is far more complicated than you realize."

"Complicated? Fuckin' A, Colonel. Men are dead. There's a cover-up. Damn straight it's complicated. And now it's deadly."

"Watch your language in this office, Major."

Hannah snapped her jaw shut, biting off her next tirade. Seething, she plastered on a decent facsimile of a poker face.

"I'm handling the situation, Major. You're close to your maternity leave. You should be more concerned with the birth of your child than this other stuff. Have you decided to inform the father yet?"

Heat flashed across her skin, followed by icy cold. Had he figured out Mac was the father? No, she wouldn't go there. The colonel was her mentor. He'd taught her almost everything she knew about working behind the scenes. And she'd made damn sure to keep her relationship with Mac out of the office.

"It might be wise, in fact, if you took early leave."

What the fuck? Was her CO conspiring with Mac now? She breathed through her anger and ignored the twinge low in her belly. "Are you insinuating I can no longer do my job, Colonel?"

Bradshaw hurried to placate her and Hannah knew she was being handled. And resented the shit out of it.

"All I'm saying is that you have a lot on your plate. I'm investigating the helicopter crash, Major. All information gathered to this point indicates it was just what it appears—a tragic training exercise caused by a malfunction in the helicopter's tail rotor, possibly from a bird strike. This country needs the Sixty-ninth. Despite your personal feelings in the matter, the men assigned do necessary work. Secret work."

Secrets. That's what it came down to. Fucking secrets.

Eight good men were dead. Eight Wolves. Who was next? Mac? The others in his unit? Not on her gawddamned watch. Colonel Bradshaw wanted secrecy? She could damn sure give it to him.

"You're right, Colonel." The words soured her stomach but she sounded so sincere saying them. "I have a few things to clear off my desk. I'll take a few days to close those files and then take leave."

"I think that's a smart decision, Major."

She saluted, pivoted and headed toward the door. She had her hand on the knob when she looked back over her shoulder. "I'll resign my commission before I go on maternity leave."

Bradshaw looked shocked and his mouth worked a moment before he formed words to go with his thoughts. "Don't resign yet. Wait until after the baby comes. You might decide you want to come back. Your job will be here for you when you come back."

"Not when. If."

"You'll be back."

CHAPTER 17

TIME WAS RUNNING OUT. Hannah had covered her tracks as much as she could. Bradshaw would suspect, but he wouldn't be able to prove she'd transferred support staff and either separated or transferred the operational units of the 69th. Besides, he hadn't given her a direct order and Secretary Mathis had tacitly agreed with her actions.

Her low back twinged and she shifted in her chair. She'd awoken that morning with a dull ache low in her abdomen, right at the tops of her thighs. This back thing was new.

She'd dotted all the *I*'s and had one more *T* to cross. The paperwork just needed the Secretary's signature. She dropped it into an envelop marked "Interoffice Mail" and waddled over to the Secretary's office. He'd made her promise to stop in to say goodbye before she pulled an Elvis and left the building. Maternity leave started tomorrow. She wanted a couple of weeks to…what did the books call it? Nest. Yeah, she wanted to nest before the Alien arrived in the flesh. She was four weeks away from her due date.

Tala was supposed to arrive with some sort of witchy-wolfy midwife person to help with the birth. This had been an on-going bone of contention—one of many—between her and Mac. He was downright adamant that she couldn't take drugs during the birth. Tala, who she'd come to respect and like, said the same thing. The chance of killing the baby was one she didn't want to take. They'd arranged for an alternative birthing center, against her OB's objections.

Timing it precisely, Secretary Mathis's assistant was on his coffee break when she arrived. Hannah slipped the envelope into the in-box. The paperwork clearing Fort Lyle Smith to be added the BRAC list would be signed, sealed, and delivered to Congress at the next hearing. She was about to knock on the door to the Secretary's office to say her goodbyes when the first real pain lanced across her stomach.

"Oh, Jesus H. Christ," she gasped. "Too soon. No. Too soon." The agony doubled her over and robbed her breath. Fuckfuckfuckityfuck. Mac was back at Fort Lyle. Panic drove her to her knees, hard, and a little voice in the back of her head got snarky by pointing out that would leave a bruise.

"Major Jackson?" The Secretary's aide had returned and was now kneeling next to her. "Ma'am? Are you okay?"

Oh hell no, Hannah wanted to scream. She was never going to be okay again. "Mac. Gotta call Mac."

The aide looked confused. "Let me call for medics. And nine-one-one."

She gripped his arm as another wave of pain racked her body. "No. Mac. I need Mac." She panted through the pain. "Phone. Give me a gawddamned phone."

Hannah managed to punch in the numbers to Mac's SAT phone. He answered on the first ring.

"What's up, babe?"

"Need you," she panted. "Too soon. It's too soon, Can't stop the pain." She dropped the phone as another contraction hit.

The aide picked it up. "Ah, hello? Who is this?"

"Command Sergeant Major Ian McIntire. What the hell is wrong with my ma—Major Jackson?"

"Oh, this is Lieutenant Stephens. I work for the Secretary of the Army. I think she's in labor. Or something. The major I mean. Not Secretary Mathis."

Mac reeled off instructions of where to take Hannah even while he was marshaling his own troops.

When Sean landed the chopper in the parking lot of the birthing center, Mac was grateful to see Tala waiting. She, and a Navajo midwife familiar with Wolf births had been in Alexandria for a week. Wolf pups had a habit of coming early and neither Mac nor Tala wanted to take a chance with a human MD. Nakai had called her in flight and the older Wolf was right behind Mac as they off-loaded, followed quickly by Lightfoot. Sean took off as soon as they'd cleared the rotors. He and Danny would be back with ground transportation.

"She is very brave, Mac," Tala told him as she led him to the birthing room.

"It's too soon, Tala."

"Yes. But your son is strong. So is his mother."

Nakai and Lightfoot peeled off for the waiting room while Mac headed back to Hannah's room. He opened the door and only Wolf reflexes kept him from getting beaned by a plastic mug. "She's feeling a little feisty," he muttered before easing into the room.

"Gawddamnmutherfuckitshitandpiss, Sergeant Major. Took your own fucking time to get here."

"Hi, darlin'. I'm fine thanks, and you?"

"Shut up, Mac. Just fucking—" A sound ripped from her that couldn't be human.

Mac wanted to howl along with her. Her pain beat at him like a heavy weight boxer going twelve rounds for the championship. He didn't know what to do. Afraid to touch her. Afraid to stay. Afraid to leave. His wolf took over, forcing him across the room to gather his mate into his arms. He settled on the bed, held her, rocking, murmuring soothing sounds against her tousled hair. The contraction passed and Hannah relaxed, even though she trembled in his embrace. Crap. Was she still scared of him?

Hannah shifted closer, turned her face to his chest and clutched his fatigues. "Too soon," she whimpered. "Not time. What if something's wrong?" A shudder rocked her body. "What if we lose him?"

The knot in his gut unwound. We. She was thinking of them as a couple. "We won't, darlin'. Tala came early because pups come early in our world. You're strong. You're the strongest damn woman I've ever met. We'll do this. Together."

She bit back a choked cry. "Are we? Are we together?"

Holding her gently, he set her back just far enough he could see her face—and she could see his. "Yes, Hannah. You and me. Always. We're a pair. The two of us. There will never be another woman for me. No matter what happens. I love you. Even when I'm so pissed off at you I want to do something stupid, I love you with everything I have, everything I am."

Over the next few hours, he had to remind himself of that. Hannah achieved new heights of inventiveness with her cussing. The midwife and Tala just watched, their expressions benign. When Hannah dozed off between the pains, Mac would slip out. The men's room would need a facelift, thanks to his handiwork and the liberal application of his fists through drywall.

Bravo team waited, patient as the hunters they were. Delta team had already disappeared into the tangled web of bureaucratic red tape. Bravo was the only active duty Whiskey team still on the books and it was just a matter of days before they separated—from the service and from each other. Still, they stayed, solid in their support of their Alpha. These men were his pack. He owed them his life. Hannah's. The son she even now labored to bring into the world whole and healthy and alive.

He chugged a bottle of water, shoulder wedged against the door jamb between the vending area and the waiting room, and watched them. Good men. Men who would always have his six, just as he'd have theirs.

Lightfoot's eyes flicked his direction, followed by Sean shifting in his seat, Nakai smiling, and even young Danny perking up. Yes. These men were his pack and he loved them as brothers.

"Right back at'cha, boss man." Sean winked a second before his attention swiveled to the door separating waiting from birthing.

A nurse peeked out, watching the men with a touch of trepidation in her expression. "Miss Jackson is awake." She grabbed a fortifying breath. "She...uhm...she has quite a mouth on her."

Mac laughed and everything inside eased, spewing out with the chortles. "Yeah. Yeah, she does. I'll be right in." And he would be, right after he took care of a few things.

Twenty hours later, Mac dozed in a light combat sleep, exhaustion leaving dark shadows on his pasty face. Every ripple of Hannah's pain had ripped right through him. Her eyes were bruised and she was so far beyond exhaustion that she could no longer speak or keep her eyes open. Mac was terrified he'd lose them both.

The door opened and a bright slash of light highlighted Tala as she slipped into the gloomy birthing room—the bleakness as much from emotion as lack of light. The older woman placed gentle hands on Hannah's stomach and her sharpened gaze collided with Mac's weary one.

"I will fetch Azee. It is time." Tala watched Mac's expression morph from fatigue to wariness. She offered him a smile. "She will do this. You are blessed, Ian McIntire, by the strength of your woman and by your love for her."

Two hours. It still took two hours of pleading, coercing, yelling, berating, and threats before Hannah gave a last gasp, a final push, and their son appeared in the world, squalling and squirming, and with every evidence of being healthy despite his early arrival and brutal birth. Mac cradled Hannah, his tears mixing with hers.

"Baby, aw fuck, baby. I didn't know it would be this bad. Brave. You're so damnned brave and wonderful and I love you so gawddamned much I would have died if something happened to you."

She murmured something, all but asleep from her ordeal. And it had been an ordeal. For him, sure, but far more for her.

"What, darlin'? What did you say?"

"Tired." She whimpered the word. "Hurts."

"Shhh, baby. I know. I know. Sleep now, Hannah. Sleep. You're safe. I'm here. I've got you. Always. I love you."

"Mmmmloveyou. Liam. Name 'im Liam." Her words slurred together and she went lax in his arms.

🐾🐾🐾🐾

HANNAH STARED AT Mac's hands. They were twice the size of hers. Long fingers with scarred knuckles. Square, blunt nails. Calloused. Rough palms. Strong. Capable of killing in a heartbeat. Yet he held their son in those massive paws displaying a tenderness that stole her breath. And her heart. In that singular moment, as she watched the gruff Wolf gaze in awe at the tiny baby in his hands, she was lost. He owned her heart and soul now. They both did.

She'd loved him before—or thought she did but this all-encompassing need to see him, touch him, love him would drive her to her knees if she'd been standing.

Liam waved his tiny fist as Mac settled their son more snugly in his arms. With his index finger, he smoothed the dark fluff on the baby's head.

"Good morning, baby."

Hannah smiled as Liam cooed.

"I'm talking to you, darlin'. He's been awake for two

hours already." His gaze lifted from their child to meet hers, searing her soul with the emotion in his expression.

"We did good work."

"Yeah, darlin', we did. How do you feel?"

She started to laugh but choked it off when her whole body rebelled with a painful twinge. "Yeah, don't ask. I'm in a good mood. If I'm reminded what giving birth to a fucking basketball is like, you ain't gettin' sex ever again, slick."

He laughed for her, the sound startling another coo from Liam. "No sex for at least six weeks anyway. But lots of snuggling, darlin'. Lots and lots of hugs and kisses."

"Okay. I can deal with that."

Mac continued to watch her and cleared his throat. "There's something else you need to deal with."

Her brows knitted together, leaving her forehead crinkled. "What?"

"We're getting married. Now. Today."

"Married?" Her voice squeaked but her gaze remained level. And cool.

"Yes. Married. You're mine. You always have been. And I'm yours. I want it formalized. I want the whole damn world to know we belong to each other. You have a problem with that?"

Her face screwed up, eyes slitted, nose wrinkled, lips tight and snarly. "Not exactly the most romantic proposal a girl's ever received."

"You want romantic?" Mac carefully placed Liam back in the crib, strode to the bed, and dropped to one knee. He held up a ring. "Marry me, Major Darlin'. Marry me for now and always." He didn't give her a chance to say no by grabbing her hand and sliding the ring on her left hand. "There."

"What? That doesn't make us married."

"No, it doesn't. We have to go to the courthouse to get the license. But we'll have the ceremony. We'll make our promises. And we'll belong to each other. Officially."

Her expression smoothed out, her eyes heated. "Oh." She blinked several times, her gaze locked on his face. "Well." More blinks before a smile tugged at the corner of her mouth. "Okay then."

CHAPTER 18

Three years later...

LIGHTFOOT AND SEAN sat on opposite ends of the ER waiting room while a toddling Liam charged from one to other. They both felt lucky they'd been nearby when Mac called. Lightfoot had been in DC for meetings at the Bureau of Land Management. Sean had been in Alexandria on a job—setting up the demolition of an old warehouse. As soon as Mac tagged them, they knew what was happening. Sean had reached out and even now, Nakai and his mate Tala were on their way from New Mexico. Hannah would need Tala. Danny Keegan, their other former squad member, was in the middle of the Gulf of Mexico on an oil rig. Captain Harjo was in the middle of the sandbox. Again.

"DA!" Liam pivoted in mid-run and charged the doors segregating treatment rooms from the waiting area.

Mac scooped up the little boy and buried his face in his son's shoulder as he fought for control. He couldn't go to pieces. Not yet. Liam needed him. Hannah would need him when she woke up from the sedative. The presence of the two Wolves pricked the hair on the back of his neck and he raised his ravaged face to them.

"Fuck, Mac. We're sorry." Sean touched his shoulder, a gesture of solidarity and compassion.

"Nakai and Tala will be here later today." Lightfoot, though his face remained stoic as ever, bit out the words. Emotion vibrated in his voice.

"Little girl," Mac choked out. "She was perfect. Ah, God." Tears clogged his throat and he couldn't speak. He could barely stand there, his son wrapped securely in his arms, comforted by two of his best friends. "There was so much blood."

"Hannah?"

"She's sleeping. They...I almost lost her." He sagged then, almost went to his knees, would have if Lightfoot hadn't grabbed Liam while Sean put his broad shoulder beneath Mac's arm to support him.

Liam fussed and squirmed in Lightfoot's arms, reaching for his father. "Da! DA!"

"Shhh, little man." Jostling the toddler on his hip, Michael backed away. "Your dad needs a minute." The child quieted as he reared back to stare up at Michael with eyes so much like his father's. The boy patted Lightfoot's cheeks.

"Da?"

"Your dad's right over there. Why don't you and I go see the big horse." He nodded to Sean and headed out the double doors that swished open at his approach. Outside, the sun blistered a hot summer sky. Crossing the street, he carried Liam to the swath of grass surrounding Washington Circle and the large sculpture of George Washington on a horse.

"Down. Down now!"

"Okay, little man." Michael squatted, steadied the boy on his feet and then rocked back on his heels to watch.

Inside the ER, Mac listened while a nurse explained that Hannah was being moved up to a room and he'd be allowed back in to see her shortly. Sean thought he might have to physically restrain Mac until his former commander blew out a breath, scrubbed his palm over the top of his head, and simply nodded.

After the nurse, her crepe-soled shoes making no sound, disappeared beyond the imposing metal doors, Mac turned to face Sean. "What do I do? How do we survive this?"

Mac tried to remember to count his blessings. Liam was healthy. They'd lost another child just after conception—one he hadn't told Hannah about. She'd thought the heavy period was normal. He'd grieved, as Wolves did, and made sure he was away during her fertile periods. But they'd slipped up and she'd gotten pregnant again. Had carried this one for seven months. Their baby girl never took a first breath when she came out into the world.

And the blood. Hemorrhaging. The doctors wouldn't let him in the treatment room. Hannah's blood slicked the floor and he'd wanted to rip the doors off to get to his mate. If Lightfoot hadn't reminded him of Liam, of his son, he would have gone berserk. If he ever lost Hannah, he would. Scorched earth. He'd leave nothing standing.

"She's strong, Mac. You both are."

"This will kill her, Sean. Her heart will break and there's no way I can put it back together for her."

Sean squeezed Mac's shoulder. *Yeah, just like yours is doing right now.*

Mac raised his head, stared at the other Wolf, nodded. "I need to go sit with her."

"Roger that, boss. Lightfoot'n I will bring up Nakai and Tala when they get here. And Liam. He's gonna want you and his mom."

🐾🐾🐾🐾

HANNAH LAY ON her side, back to the door and the people gathered in the room talking in hushed tones. Fucking doctors. What good were they? Didn't they realize she could hear them? Nonviable fetus. Still born. That wasn't a fetus. That was her baby. Her baby girl. Liam's little sister.

She was angry. So fucking angry. No amount of drugs could dull the rage firing through her blood. Seven months. She'd been so damn careful for seven months. Two. She'd lost two babies now. Mac didn't know about the other one. A week old. Maybe. She'd known as soon as her period hit that something had happened. She'd spent all her love on Liam. And tried not to resent Mac because damn him all to hell, she loved him. And she didn't want him to hurt like she'd hurt. She had pulled away from him, from intimacy with him. Liam. She'd claimed him as her excuse. An active toddler who left her exhausted.

Wanting to curse and scream, she bit her tongue, pretended to still be unconscious. Smoothed her breathing and her heart rate when the medicos stopped talking to check the fucking monitors. She'd been so careful. After Liam, she didn't go back to work. She wasn't a milk-and-cookies kind of mom but she didn't go back, resigned her commission, became a stay-at-home mother. Twice now, she'd been careful, done everything in her fucking power to keep the babies growing inside her safe.

But she didn't. She didn't keep them safe. Hell, she'd worked right up to the day she'd gone into labor with Liam. She'd left the Pentagon for the birthing center, met there by Mac and the Wolves. Fucking bunch of pansies when it came to pregnant women and babies. They'd all cooed and held Liam. He'd been a gift to them all, she realized now. Her gift to them, a reminder that they could have...normal. But this wasn't normal. This aching void in her chest was too hurtful to be normal.

The doctors left, followed shortly by the two nurses. She opened her eyes then, stared out the window. She looked out toward the southeast, toward the Mall, though she couldn't see beyond the buildings on the next block. Work. She needed to get back to work. She could find herself again in the mundane tasks of adding up numbers, find a way to hide from the pain. She would tug on the Secretary if she needed to. She didn't want the rank, the uniform. Just the work. She could be a DAC. Department of the Army-Civilian. She'd laugh if her chest didn't hurt so bad.

🐾🐾🐾🐾

TALA, LIAM FIRMLY in her arms, shooed her husband and the other two Wolves out of the room. Hannah's voice raised in anger behind her and Mac's snarling rumble raised the hair on her arms. None of them should witness this fight, especially the little boy with tear-slick cheeks. He didn't need to hear the words his parents slung at each other, every one meant to wound, to slice and bleed the other.

Wolves. Their passions ran deep, especially mated pairs. Hannah was stronger than most, as much an alpha as her husband. She could only pray they didn't injure their hearts so deeply they killed what was between them.

"Come, Liam. I want ice cream. I think you want some too, little man, yes?"

The boy in her arms nodded, his child's face solemn as he peeked over her shoulder at the closed door.

"I think ice cream is good. For all of us." Nakai deftly herded Sean and Lightfoot away. "Leave them be. This is a river they must cross alone. We cannot help them. If one starts to drown, the other must throw the rope to save. This is not up to us."

🐾🐾🐾🐾

FOUR MONTHS LATER, Hannah walked into General Bradshaw's office. He'd gotten his first star while she'd been off playing mommy. He wore a smirk and didn't rise as she approached his desk.

"Major."

"Not any more, General. Congratulations, by the way."

"I told you so."

She just managed to keep her eyes forward despite the insane urge to roll them. "You always did like getting the last word in, General Bradshaw."

"Are you settling in?"

"Yes sir."

"Thoughts?"

Resisting the urge to remain at attention, she shifted her feet and relaxed her shoulders. "It's not the BRAC Commission."

Bradshaw laughed—a deep, cheery sound—and his eyes lit up. "I'd think not. The Defense Security Service has a much...broader mission. What are your thoughts on Director Talbot?"

Hannah's internal radar went off. "My thoughts, sir?"

"Don't dance around it, Hannah. Can you work with her?"

"I've only met her once, sir. She seems very...capable."

The general leaned back in his chair and steepled his fingers. "I want you to understand your role in the agency, Hannah."

"I'm assigned to counterintelligence, general. I figure that spells out my mission pretty clearly."

An expression flickered across his face, one gone so quickly Hannah didn't have a chance to decipher it.

"How does your husband feel about this?"

The question rocked her back on her figurative heels but she maintained her posture and demeanor. "The choice is mine, general. It always has been."

🐾🐾🐾🐾

Seven years later

MAC ENTERED THE Alexandria house through the garage. Liam was happily away for his camping weekend with his best friend. Hannah was home, the sour apple smell of her annoyance overlaying the other scents. Eleven years they'd been together and he knew her as well as he knew himself. Work. Something had happened at the DSS and while she might have shrugged it off, she still dragged the last dregs of it home. He caught another whiff—all Hannah. Rich, spicy. Cloves and jasmine washed in rain. He wanted her, as evidenced by the tightening in his groin.

He found her in their bedroom. She'd stripped out of the suit she'd worn that day and currently wore nothing but a tank and gym shorts. Work clothes and her shoulder holster had been tossed carelessly on the bed. She glanced over her shoulder, acknowledged him with a flaring of her blue eyes. Annoyance, and beneath it, beneath the surge of her arousal, he scented burnt toast. Anger. But not at him. Still, he made a handy punching bag. He would push her buttons, tease the mad until she unleashed it and let it go. Then he'd have her, as she would have him, the give and take of their lovemaking as comfortable as old sweats and as sharp as nails.

"I see what you're thinking," she snarled, turning and backing away. "No. I don't have time to play."

"Who's playing, Major?"

"Not me."

"Good." He stalked toward her, ripping his T-shirt over his head. "Me either." He cornered her against the wooden foot board of the bed and ran a hand over her butt, along one muscled thigh. She pushed at his chest but he flipped her onto the bed, following quick as a snake, pressing his body to hers, his mouth searching and finding its mate in an explosion of need that rocked them both to their cores.

Hannah fought, squirming beneath him before surrendering, arms wrapping around him as she met him, her passion turning greedy, reckless, unfettered. She dragged short nails up his back, scraping along his skin before she dug fingers into his shoulder muscles. She craved his body—always had, always would. The weight, the shape, the glorious heat radiating from him. He pressed against her, pinning her down. Her heart slammed against her ribcage and she couldn't breathe as his clever fingers found her, teased her legs apart, found the heat and depth of her. One finger, two, and she quivered, unable to catch her breath. Everything inside her clenched and she was up and over, spiraling on a wave of joy.

He felt her release, that shuddering surrender followed by a sigh. But he wasn't done. This wasn't enough, not for her, not for either of them. He ripped off her tank, knew his hands were rough. Didn't care. He was wild with need, wanted her desperate for him, wanted— needed—her with him in the delirium.

She followed. Her body came alive, her panting whimpers as eager and mindless as his own. Her hands turned as rough, grasping, taking, leaving her mark on his skin as he marked hers.

No longer a patient hunter, he had no time for tenderness. Not here. Not now. There was only room for wanting her. Only voracious, urgent need devouring all thought, demanding to be quenched. Mac set the wolf in him free, and its mate—his mate—Hannah met them both, ferocious and relentless.

Pushed to feral excitement, they stripped each other of the few clothes left between them. Skin to skin, he drove into her, hard and deep. She gasped at his invasion but he didn't care, shoving up her knees, wanting her to take more. To take all. Take him.

Hannah cried out as pleasure slashed through her with burning claws. Her hips pistoned against him, the slap of sweaty flesh drowning out the sounds of their breathing. Her hands gripped his shoulders, anchoring her. His squeezed her butt, lifting her, changing the angle so he could drive deeper. Fast. Faster. Even faster still. Hannah's cry of release came in desperate sobs as his echoed hers and he choked out her name.

Later—whether minutes or hours, her hands slid limply to the bed. Her breath rasped as she gulped air. Surprised her racing heart didn't leap from her chest to pirouette around the room, she inhaled Mac's scent, drawing it into her body as she had his cock.

"Christ on a cracker with raspberry jam!" she managed to huff out.

Mac started to laugh, discovered he didn't have the breath for it. He'd collapsed on top of her. He meant to roll off, let her breathe—and him too, and he would. Soon. Or maybe in a day or two.

She shoved at him. "Move."

"I don't think I can." He waited another moment, gathered his energy. With effort, he slipped out of her, and rolled off. He lay on his back staring at the ceiling, mirroring her posture. "I vote we stay here."

"Forever?"

"It's an option."

She managed to roll to her side, tuck her head against his shoulder. "Have I mentioned lately that I love you?"

"Once or twice."

"Good. Yeah, that's good. Should hold you awhile." She mumbled something else as her eyes drifted shut. "Pups. Remind me wolf pups when we wake up. Like next week, 'kay?"

CHAPTER 19

MICHAEL LIGHTFOOT RAISED his head to the moon and howled. The silvery crescent carved a grinning bite out of a midnight blue sky sprinkled with twinkle lights. Off in the distance, cushioned by the humid air of the early summer night, an answering howl echoed. Wild wolves hunted tonight and he wanted to catch up to them. The uncompromising need to hunt would come with the full moon. For now, he was content to run with the pack, his nose filled with the scents of the forest.

A branch snapped and the sound ricocheted like a gunshot. He dropped to a crouch and waited, all his senses open and questing for the source of the noise. His sensitive ears picked up the rustle of cloth and a soft thud of footfalls in the thick carpet of leaves. He lifted his nose and sniffed. Human. His teeth bared. Why was a human female here deep in the forest, especially this close to the pack's den? One lone female wolf remained with the pups, making her and the little ones vulnerable. The fur rose on his ruff and a rumbling growl echoed in his chest. He slipped through the forest, getting between the den and the woman. He would not leave the beta female to defend the pups alone.

All senses attuned to every smell and rustle, he stalked the human. Her scent wafted on the breeze, sighing and whispering a siren's song through the pine boughs. He shook his head and fought the urge to sneeze, feeling almost desperate to get the woman's scent out of his nose. More curious now than apprehensive, he watched her drop into a hollow behind an old tree fall. Canvas grated as she reached in her bag for something. He stiffened, teeth bared, ready to charge if she pulled out a weapon. No gun but he didn't relax. The camera in her hand could be almost as dangerous to the pack as a firearm. His sharp ears picked up no whir or click. She didn't take pictures but simply watched the den through the telephoto lens.

The beta lay in front of the small cave tolerating the playful nips and mock attacks by the pups. Michael counted them and froze. Two were missing. He counted again. Raising his nose, he sniffed the night breeze. He caught no hint of the missing wolves. One of the youngsters strayed and the female growled. When the pup didn't respond, she shook off the others, pushed off the ground and trotted over to him. She nosed him back to the group and stood gazing around the woods. Her nostrils flared as she tested the wind. The female whined softly and honed in on his position. His scent would be familiar. She turned her head, now staring at the log the human hid behind. This time the wolf growled. She backed toward the den and when the pups didn't respond, she whirled and nipped at them until she'd herded all of them into the small cave and ducked in after them. Her shadowed bulk remained visible to his eyes where she guarded the mouth of the den with silent menace.

The woman sighed softly and shifted position. His ears caught the brush of skin against canvas as she put up her camera. Then he heard something else. Men. Three of them. And they carried guns, the stench of gunpowder and oil unmistakable. The woman heard them too. She retrieved her camera and hunkered deeper.

Torn, Michael decided the woman was the least danger to the den. He padded off, circling around to follow the men.

"Are you sure the pack is gone?" The voice sounded high and squeaky.

"Yeah." Gruff, this voice sounded more snarl than anything.

"The pups are old enough they should be alone. We're supposed to get at least three more if we can't grab all of them." Excitement tinged the third voice.

"You two'll have to haul 'em. I need my hands free to shoot." The second man again. Michael knew who to hit first.

Before he could react, blinding pain hit him out of nowhere. A sharp crack reverberated. His brain scrambled to name the sound. Gunshot. He howled to alert the female and call the pack, then darted deeper into the woods. Excited shouts followed the shot, along with heavy boots pounding behind him. A burning throb ate through his chest and blood slicked his left leg. The heavy caliber bullet had torn through muscle but missed anything vital like his lungs or heart. If he could lead the hunter away, then maybe the female could keep the pups safe until the pack returned.

Howls filled the night and a savage grin curled his lips. The pack was closer than he'd thought. He circled to the west, headed back toward his clothes and his own weapons. He might be wounded, but he was far from defenseless.

🐾🐾🐾🐾

LIZ GRAHAM STIFLED her scream when the gunshot shattered the still night. Panicked, she watched the mouth of the small cave where the wolf had hidden the pups. Through the viewfinder of the special infrared camera, she could easily see the female guarding the den. Two men entered the small clearing, stumbling and sliding down the low embankment.

"Shit. There's a full-grown wolf in there. How are we going to grab any of the pups?"

She needed to take pictures, to get evidence but the sound of her camera might carry and alert the thieves. Men. Criminals. She didn't know what to call them.

The second man pulled out a pistol and pointed it toward the cave. His hand shook and he offered it to the other man. "Here. You shoot her."

"Hell no. I didn't sign on to shoot anything. We're just supposed to nab some more little wolves and make sure they get to the lab."

The wolf growled and the two men backed up. Liz knew what she needed to do. She could hear someone else crashing through the woods. It sounded like he was chasing something and was probably the hunter in the group. Neither of these guys were the outdoorsy type. They were science nerds. Like her. But where she wanted to protect the wolves, they were here to harm them. She'd bet a month's salary—not that she made the big bucks working for the state of Wyoming—that these guys had stolen the two missing pups. Gripping her camera tighter, she crawled to the end of the log, prepared to confront them. If she used her flash, maybe she could blind them long enough to grab the gun or something.

A branch cracked beneath her. The men whirled. She clicked the button on her camera and the flash fired. She clicked again, her finger mashing the shutter button as fast as the flash recycled.

Another gunshot echoed in the woods. She screamed reflexively. Throwing caution to the wind, she scrambled down into the hollow and tackled the man with the gun. He fell backwards with an "oof" as her shoulder jammed into his solar plexus and drove the air from his lungs. The gun went flying.

The man yelped and cussed but scuttled away from her.

"Get the hell away from here!" She crab-walked backwards, putting herself between the two men and the mouth of the cave. "I'm going to the authorities. I have your pictures!" Her fingers crunched through leaves and encountered something hard and metal. The gun. She snatched it from the leaf litter and held it in front of her with both hands. Did it have a safety? Guns had safeties, right? Terrified they'd call her bluff, she stiffened her arms to hold the gun steady. "I know how to use this. Now get the hell away and don't ever come back here!"

One man turned tail and ran, crashing into a tree trunk before he fought his way past to disappear behind the curtain of darkness. The second gaped at her before he scrambled to his feet and followed. Liz lowered the gun, shaking so hard she couldn't hold it out any longer. Tears streaked her face, a combination of fear and anger. Inhaling deeply, she brushed the moisture off her cheeks with the back of her hand. And then she discovered she was in even deeper trouble. A large man with a scraggly beard and a very big rifle stood at the top of the embankment. She froze.

"You might scare them science sissies, little girl, but you don't scare me. If I shoot you out here, ain't nobody ever gonna find your body. The wolves'll have a good dinner and the crows'll eat anything that's left." He leered and walked toward her. "But we can sure have some fun before I slit your throat." He fiddled with his belt buckle as he advanced.

Liz scrabbled backwards and then remembered she had a gun too. She lifted it. "Stay away from me!"

He laughed, a dark, ugly sound that turned her insides to liquid. "You ever shoot a pistol before, girlie?" His lips stretched into a parody of a smile. "Didn't think so." He stripped off his pack and dropped it. Holding his hands out to his sides, the rifle pointed away from her, he mocked her. "Here. I'll even give you the perfect target. Go ahead and pull the trigger."

She did. And nothing happened. She gasped and fresh tears pooled in her eyes.

"You think I'd be stupid enough to give them pussies real bullets?" He propped the rifle against his pack and advanced toward her.

Liz pulled the trigger again. And again. It clicked hollowly each time. She fumbled with it, looking for a safety button. Finding it, she moved the lever to the opposite direction, pointed the gun, and pulled the trigger again. Still nothing.

Just before the man reached her, something dark and furry leaped from the shadows behind her. A wolf! The animal snarled and attacked. Swearing, the man whirled, snatched up his pack and rifle. He used the butt of the weapon like a club as he slowly backed up the embankment in a controlled retreat. Howls, close enough to raise the hair on her arms, echoed the racket the man made while he thrashed through the underbrush and fired randomly. Shaking, she dropped the gun to the ground and wrapped her arms around her legs. She rested her forehead against her upraised knees and struggled to control her breathing. She gasped and shuddered every time she heard another gunshot.

"Pleasepleaseplease," she whispered. "Don't let him come back. And don't let him hit any of the wolves."

She sat for what seemed like an eternity before all man-made sounds ceased and normal forest sounds returned. The hair prickled on her arms again and she raised her head with utmost care. A ring of silent wolves, muzzles curled into snarls, circled her. Their teeth gleamed in the shifting moonlight. She swallowed hard and worked to control her trembles. The biggest wolf, the one she'd identified as the pack alpha advanced on her, his legs stiff and ears perked forward. Why had she turned loose of the gun? It didn't have bullets, but she could have thrown it at him and maybe gotten back to her camera. Perhaps the flash would scare them off until she could retreat.

"Please," she whispered. "Don't eat me."

"Wolves don't eat humans. Usually."

She jerked and raised her head. A man in a dark uniform stood just beyond the circle of wolves. Her mouth opened and she tried to form words but nothing came out. At least nothing coherent.

"You want to tell me where the missing pups are?"

She blinked, her jaw opening and closing but her tongue was stuck to the roof of her dry mouth. "I...they..." She swallowed and tried again. "Those men. They have them. And came after more. I...I have a photograph of them. I think."

"You think?"

Why did he have to sound so amused? And how could he be standing there so casually with a pack of angry wolves at his feet. "Who are you?"

"I'm the one asking questions. Why are you here?"

"I'm Liz...Elizabeth Graham. Doctor Liz Graham. I'm a wildlife biologist with the state of Wyoming."

"Really." His voice sounded both wry and disbelieving.

"Really. I...I have ID in my backpack. I've been studying this pack. But tonight... Two of the pups were gone. I thought maybe they'd gotten ill and died, but neither was a runt."

The alpha wolf growled again. She tucked her chin, blinked, but stared at the animal. "No offense. I know this is your litter, but there's always a runt." The words tumbled from her mouth without thought. Yeah, right. Like the wolf could understand her, but she'd always had the feeling wolves were far more cognizant than humans realized.

The man laughed and her gaze darted back to him. "Well there is." She took a deep breath. "I didn't know anyone else had found the pack, but obviously they did." Her bottom lip quivered and everything around her looked all swimmy like she had her eyes open underwater. Tears filled her eyes. Again. "Did I lead them here? Oh, god. Please, not that. Don't let this be my fault." She blinked hard to clear the moisture and then she noticed the dark stain on the man's shirt. Blood? He was

149

bleeding and the wolves ignored it? It couldn't be blood. "Are...are you okay?"

"No. The asshole with the rifle shot me."

She squeaked and surged to her feet, freezing when the alpha advanced on her, mouth open, canines gleaming, a growl rumbling in his chest. She held her breath.

"Stand very still," the man ordered. He didn't have to tell her twice.

He stepped through the ring of wolves, his hand dropping briefly to the head of the alpha. As he approached, she got a better look at him. Close-cropped black hair above piercing eyes that also appeared black. Dark-skinned with high cheekbones, a hawk nose, and a strong jaw, he towered over her. She resisted stepping backwards. She recognized the uniform now. Dark woodland camouflage pants and boots topped with an olive tan shirt with a U.S. Forestry Service patch. A forest ranger. She relaxed just a little.

"Give me your hand."

She offered him her right hand without stopping to consider his order. His strong fingers closed around hers and she had the impression he could crush her more delicate bones if he wanted. With surprising gentleness, he gripped her hand as he scooped the gun off the ground and shoved it into his belt.

"Slow now. Stay with me."

He led her toward the wolves with a soft tug and she followed, her heart rate spiking. He led her through the pack, pulled her up the incline, and snagged her camera strap as they reached the top. He passed it over wordlessly and she started to turn her head.

"Don't. They're watching. We need to grab your bag and keep moving."

She nodded wordlessly and as they passed the hollow behind the tree fall, she dropped to one knee to grab her camera bag. He pulled her back to her feet and continued on through the woods, surefooted and swift. She almost had to run to keep up with his long-legged stride. Every time they came to a moonlit space, she glanced down at his side. The stain kept growing.

"You're still bleeding." The words came out between panting breaths.

"Is this where I say d'uh?"

"I recognize sarcasm when I hear it," she muttered. And he didn't even sound winded. That was so unfair. She wasn't in bad shape. She hiked. She even jogged. Sometimes. She gritted her teeth and did her best to match his pace. The grip he maintained on her hand pulled her along in his wake. Her toe caught on a branch and she stumbled. He jerked her up and she collapsed against him. He grunted and winced at the contact.

"Look, you need a doctor. My car's…" She trailed off as she planted both feet and stopped, looking around to get her bearings. "Uhm…Actually, I have no clue where it is from here."

He smirked and nodded in the direction over her shoulder. "It's about two miles that way. We're closer to my place. And no, I don't need a doctor. It's a through-and-through wound. I just need to clean it out and stop the bleeding. I'll be fine." He gave her no time to protest, simply turned and towed her along as if she weighed no more than one of those tall, skinny fashion models. She almost giggled. That certainly didn't describe her. At all. At five foot two in her bare feet and a body more suited to an Old Masters' painting than the fashion runway, this was a totally new feeling for her.

Liz tripped again and the ranger tucked her closer to his side. "Can you see in the dark or something?"

"Or something."

This guy was a man of very few words. And she'd be darned if she was going to whine or ask him to slow down. She soon caught sight of a light flickering through the trees. She let out a sigh of relief but a moment later, the ranger had her shoved up against the rough bark of a tree trunk.

When he spoke, she as much felt the words as heard them, he was so quiet. "Don't move."

His breath teased her ear as she found her nose buried against his chest. She inhaled sharply and shivered as his rich, warm scent filled her lungs. A combination of pine needles, wind coming off fresh snow, and beneath it all, a spicy musk that was all male, his fragrance did funny things to her insides. She closed her eyes and inhaled again but he'd disappeared. She froze except for the slight movement caused by craning her neck to peek around the tree trunk. A shadow moved between her and the cabin. She blinked. Had she actually seen anything or was the movement a stray cloud drifting across that grinning moon? Minutes passed but no matter how hard she strained to see, nothing else moved in the dark.

"Let's go."

The scream was out before she could clap her hands over her mouth to stifle it. She balled up her fist and struck out blindly. "Don't sneak up on me like that!" His chuckle teased her ear and her girly bits all noticed how close he was. And then he disappeared again.

"Coming?"

She muttered but she wasn't sure if she was chastising him or her rebellious parts. She carefully picked her way across the uneven ground and then let out a little huff of air in relief as her feet discovered smooth grass and then a gravel path. She followed him up on the porch and waited as he unlocked the door.

Once inside, she glanced around—curious yet nervous. The main room looked comfortable enough with furniture designed for a man. The decorating was sparse, much like the man, now that she got a look at him in the soft light of a floor lamp.

"Have a seat. I'll be back after I get cleaned up." He gestured toward the couch and headed under the stairs toward what she figured was a bathroom. He shed his shirt as he went and she was treated to a glimpse of broad shoulders, a muscled back, and blood. She choked back a whimper. He paused at the door, turned, and tossed his shirt toward the kitchen sink. It missed but he ignored it, stepped into the bathroom, and shut the door behind him.

Despite feeling a little green around the gills, she turned a slow circle, partially to ignore the bloody clothing. Nothing of a personal nature hung on the walls. A few books occupied a battered, wooden bookcase and she wandered over to check them out. The first book she picked up surprised her. "The Art of War, by Sun Tzu." She read the title aloud doing her best to disregard the bloody shirt on the floor. The shirt would stain if not rinsed out. Even with the queasiness dancing in her stomach, she felt compelled to help out somehow. He had saved her from the wolves after all. And the hunter. She slipped over to the door and pressed her ear to the wood but couldn't hear a thing. She knocked timidly.

"Uhm…can I help with the bandage or anything?"

"I'm fine."

His voice sounded muffled but she got the distinct impression he hovered just on the other side. What had seemed like a thick barrier of heavy wood now seemed a little too flimsy for comfort. She inhaled deeply to get her imagination under control and backed away. The shirt tangled around one of her feet and she stooped to pick it up. Holding it with two fingers she scurried to the sink and dropped it in. Turning on the cold faucet, she waited while water soaked the shirt. When the water no longer looked pink, she turned it off, picked up the shirt and twisted it between her hands to wring it out. She shook it a little and held up it. Two things happened simultaneously. The bathroom door opened and she realized there were no bullet holes in the shirt.

CHAPTER 20

"WHAT ARE YOU doing?" Michael watched her stiffen and the scorched-milk stench of her fear clogged his nostrils. She turned slowly and held his wet shirt out in front of her like a shield.

"N-n-nothing. I just rinsed the b-blood out."

He stared at her, wondering why she was suddenly so terrified. Emotions flickered across her face and he hid his grin. Playing poker with this woman would be easier than taking candy from a baby. His shirt didn't have bullet holes and now she was wondering if maybe he was one of the bad guys. Just to test his theory, he stepped closer. She scurried backwards until her butt banged up against the counter.

"You st-stay right there, buster."

Buster? He snickered. "Can you put the shirt back in the sink so it doesn't drip all over my floor? If you promise not to panic, I'm going to reach into my hip pocket and get my ID. My name is Lightfoot. I am a ranger." As promised, he pulled out his photo ID and held it up.

She squinted at it. "I can't see it."

"Then come closer."

"How dumb do you think I am?"

His brow arched. "Really? I'm assuming that's a rhetorical question. Here..." He turned and padded toward the kitchen table. He tossed the ID on it and backed up into the living area. "I won't move while you check it." Trying his best to hide his smirk, he watched as she sidled over, snatched the plastic tag and scuttled back into the kitchen. She'd at least returned his shirt to the sink. He winced at the stitch in his side. His wound was knitting. Wolves didn't heal instantly, though their DNA helped heal them faster than a normal human.

"Dr. Graham, right?"

She nodded, still comparing his face to his photo. "You really are a ranger and not one of them?"

He'd guessed her train of thought correctly. "I really am. I'm a wildlife management officer, to be precise. I've been watching that den since the pack was relocated here. This is their first litter. How did you find them?"

She relaxed a little and pushed her hair back, hooking a loose strand behind one ear. "I'm doing a genetics study on native populations. When I found information about this pack, I started looking for them. I've been studying them since before the pups were born."

His brow furrowed. How had he not sensed her presence? Had not caught her scent? He inhaled, his nostrils flaring. She smelled of sweat and the acrid tang of fear but there was also a hint of... He sniffed again. Coconut? He wanted to sneeze but didn't.

"Who are those guys?"

He tilted his head to watch her. "You tell me."

"I don't know. But...wait!" Looking like a light bulb had gone off inside her head, she dashed toward the door.

The growl rumbled in his chest before he could stop it and with the preternatural speed of his kind, he blocked her way. She slid to a stop, her eyes wide with fear. She swallowed and he watched her throat work. He wanted to bury his nose in the soft hollow where her throat and jaw joined. He wanted to bury his dick between her legs. Her fear registered at the same moment as his consternation.

Fuck. She wasn't fertile yet but she would be soon. He needed to get her out of here and far away from him. He hadn't had a woman in a very long time and he didn't plan on enjoying this one.

"H-h-how did you do that?" She swallowed again. Her breasts rose and fell as she sucked air into her lungs.

Michael forced his eyes to her face. "What are you doing?" Her eyes widened even more and he swore under his breath. He didn't mean to growl but damn if his wolf didn't want her. She was short; if he held his arm out, she could walk under it without ducking. She was compact and curvy in all the right places. He had big hands and women with skinny butts turned him off. Hers would fill his hands as he backed her up to the wall and held her while she wrapped her legs around his waist and...

"R-Ranger Lightfoot?" Her voice quivered and the sulfurous stench of rotten eggs joined scorched milk as her fear edged toward terror.

Her scent choked him so he closed his eyes. Still, her face was burned on his retinas. Brown hair he'd first thought mousy shimmered with golden red highlights. He breathed deeply and opened his eyes, his gaze colliding with hers. No longer muddy green, her eyes reminded him of the color of Irish moss but her pupils dilated as she watched him, wary and nervous.

"I'm sorry, Dr. Graham. I'm running on adrenaline and my...military training kicked it. Where are you going?"

She blinked a couple of times, as if she didn't believe him but cleared her throat and answered. "My camera bag, there by the door. I-I used the flash to surprise those two guys. I may have actually gotten a picture of them, though it'll be in infrared. I was just going to get it. It's digital. We can look right now. I didn't recognize them but we could give the images to the police."

"Police?"

She nodded, less afraid now. He backed away from the door but still watched. His wolf had no intention of letting her leave.

"We have to call the police and report this. You were shot for goodness sakes! And I think they stole the two missing pups. I—" She paused as she dug out her camera and then glanced up at him. "I don't think they plan on selling the pups. I think they plan on using them for...I don't know...some sort of experiment or something."

The last people he needed to get involved were the police. He'd been shot, but the wound would be mostly healed in a couple of days and that would be hard to explain. Michael breathed deeply, partly to calm down, partly to let her scent fill his lungs to appease his wolf. If Liz's theory was correct, he had more than poachers to worry about. His Army unit had been disbanded because of a group of scientists working covertly with the government. Several teams like the 69th Special Operations Group were decommissioned and all records buried deep in the bowels of the Pentagon. Which in this day and age of computers and public information requests didn't mean a damn thing.

"Here. A moment. Let me click through the frames."

Her voice called to him and his wolf stretched lazily. Despite his best intentions, he stepped closer but concentrated on not crowding her. Liz was already spooked. He didn't want to send her running into the night. He watched over her shoulder, which wasn't hard given their height difference.

The first few photos showed the pack lounging around their den and the pups playing with each other and the juvenile wolves. He easily distinguished each pup based on their coloration and the personality they exhibited and picked out which two pups were missing—the biggest male and the most curious female. He couldn't figure out how the humans got so close to the den. The pups were almost old enough to be left alone while the pack hunted but for now, a beta female stayed close when the pack hunted. He'd go back in daylight and scout around the den to see if traps had been set.

Liz gasped and he focused his attention on the view screen of her camera. It was blank. She frantically pushed buttons but the screen remained dark.

"I don't understand." She almost wailed. "I know I fired the flash. Why didn't the shutter click? Even though this is infrared, there should be light splotches at least. I should have caught their faces!"

A growl rattled around in his chest ready to force its way between his clenched teeth. Maybe she was one of the thieves after all. He swallowed the sound and schooled his expression. "Maybe they weren't there? Maybe you invented them to cover your ass." He leered down at her. "And a mighty fine ass it is." A sardonic smile curled across the lower half of his face but his eyes remained expressionless on purpose.

She stepped backwards and clutched the camera to her chest almost as if it might protect her from him. Fat chance of that. Her skin flushed and she swallowed hard again. Several times. But she never blinked. Her gaze didn't challenge him—a very wise decision under the circumstances. She looked more like a wounded deer. Prey.

"I-I need to go. Whether you believe me or not, my supervisor needs to know that someone is poaching the wolves."

"Federal land, baby. State doesn't have jurisdiction."

"I still need to go. You can't keep me here."

"You plan on hiking back to your car?"

Liz lowered her eyes further and half-turned from him to stuff her camera in its bag. "If I have to. And before you get all smirky, no. I don't know where my car is from here. But I saw your Jeep outside so there has to be at least a fire road. I'll simply follow it down the mountain." She slung the bag over her shoulder, inhaled deeply, and raised her gaze to meet his. "I'm sorry you got hurt. You really should see a doctor."

She sidled toward the door but he made no move to stop her. Obviously feeling a little braver since he remained still, she reached for the door knob, turned it and pulled the door open. She peered out into the darkness and then fumbled in her bag again. She dug out a flashlight and clicked the button. The weak light formed a pale circle on the floor. The batteries likely wouldn't last the whole distance back to her car or down the mountain on the access road that ran between the main ranger station and his cabin.

Folding his arms across his chest, he waited. She thumped the shaft of the flashlight against her palm and the pool of light at her feet brightened perceptively. She glanced over her shoulder but he couldn't read her expression beyond determination with a hint of fear. Liz stepped through the door. His wolf reacted to a metallic click before the man could catch up. He slapped the light switch next to the door, plunging the house into darkness. His other arm circled her waist and his body drove her toward the rough wooden planks of the front porch. Michael rolled so she landed on top of him.

"What...?"

He knocked the flashlight from her hand a microsecond before what seemed like an angry wasp whizzed by and slammed into the log wall of the cabin behind her head. Reversing direction, he rolled them back toward the door and inside, kicking the door shut.

"Keep your head down," he hissed.

One of the front windows shattered and glass rained onto the floor not far from her. She stifled a scream and pulled her legs to her chest so she formed a tight, little ball. Absolute terror kicked in all sorts of survival instincts and hers seemed to be working.

He put his mouth next to her ear. "Liz, you need to crawl over under the stairs to the bathroom. Get inside, lock the door, and hunker down in the bathtub. It's cast iron and deep." More bullets thwacked into the outside wall. He felt her wince and noted the low keening moan she swallowed. "That's the safest place in the cabin."

"You aren't coming with me?"

Her voice quavered. He couldn't tell if it was from fear or worry for him, and he didn't have time to think about it. "No. I'm going hunting."

She shuddered as she watched the face of his humanity drop away. He turned into a predator right before her eyes. He was a predator—in human or wolf form. A former Army sniper, he never missed anything he targeted in his crosshairs. He listened, head cocked toward the door, before giving her a push. "Go."

He moved as she scurried across the floor. As the bathroom door closed, he loaded his sniper rifle. A moment later, he set a high-powered spotlight so it would shine out the broken window but would take an expert marksman to knock out. Michael suspected the shooter had night vision goggles. Had Liz been there to see him, the wolfish grin on his face would have scared ten years off her life. He had his own brand of night vision. He clicked on the light, dashed across the room and out the back door, fading into the shadows behind his house.

This is what he knew best, this elemental surge of power and hunger for the hunt. But this time...this time something else, some other emotion tinged his senses. Liz was in danger. And that was unacceptable. Michael didn't want to examine that feeling too closely. Not now when the distraction could get them both killed. He snarled. If anything happened to Liz, he'd be ripping heads off and shitting in the holes that were left. He circled through the woods, all his senses attuned to the barest sound, a mere glimpse of movement, a whiff of stench from those who dared threaten his mate.

Mate? Oh, shit. No. Not now. He didn't have time to be moonstruck. He focused on the task at hand. If he didn't take out the shooter, or shooters, she wouldn't survive long enough for him to confirm or deny. For a brief moment, he remembered when Mac had found

Hannah in the midst of a dangerous black ops mission. His commanding sergeant and the Army major who'd stolen Mac's heart managed to survive it. He and Liz would survive this.

Someone thrashed through the undergrowth up ahead. Michael paused, all his senses open. A familiar stink filled his nostrils. The man who'd shot him was back. And he'd brought friends—at least two but their scents were unfamiliar. Glass glinted through some low branches off to his left. He sighted in and a man's face, with night vision goggles shoved up on his forehead, swam into view. The spotlight had worked, temporarily blinding him. Michael's finger caressed the trigger. One gentle pull and the man's face would explode. Sinews and tendons tightened almost imperceptibly. This man dared threaten Liz. This man wounded him. If he killed him, dragged his body deeper into the woods, no one would ever know. Except him. He would know. The barrel of his rifle shifted a millimeter and he squeezed the trigger.

The bullet thwacked the tree trunk next to the man and bark splattered, hitting him in the face and drawing blood. With a muffled curse, the man dropped liked he'd been pole-axed but Michael never lost sight of him, following the guy's fall through his scope. Cloth rustled to his right and he listened intently. The other two had followed his muzzle flash and now attempted to sneak up on him. He melted into the shadows once more and circled around behind the man he'd "barked." These men thought they were playing cat and mouse. Little did they know it was wolf and hare. As long as they followed him, Liz remained safe in his house.

"What the fuck, man?" The voice whispered on the soft night breeze. "He's a freakin' forest ranger."

"Can't shoot worth shit, can he?" That voice belonged to man he'd shot at. "I wouldn't have missed."

"You already did, asshole. More'n once. As long as he's out here, the girl's alone. We need to get to the cabin and snatch her."

Michael saw red. Literally. He choked off the snarling growl and had to swallow a howl. He'd kill them if they touched Liz. He measured his breathing, regained control, let his training kick in to override his instincts. He wanted to kill them but knew he couldn't. He needed to find out who they were. Why were they here? But more important, who the hell did they work for? Time to get answers.

Homing in on the voices, he reloaded his rifle. The tranquilizer darts he had would take down a large elk. At the moment, he was sorry he wasn't loaded for bear, but he needed them alive to answer questions. Sighting in on the first man's chest, he elevated the barrel slightly, squeezed the trigger, and smiled when the man slapped at his shoulder. His target gasped and then his eyes rolled back in his head. He melted to the ground as his knees gave way. Michael had reloaded and had the second man in his sights before the first hit the ground. That man quickly followed his buddy to dreamland, which left the third man. He slipped through the forest, intent on his final target. He found the man creeping toward the cabin. Michael stretched out on the moss-covered ground and took aim.

The hairs prickled on the back of his neck but the warning came too late. Pain exploded in his head. Skyrockets burst behind his eyes before darkness surround him. He'd failed. He hadn't protected his mate.

I'm sorry, Liz.

CHAPTER 21

LIZ HUDDLED IN the old-fashioned claw-footed tub, shivering. Terrified, she jolted at each creak in the log house, at every sighing breath of wind outside. When a gunshot echoed outside, she clapped her hands over her mouth to stifle her scream. She knew she shouldn't trust the ranger. Michael. He was so...strange. Intense. His dark eyes had bored into her very soul, stripping her bare, his distrust evident in his expression. But at the same time, he'd seemed to protect her. When he tackled her on the porch, he'd twisted at the last minute to cushion her fall. She remembered his muffled oath, had felt him wince, and realized she'd landed on his injured side.

His first thought had been to protect her. And now he was out there with those terrible men. If men would steal wolf pups for nefarious reasons, what would keep them from killing Michael? He'd already been shot once.

She strained to listen. Were those more gunshots? The sounds were muted, a thud rather than a sharp report. A silencer? She choked back a nervous cry. All she knew about identifying the sound of gunshots and silencers came from some Foley artist adding sound effects to a movie. She didn't do guns. Hated the things, in fact.

A sharp cra-ack sounded much too close for comfort and her heart leaped against her ribcage. She tried to breathe, to swallow around the fear clogging her throat. That *was* a gunshot. She was positive of it. What was going on out there? Was Michael all right? Should she call for help? But who would she call? She didn't even know if Michael had a phone but surely he had a two-way radio or something. He had to have some way to contact the ranger station and the outside world, right?

She screwed up her courage and poked her head above the rim of the tub. Her eyes had adjusted to the dark and she could see vague shapes in the bathroom. Creeping over the edge, she crouched on the floor and held her breath, listening. All she heard was the pounding of her own pulse in her ears. She let out a slow puff of air and crept to the door. Pressing her ear against the smooth wood, she listened again, remembering to breathe softly this time. Something creaked out in the main room. A floorboard maybe? Liz fought the urge to hold her breath. A second creak echoed, above her head this time. Someone climbed the stairs to the sleeping loft. She pressed her knuckles to her mouth and abandoned the door. As frightened as any mouse, she scurried back to the tub and tumbled into it.

Pleasepleasepleaseplease. The plea reverberated in her head. No light shone under the door so maybe this room would stay hidden. Somebody now stomped around the room above her head. Whoever it was most likely didn't belong here. She'd bet money Michael lived alone. He didn't seem like the roomie type.

Why did she trust him? Just because he was sexier than all get out? He was definitely that. Tall, but to her every man was tall. Broad shoulders. Muscled chest and back. A butt that filled out those camouflage pants and thighs that flexed when he walked. Normally, she liked long hair on a guy. Hey, she was a Cali girl by birth, but his close-cropped hair fit his chiseled face. Chiseled? Okay, she'd been reading way too many romance novels.

Since she wasn't dating anyone, who could blame her? The scientific part of her brain understood she was focusing on trivial things to keep her fear at bay. The scared part of her didn't care. She just wanted to get away and be safe.

Liz strained to listen, berating herself silently for acting like some dumb teen star in a slasher movie. The floor above her head creaked again and she followed the sound of heavy steps clomping down the stairs. Maybe it was Michael after all and he was just checking things out to make sure no one snuck in while he was gone. The door to the bathroom banged open and a flashlight blinded her. Or maybe not.

"Stand up."

That disembodied voice demanded immediate compliance but she didn't move. What could they do, shoot her? Then she remembered the sound of gunshots and shattered glass. Oh, yeah, they could do exactly that. She held up her hands so they'd see she was unarmed and then braced on the tub's rim to steady her shaking knees as she stood.

"Who—"

"Shut up." A hand appeared from behind the light, grabbed her arm and jerked her out of the tub. She scrambled to get her feet under her. The man didn't give her much time. He marched her out of the bathroom. "Got her. What about that ranger?"

"Dead."

Liz couldn't breathe for a minute. Dead? How could Michael be dead? What was so important about those wolf pups that these men would kill a forest ranger over them? Did that mean they were going to kill her, too? Her mouth worked as she tried to form words but nothing coherent came out, only a scared whimper. Men moved through the darkness, heavy-footed and cursing as they bumped into furniture. The odor of alcohol filled her nose even as her ears identified the sound of something being poured. Booze? Or something more sinister? Were they going to burn down the cabin? It'd been a dry season. Burning the place would start a forest fire. All the animals... She flailed at her captor as another thought struck. Did they plan on leaving her in the house to burn with it? Fire. Her biggest nightmare. Her biggest fear.

Her fist connected with the man's face and he grunted. When his grip loosened just enough, she jerked free. Liz collapsed but didn't stop moving, crabbing on hands and feet for the door. She scooted through it, straightened as she jumped off the porch, and took off for the woods at a dead run. Her whole body tensed, waiting for a gunshot to her back. None came. Head down and running hard, she didn't see the man until she ran into his solid form—and bounced off.

She landed on her butt, all the air knocked out of her lungs. Struggling to breathe, she stared up at the huge form she'd hit. And screamed. His meaty fist aimed at her face and she closed her eyes. The force of his punch snapped her head back. As she slipped into darkness, she wondered if he'd broken her neck.

🐾🐾🐾🐾

LIZ GROANED BUT didn't open her eyes. She hurt all over and a supernova exploded behind her closed lids. Her head pounded in time to her thudding pulse. Something small and cold nudged her cheek. She batted her hand in annoyance and connected with fur. A sharp whine, much too close to her ear, caused her to wince. This was the worst hangover ever. Even her hair hurt. Something warm and damp licked her cheek. She didn't have a dog. She didn't even have a goldfish. And she hadn't been drinking!

Her memories rushed back and she sat bolt upright. Starbursts blinded her and the sound of little claws scrabbling away from her on a bare floor grated like chalk on a blackboard. She closed her eyes against the sparkles and crossed her legs Indian style to sit more comfortably. She propped her aching head in her palms as memories rushed in to fill the void. That sorry son of a bitch hit her. She winced as her exploring fingers found the lump and the tender flesh on her cheek.

Something whined again and when she opened her eyes this time, she could make out shapes in the room—not like there was much to see. The small room looked like it might have once been a laundry room. There was one door holding a tiny window at eye-level and another window high on the opposite wall. She couldn't see much outside. It was still dark out. Beneath that window, plumbing stuck out of the wall along with a covered hole she thought might have once been a dryer vent. The linoleum on the floor looked old and scuffed.

She shared the space with two puppies. She blinked rapidly hoping to clear her vision before closing her eyes and with utmost care, rolled her neck. The muscles were stiff but the motion didn't add to the pain throbbing in her head. In fact, it seemed to ease the ache a little. She opened her eyes to find the puppies sniffing her boots. The smaller one whined and climbed into her lap.

Liz choked back her gasp as the second pup hopped into her lap, too. These weren't dogs. Wolf pups. These were the two missing wolf pups. They must have smelled the pack on her and that's why they wanted to be close. She stroked them both, her mind whirling. People bred wolves in captivity to sell. While those pups commanded four figures, there'd be no market worth the hassle of live trapping babies in the wild. And why kidnap her? Her heart clutched for a moment as all the memories rushed back. Dead. Michael was dead. She wanted to throw up and had to swallow hard to keep the bile down. She couldn't think about him. Not right now. She focused on the wolves instead. Why kill to steal the pups? None of this made sense.

The lock on the door clicked and the pups burrowed deeper into her lap. The little female tried to climb inside her shirt. She cuddled them and scrambled to the far corner. The door opened slowly. Two men stood there.

"See, told you she'd take care of 'em." She recognized him as the man with the rifle from the wolf den.

"Just 'cause they'll let her get close doesn't mean they'll eat." She'd never seen the bigger man before but he scared her far more than the first.

"Hello. I'm right here. What is going on? Why am I here? You better let me go right now! If you do...I...I won't tell anyone."

"Too late for that, girlie."

Girlie? Who the hell was the jerk calling girlie?

"You better hope those pups stay alive. That's the only reason you're not singing with the angels."

"Ha. Shows what you know. I can't sing."

The jerk laughed. "You do have a mouth, girlie. I think we'll have lots of fun." His leer left little to her imagination and reminded her of his previous plans for her.

"Put your dick back in your pants." The bigger man—the one who'd hit her—looked bored. "She's not here for that. She's here to look after the pups so we can deliver them alive and well. You clear on that, shithead?"

"Jeez, dude. Don't take it personal."

"Nothing in this job is personal."

Liz could well believe that. The man's expression never changed. He appeared cold, aloof, and in complete control of his emotions. Mercenary. The man was a mercenary. The cold lump in her chest confirmed her assessment.

A third man appeared carrying a plastic bag marked with a convenience store logo. "Water and dog food, boss."

She stared at the bag, trying to guess its contents from the shapes. Dry dog food? That wouldn't work. These pups were barely weaned, if at all. No wonder they wouldn't eat. "Idiots." The word slipped out.

The big man's eyes narrowed. He could be angered. She needed to remember that. "Watch your mouth."

"They can't eat that," she explained.

"There's no such thing as wolf food." The man with the bag sounded whiny.

"If they were old enough, they could eat dog food. But they aren't. They're still nursing. They need their mother."

"I'm not about to go catch that wolf bitch so you'd better figure out some way to keep them alive and healthy until they can be delivered."

Liz looked around the bare room. "I need milk. Preferably goat's milk. Or canned milk as long as it doesn't have sugar in it. And puppy chow. And canned dog food. And I need a stove or some way to heat the milk."

"Make a list."

She glanced up at the big man and calculated how far she could push. "I need to go to the grocery store to get the right stuff." Her gaze slid over to the doofus with the sack and she waved a negligent hand. "Even spelling everything out, I doubt this guy could get it right."

The guy in charge laughed and she breathed. So far so good. If she could get out in public, she wasn't afraid to make a scene. The big man stared at her as if assessing her motives. He wasn't as dumb as he looked and she'd do well to remember that.

"I'll take you. And if you make one peep or try to get away, I'll come straight back here and slit the wolves' throats. And I'll make you watch."

Her eyes widened in horror and she choked on the bile churned up by her stomach. The pups whined and burrowed closer, sensing her fear.

"Get up and go wash your face. No need to call more attention than necessary."

She moved the pups carefully and pushed off the floor. She wobbled a bit, overcome with dizziness. She braced a hand on the wall until her vision cleared. The pups clamored around her feet, shivering in their fear. She bent and gathered them into her arms. "Do you have a big box or something to put them in? Being out in the open like this is stressful for them. They need a place to nest."

"Nest? They ain't chickens." The smaller man guffawed at his stupid joke.

"Shut up, dickhead. Go find a box."

"And a blanket. Or a towel. Something soft."

Liz didn't move. She cuddled the pups and tried to stare down the big guard. Stupid on her part but she felt better for the attempt, like she was less a victim and might actually have a say in her future. The second man returned with a plastic tub deep enough to keep the pups inside. He tossed it her direction and she ducked instinctively. The thing bounced with a hollow thump and skittered on its side to the far wall. She righted it with her foot and lowered the pups into it.

Glancing over her shoulder she started to ask about a towel but stopped when she caught both men leering at her rear end. She stripped off her jacket instead and made a nest for the pups. They sniffed the material and then settled on it, curled in together. Liz straightened and faced her kidnappers. "You said something about me cleaning up?"

Thirty minutes later, when the big guard removed the blindfold he'd placed on her before leading her to the vehicle, she stood in a dimly-lit parking lot. The small grocery store looked mostly deserted, not that she could do anything overt anyway. With luck, there would be video cameras in the store. She planned to plaster her face on every single one of them. When she didn't show up for work, somebody would come looking. Hopefully.

Big Dude fisted the back of her shirt and marched her toward the front door. "Not a word out of you, remember?"

She nodded, but didn't say anything figuring now was not a good time to test his sincerity. She grabbed a shopping cart and with him shadowing her, started down the aisles, looking up as much as possible seeking security cameras. She dragged her feet, figuratively if not literally. The longer she was there, the better the chance someone would notice her battered face and Big Dude's threatening manner.

By the time she was through shopping, her cart was full. Paper towels, puppy food—dry and canned, evaporated milk, baby bottles, and one carton of goat milk. She hoisted the items onto the conveyor at the checkout lane. The bored cashier never even looked up though Liz wasn't sure she'd have the nerve to even mouth that she needed help. The total rang up and she reached into her back pocket for her debit card without a second thought. The clerk was about to take it from her when Big Dude knocked it out of her hand with a growl.

"Cash."

Stunned, she stared at him for a long moment. "I-I don't have any."

He dug a bill out of his pocket and tossed it at the clerk. "Keep the change." He glared at her, grabbed the bags and shoved two into her arms. "I'll get your card."

Her heart sank, albeit she felt a little relief. While she might have been traceable if it was left behind, she wasn't completely sure that the clerk or a customer wouldn't have jumped at the opportunity to drain her account.

The clerk unfolded the bill and held it out. "Yo, bro. This is only a fifty."

She stared at the clerk like he'd grown a second head but he only had eyes for Big Dude. Big Dude stared at the clerk, too.

"Your total was $84.39." Did the guy have a death wish?

"Tough shit."

Big Dude grabbed her arm and hustled her out the door. She glanced back over her shoulder. The kid had grabbed the house intercom phone and was making an announcement into it. She cringed. She hadn't done anything wrong. She'd kept her part of this devil's bargain. Would he still kill the pups? He dragged her across the parking lot but she managed to stay on her feet and keep hold of the grocery bags. He all but threw her into the back seat of the SUV.

"Keep your fucking head down or else."

She already knew what that *or else* entailed. She obeyed, crouching on the floorboards and bracing her body between the seats as he drove like a maniac. If she survived this ride, she was going to beat the crap out of the guy. Sure she was. A girl could dream, right?

CHAPTER 22

A ROUGH, DRY tongue rasped against his cheek as the scent of wet wolf permeated his nose. Michael kept his eyes closed, reaching for the dream of womanly curves and hair that smelled of coconut. But why was he lying in the woods, half-dressed, in a rain storm?

The wolf licking his face whined. He'd been hunting with the pack. No. Men. Hunters. LIZ! Memory flooded back. He sat up and promptly rolled to his hands and knees as dry heaves racked his body. Stars burst against his retinas and his head throbbed with pain. A warm trickle trailed from his temple and his nostrils flared at the hot, coppery scent of his own blood.

He checked the diver's watch on his wrist. He'd been unconscious for most of the night. The wolf nosed him again. Switching positions with great care, Michael sat and combed his fingers through the wolf's thick pelt. "Wish you could talk, big guy." The words tumbled out thick and jumbled. He touched his fingertips to his temple to discover raw, jagged skin, half-congealed blood and another flare of pain. He'd been shot. Again. And left for dead. Big mistake on the part of the hunters.

Using a nearby tree, he managed to lurch to his feet. He leaned against the rough bark until his head cleared of dizziness. Breathing through the pain, he pushed off the trunk and stumbled back to his cabin. Shards of glass glittered under the intermittent flashes of lightning. The door hung on bent hinges, creaking as the wind waved it back and forth. He crept to the front porch, ears attuned to any living thing inside. Nothing. No sound of breathing. His nose twitched at the odor of alcohol laced with oak. Damn. That was sixteen-year-old scotch. He sniffed again. No scent of fear or adrenaline. No thumping hearts. Liz was gone. Taken.

The wolf cringed back as Michael growled, the man more beast than human at that moment. He searched the house, playing out the scenario in his mind. The good news was that he caught no whiff of Liz's blood. She'd left here in one piece. The bad news was he had no idea where they'd taken her. Padding into the bathroom, he discovered the lights still worked. He examined his wound in the mirror, cleaned it again and slapped a bandage on it. He probably had a concussion and that would preclude him from shifting. And needed stitches, too, since he couldn't shift.

Gripping the handrail, he hauled his protesting body up the stairs to change clothes. If he was to find Liz, he'd have to start in town. In moments, he'd pulled on a uniform, slipped boots on, and headed back downstairs. He grabbed keys and his phone, patted the wolf and headed to his SUV.

Down in Northpark, flashing lights drew him like a moth to the one grocery store in town. As Michael parked, he noticed the town constable inside talking to the clerk. Neither of them were the brightest crayons in the box but from the wild gesturing, he figured something fairly serious had happened.

As he stepped inside the clerk was explaining what the shoplifter had taken. "Goat milk. I mean, really? Who drinks that shit? And puppy chow. The guy gave me a fifty. Had the balls to tell me to 'keep the change.' The woman with him tried to pay but he wouldn't let her."

"What did she look like?" Michael butted into the conversation without a second thought.

The clerk shrugged. "Didn't pay much attention, Ranger Lightfoot. She was short and had a big ol' knot on her cheek, like she'd been hit with a two by four or something."

Michael managed to keep a snarl from showing in his expression. "What about the man?"

Constable Gunderson stared at him, his mouth working like a guppy. "You can't just—"

"Yes, I can." He cut the other man off. "I was attacked up at my cabin last night and a state wildlife biologist was kidnapped. Do you have surveillance footage?"

Bug-eyed, the clerk nodded. "Yeah...but I can't leave the register to take you to the office."

"Constable Gunderson will watch it while you're gone. Let's go." His tone left no room for argument.

Thirty minutes later, he had a picture of Liz's kidnapper firmly entrenched in his memory, along with Liz's battered face. He'd kill the sonavabitch for hurting her. He had to admire the doc, though. She'd managed to get her face plastered on every camera in the store, along with all the items she'd placed in her basket. Wherever she was, he figured he'd find the wolf pups, too. Two birds, one shot. He left after taking cell phone pictures of both Liz and the man with her from the surveillance monitor.

Sitting in his vehicle, he emailed the photo to Ian McIntire, his NCO from Army days. He'd bet money either Mac or his wife, Hannah, could figure out a way to run the photos through a facial recognition program. Michael would learn if Liz was on the square and with luck, who the asshole was. In the meantime, he needed to find the big black SUV captured on the store's cameras. Cruising the motels and cabins around town, he came up empty. That could mean they were on the road or that they were holed up in one of the remote cabins sprinkled across the mountainside.

The sun was up now, sparkling through the branches of the pine trees circling Northpark. The rain hadn't followed him down the mountain. He parked outside the one real estate office in town. If anyone knew about strangers in the area, Monica Presgrove would. The woman was a complete snoop. The "Closed" sign showed on the door so he settled in to wait.

A tap on his window made him jump. He'd dozed off without realizing it. Monica stood outside, holding two cups of coffee. He rolled down the window.

"You're up early, Ranger. You drink your coffee black, right?"

"Yes, ma'am." He accepted the Styrofoam cup from her and inhaled deeply. The scent of caffeine was almost as bracing as swallowing the stuff. She backed away so he could open his door and step out.

She blanched as she saw his face full on. "What in the world happened to you?"

"Long story, Miz Presgrove. I need to know if you've noticed anyone suspicious hanging around the area lately?"

She waggled her finger at him. "No, you want to know if I've leased a cabin to someone who wants to stay out of sight. As a matter of fact, a group of fishermen leased Lone Pine Cottage last week."

He waited for her to enlighten him. She cleared her throat, sipped her coffee, and gestured for him to follow her up onto the porch of the old Victorian house she used for an office. She settled in the porch swing before she continued. He bit back his impatience. This was the way Monica worked and he couldn't rush her.

"Problem is, ranger, they didn't have any fishing gear. Guns? Now those they had. In spades. I mentioned that hunting season didn't start for a couple of months and the man who seemed to be in charge insisted they were here for the trout."

"Seemed to be?"

She offered him a sly smile. "The big scary hulk who stayed in their SUV had everyone cowed."

He held out his cell phone to her. "Him?"

Her forehead crinkled in surprise and she and nodded. "Yes. I do believe so. But there was no woman with them. Just two skinny little geeks, the big guy on your phone, and three guys cut from his cloth."

"What're the terms of their lease?"

She opened her mouth to protest his question but obviously saw something in his expression that changed her mind. "A month. Cash up front. Option to keep it for another two months."

"Thanks, Miz Presgrove." He turned to leave but she called him back.

"Ranger Lightfoot? Don't go up there alone. The geeks are trivial but those other men? They mean business." She blinked and tilted her head, watching him with far too much knowledge in her eyes. "Like you."

"Like me?"

"Yes. They are dangerous men. But unlike you, they don't care which side they're on, just so long as there's money involved and they get their share."

He stared at her a long moment. "That's very astute, Miz Presgrove."

She laughed, the sound a gay twitter. "I wasn't always old and I wasn't always a real estate agent in a one-stop-light town." She met his quizzical stare with a wink but then grew serious. "These guys are not to be trifled with, Ranger. Please take back up with you. Call the sheriff. Get some deputies."

His phone beeped before he could respond—Mac calling him back. He thanked her quickly and returned to his car before speaking. "Did you find something?"

"Your doc is just who she says she is. A wildlife biologist with a background in genetics employed by the Wyoming Division of Wildlife Management. The dude? Bad news, Lightfoot. He popped up all over the place and not in good ways. At the moment, he's employed by Black Root Security."

"Damn."

"Double damn, man. You can't take on these guys alone. Want me to send up the Bat Signal?"

He shook his head then realized Mac couldn't see him. "No. I need to scout the terrain first. I'll be in touch."

Mrs. Presgrove remained on the porch watching him. He offered a small wave before climbing into his SUV. He headed down the street and almost chuckled as Constable Gunderson parked in the spot he'd just vacated. He hoped the real estate agent would keep the man occupied until he could get out of town and cover his tracks. He headed home to get the gear he would need for a reconnaissance mission.

🐾🐾🐾🐾

LIZ CURLED UP and braced as best she could against the bumpy ride. If the driver didn't wreck, he'd probably kill her once they got back to the house. Either way, she figured she was about to die. Looking back, she'd led a miserable life not worth recounting. No flash of clarity, no moments of heart-breaking remembrance, nothing to note she'd lived her life well. One of two things—she wasn't going to die today or the poets were wrong. She prayed it was the former. She didn't doubt for a minute that the man in the driver's seat would kill her and the wolf pups without a second thought.

A ripple of grief moved through her soul. Michael was dead. Why did her heart lurch and ache when she thought of him? He'd been a jerk. He'd also saved her life at least once. Okay, more than once. And he'd died trying to save her again. But there was something else, some deeper connection. The feel of his arms wrapped around her, the strength of him, even the way he smelled—wild and rich like he'd never been touched by civilization.

She had to physically shake her whole body to get her thoughts back on track. Her office wouldn't miss her for several days. They knew she'd gone into the field and wouldn't expect her back. Michael was... She couldn't voice the thought. He couldn't be dead. That was just wrong in ways she didn't want to think about. Blinking back tears, she inhaled deeply. Nobody would save her but herself. And she was determined to save the pups, too.

Liz hadn't worked out all the details but these thugs weren't stealing the pups to be sold. There was something darker at work here. And if she wasn't careful, she'd end up a casualty of war. She inhaled again, working past the pain in her chest. War. Yes, that's exactly what this felt like. She was a prisoner of war, but she wasn't a total girlie girl. She might be small but so was Mighty Mouse. And Speedy Gonzales. The Roadrunner was smarter than the coyote. She just needed to think smarter. Big Dude had messed up back at the grocery store. The clerk would have notified the authorities. Her face—and his—was on the security tapes. She'd gladly get arrested for shoplifting.

The big vehicle rocketed around a tight curve and she was thrown against the opposite door with enough force her shoulder popped. Pain radiated but she could still move it. That contact would leave a bruise for sure. She shifted slightly to brace better but the SUV slowed for a long climb along a bumpy road. As ready as she was to get back to the wolves, she wasn't quite prepared for the ride to end. She didn't have a plan yet.

Big Dude climbed out, opened the door, grabbed the collar of her shirt and yanked. She spilled out on the ground at his feet. Moments later, he jerked her upright, shoved some bags into her arms and hustled her toward a sweet, Victorian-style cottage. Her brain scrambled to catch up, completely unable to wrap around the concept of these mercenaries staying in an ivy-covered cottage. A giggle welled up from deep in her chest but she swallowed the hysteria creating it. Hysterics could come later. Right now, she needed to remain focused.

She didn't have much chance to look around as Big Dude hustled her toward the back and the little room where she'd awakened. She could hear the puppies whimpering as one of the other guys opened the door. A meaty hand shoved her between the shoulder blades and she ended up on her knees. More bruises to add to her collection. She bit back an angry reply as the door slammed shut behind her. For now, she was alive and so were the pups.

Crooning to them, she lifted them out of the box and cuddled them. Both tried to lick her face and burrow into her shirt. The male eventually squirmed loose and rooted around in the sacks. She needed to get food into them. But she also needed something to heat the milk and make a warm mash of the dog food. Before she could yell at her captors, the door opened. One of the guards held a microwave and a few plastic bowls. The male pup chased after him as he strode across the room. The man kicked the little wolf and Liz leaped off the floor, flailing at the man with her fists without a second thought.

One man grabbed her from behind, growled some orders, and held her still while another man set up the microwave and plugged it in. The little male cringed with his sister as the man stomped out, laughing. Moments later, she was free and whirled just in time to see the door close. An unmistakable click indicated the door was locked once more.

Liz opened the microwave to set the milk inside and found an old-fashioned can opener. She used it to open the dog food while the milk warmed. Mixing some kibbles with the canned food, she set it in the oven to heat while she tried to bottle feed the pups. They suckled hungrily, like they hadn't eaten in days.

After the pups were sated, they settled in the box for naps. She'd turned it on its side so it was more cave-like. They snuggled together on her jacket and were soon sound asleep. Now that things were quiet, she realized she hurt. All over. She bet her bruises had bruises. Even so, she had no time to relax. Creeping to the door, she pressed her ear against it. Silence. No TV. No radio. No conversation. Were her guards still here? She gripped the door knob. The thing wouldn't move, not even to rattle.

She lay down in front of the box and attempted to get comfortable. Worn out, her body decided the hard floor wasn't so uncomfortable after all. Her eyelids drooped and she didn't suppress the yawn stretching her jaw. She and the pups were still alive. That was enough. For now.

CHAPTER 23

MICHAEL LISTENED, THE voice whispering from his cell phone both familiar and comforting.

"Tala and I are in Teton Village. One of the grandchildren has a timeshare condo. What is going on, Wolf? I have been up all night thinking of you."

"You are always too wise, Nakai. A lot of shit has happened. Can you come?"

"We are an hour away. Can it wait?"

"No, but I will wait for you. I need your wisdom."

"What is her name?"

Michael choked and had to clear his throat before he could speak. "How do you know a woman is involved?"

Nakai's low chuckle grated on his nerves. "We will talk but now I drive fast."

"Thank you."

He clicked off the phone and went back to work. The men who invaded his cabin wanted one thing—the woman. They'd also tried to burn the place down. He'd been in too big a rush to notice earlier. They'd emptied several bottles of excellent scotch and left a pile of papers smoldering. His gun locker remained undiscovered. Had they found it, they might have gone back to make sure he was dead. Lucky for him, they just assumed the worst.

Unlucky for them. He'd find them. And it would be ugly when he did. They had much for which to atone.

When Nakai and his wife arrived, Michael was on the porch waiting for them. Tala took one look at him, kissed his cheek, and passed into the house without a word. He heard her bustling in the kitchen.

"Tell me about the woman?" Nakai was not one for preambles.

Michael stared at him. "I still want to know why you think there is a woman."

The old Indian's face crinkled into a smile. "You are moonstruck, Wolf. But there is more than that." He nodded toward the arsenal Michael had assembled.

"It is a long story, Nakai. I will tell you as we drive."

Tala appeared at the door, wiping her hands on a dishtowel. "You bring her home. I will have food ready."

Nakai kissed his wife, picked through the weapons and then gestured for Michael to lead the way.

In the SUV, Michael briefed his former Army teammate and finished with, "I am not moonstruck." He sounded defensive which only pissed him off even more. "This is strictly a rescue operation. Somebody took those wolf pups and somebody took her." The old man remained silent, which caused Michael to snarl even more. "What?"

"You can fight your feelings but I think this woman is under your skin. If nothing else, these men invaded your territory and took her from you. It is good we hunt. It has been a very long time for me."

Michael controlled his breathing to get a handle on his anger. Nakai was here to help, even if he didn't like the insinuations the old man made. "Do you miss those days?"

"Sometimes."

He laughed. "Yeah, me, too. Wolves are not meant to be domesticated."

The old man's face split into a grin. "Try telling my woman that. Or Mac's." The chuckle reference to Hannah McIntire created died on Michael's lips as Nakai continued, "I think these men we hunt should be glad the moon is not full tonight."

He stared into the distance, weighing his words before speaking them. The old man was very wise—in the ways of Wolves and their mates, and in the ways of men. Hannah had watched them shift and hunt on the full moon. She'd mated with Ian McIntire despite everything. She'd adjusted to life governed by the phases of the moon. Michael prided himself on his control—as a soldier, as a Wolf.

"Even if this were the Blood Moon I would not lose control. I hunt because these men violated the pack I swore to protect. They took new pups from their mother. I want to know why mercenaries now kidnap puppies." And a feisty biologist. He left that thought unvoiced but the quick glance at his passenger convinced him that he might as well have said it out loud. Nakai knew exactly what he was feeling.

"The Blood Moon is a bad time for a Wolf. Do you think this might be like what happened before?"

"What do you mean?"

"Perhaps you should call Mac. Maybe his Hannah knows something. She still works with the Pentagon."

Michael stared at the old man so long he ended up jerking the steering wheel to keep the SUV on the road. "I hadn't considered this situation might be tied to what happened back then."

"You should. When scientists need mercenaries, there is a bad moon on the horizon."

He drove in silence, pondering what Nakai had said. The more he considered the implications, the more he was convinced the old man was on to something. Why hadn't he figured that out himself? Man, living in the backwoods had really dulled his senses. He'd sent photos to Mac and Hannah to help track down the guy with Liz, but he hadn't made any connection to the situation that led to the Wolves disbanding. Black Root had been an entity that reared its ugly head later in another matter Hannah had investigated but in retrospect? Maybe. Maybe they needed to take a closer look at Black Root.

As he neared the drive for Lone Pine Cottage, he slowed. Tire tracks showed on the rutted road but tall pines hid the cottage. No smoke stained the blue sky. To all appearances, the place was deserted. But Michael knew better. So did Nakai, judging by his reaction. Michael pressed the accelerator and headed on up the mountain road. Two miles later, he steered onto a forestry access road and shifted into four wheel drive. When he reached a turn-around, he pulled off and cut the engine.

Wordlessly, the two men armed themselves and slipped into the pine trees. They might have been apart for almost ten years, but old habits die hard. They'd trained together for almost a human lifetime. They'd participated in covert missions just like this more times than either could remember. They didn't need words. Each knew what to do and Michael was glad to have Nakai at his side once more. The only thing better would be for the whole team to be here but each of them had found a new life after the Army, after Hannah helped disband the 69th. Granted, it had been for their own safety, but the whole incident and reason for the deactivation left a bitter taste in his mouth.

A deadfall above the cottage provided perfect cover. They prowled to the piled-up branches and settled in behind them to watch and wait. Wolves were patient hunters. So long as Liz wasn't in imminent danger, he would remain hidden until nightfall. Once it was dark, he and Nakai would scout the house.

🐾🐾🐾🐾

THE HAIR ON Liz's arms prickled and she had the sense she was being watched. She remained still, eyes closed, listening with all her might. Nothing. No sound but the soft whimpers of the pups. She pushed to a sitting position and just managed to suppress her groan. She only thought she'd hurt before. Stiff and aching, she tried to stretch but had to bite back a whine.

"Ow."

The pups stirred and after their own stretches, they joined her. She needed to feed them again. She crawled over to the microwave and heated more goat milk, but added a little evaporated milk with it. The goat milk wouldn't last without refrigeration and she'd need to transition to watered-down canned milk sooner than later.

Once she had the bottles prepared, the pups nosed in and latched onto the nipples, sucking hungrily. She still couldn't shake the sense someone watched. She glanced at the dirty glass square set in the door but couldn't see anyone on the other side. The outside window was set well above her head. She could see the overhang of the eaves and despite the shade, the window provided enough light to see by. Not even Big Dude was tall enough to look through it so no one could play Peeping Tom. Her stomach grumbled, pulling her thoughts away from unseen eyes to focus on something much more pressing—like starvation. She wondered if she could—or would—eat dog food if she got hungry enough.

🐾🐾🐾🐾

MICHAEL STARED THROUGH the small window on the back of the house but couldn't see anything. His instincts insisted Liz had been confined there, and might still be. The interior of the room remained bathed in gloom but the occasional shadow led him to believe it was occupied. Nakai appeared at his side.

"Four men, front room. Two on the porch."

Michael nodded. That tallied with the evidence he'd found at the wolf den and his cabin. "Back room."

Nakai's gaze flicked toward the window. He watched for a long moment. "One. The girl?"

"Hopefully."

Both men froze as the front door opened and muffled voices carried on the light breeze. One of the guards had been ordered to transport the two science geeks back to some facility. That cut their forces in half, not that he and Nakai weren't up to taking out all of them, mercenaries or not.

"We wait for dark."

Nakai nodded. Between one sighing breeze through pine needles and the next, the old man disappeared. Nakai would circle the cottage and set up an observation post on the other side. Michael settled in, set up his sniper rifle, and checked the rest of his weapons. He hoped this could remain a covert operation but if it went hot, so be it. He'd killed before and would kill again. The snarl twisted his face before he could stop it or the thoughts running rampant in his head.

Liz. Short, curvy, vibrant Liz pressed against him as he buried himself in her sweet pussy, each breath pressing her full breasts against his skin... No, his fur. He gulped and shook the thoughts from his head. Fuck. Nakai was right. Moonstruck. The need to mate couldn't come at a worst time. He clamped down on the raging hormones. He wasn't some adolescent Wolf ready to fuck everything that moved. He would not force himself on Liz. Once he got her back. Once he killed the man who dared mark her face with his fist. He would claim her then.

The growl rumbled in his chest and the birds previously chattering in the branches above him stilled. Two squirrels playing tag froze. Even the wind died, leaving a breathless stillness in its wake. The world knew a predator lurked in the shadows and that death would come with the setting sun. He cooled his anger. A few minutes later, the critters resumed their activities. He could only hope that the mercs in the cottage were not as attuned to the wildlife as he was.

LIZ CLEANED UP the corner of the laundry room and stuffed the soiled paper towels into one of the plastic grocery bags. The pups had eaten again and now nested in their box. Hungry, thirsty, and debating whether she could pee in the corner, too, she paced the room. Her skin itched and the hair on the back of her neck prickled. She could not, for her life, shake the feeling someone watched her. She glanced toward the high window for the umpteenth time. Nothing was there but the green and brown of the pine forest marching up the mountain.

A floorboard creaked on the other side of the door. She stopped pacing to face the door with the box and pups behind her. Stupid Dude opened the door and leered at her.

"Boss says to let you use the facilities." He stepped into the room. "You try anything, I'll stomp those little bastards 'til their heads splatter."

Her fingers curled into fists. She wanted to scratch his eyes out but for once kept her emotions under control. She stepped toward the door and slipped past him with minimal contact even though her skin crawled at even that brief touch. Liz trotted down the short hall to the bathroom and slipped in. She closed the door, but not fast enough. Stupid Dude shoved his booted foot between the door and jamb.

"Nuh uh, bitch. Boss says to keep an eye on you."

"That's Doctor Bitch to you, asshole."

His meaty fist raised and Liz realized she'd uttered her thoughts out loud. "Crap." She scrabbled backwards and opened her mouth to scream. Maybe someone would hear her. Maybe the "boss" would come to deal with his underling. Maybe she'd wake up and this whole ordeal would be some Mad Hatter's nightmare of a reality series.

"Johnson, let her piss in peace."

Liz barely choked back her giggle. Johnson? Oh yes, this guy was definitely a dickhead. The door closed and she had a moment of privacy. Her vocabulary had definitely deteriorated. She never cussed, never asserted herself. Staring at her face in the mirror as she washed her hands she wondered at the changes, both inside and out. She was a scientist, a geek, a bookworm. She didn't confront people. She didn't attack them with her fists. But something about those wolf pups brought out every long-buried maternal instinct she possessed. She would die protecting those little critters if she had to. She gulped, hoping it didn't come to that.

She took a chance and glanced out the bathroom window. Nothing but forest. "You're on your own, girl. You..." Her voice trailed off. Not for the first time, she felt like someone watched—not from within the house, but from outside. She scanned the tree line but couldn't see anyone. She rubbed at her arms, reminded of the other night in the woods. Her skin flushed and her nipples pebbled. Holy moly, what was wrong with her? She didn't think about sex either. Oh, she noticed men, even admired them from a genetics point of view. But she didn't get the urge to bed them. Horny was the state of her former college roommates, not her! Not only was she extremely turned on at the moment but for some inexplicable reason, she didn't feel alone.

Totally creeped out, she stepped out into the hall. Big Dude stood at the far end, massive arms folded across his equally massive chest. Head down, she scurried back to the laundry room. She found a box of cereal and a bottle of water just inside the door. She scooped up both and darted to the far corner, once more positioning her body between the door and the box. Big Dude didn't even look in as he closed and locked the door. She wouldn't starve, at least not today.

"Would a spoon with milk and sugar have been too much to ask?" she muttered.

CHAPTER 24

THE FOREST BLAZED as the sun sank behind the mountain, dipping the landscape in fiery reds and yellows. Michael felt the moment Nakai shifted to his wolf form. Once twilight cloaked the woods, the old wolf would boldly scout the cottage in hopes of drawing the men out. Michael would go in through a back window, find Liz and the pups, and spirit them away. If the men could be lured into the woods. If Liz was there... No. Every fiber of his being insisted she was inside that house. He could feel her, had caught tantalizing hints of her scent.

Shadows gathered under the trees and small animals skittered away, far more attuned to the atmosphere than the men inside the cottage. An unearthly howl froze any stragglers. Stripped down to the bare minimum of weapons, Michael edged into position. Clouds played tag with the quarter moon and he saw Nakai pad into the cleared area in front of the cottage. He worried for a moment then remembered the old wolf could take care of himself. Each of them had a mission. He focused on his— get inside, snatch Liz and the pups and get the hell away.

Nakai howled again. The front door creaked open followed by whispered voices. The old wolf growled and backed away. Two of the men followed. The third remained inside. It was now or never. Michael forced the window open and slithered through. He hit the floor and rolled to his feet, his .40 H&K automatic pistol in his hand. His nostrils flared. Liz. Her scent teased him and he followed like a bee homing in on a succulent flower.

With the sound of the first shot at the front of the house, he dashed down the hall following Liz's scent. He hoped she had the good sense to get away from the door because he slowed down only long enough to kick it in.

"Michael!"

"Get the pups!"

Thankfully, she didn't gawk at him for long. She ducked into a box and came out with a squirming bundle clutched in her arms.

"Stay behind me."

"But...how? I thought—"

"Later."

Silent, she stayed close. He led the way back to the bedroom and she slipped through the door. A bullet thwacked into the wall next to his head. He slammed the door shut, locked it, and hustled Liz toward the open window. "Get out and run up the mountain. Keep going. I'll be right behind you."

Liz clamored through the window using only her legs as she fought for control of the wiggling pups. He growled and the pups stilled immediately. She flashed him a questioning look but didn't speak. The door shattered and he snapped off a full clip before diving through the window, reloading even as he hit the dirt and rolled. Liz had already disappeared into the trees. With preternatural speed, he followed suit. He paused long enough to grab the rest of his weapons and the bundle of Nakai's clothes. Snarls and growls echoed through the trees and then a man screamed. A barrage of shots followed.

Instinct urged him to go after Nakai to cover the wolf's back, but Michael headed deeper into the pine forest. Liz huffed and puffed up ahead. She wouldn't last long. They needed to go to ground until the old man rejoined them and they could reach his vehicle to get away—despite his urge to just kill the men. In a few long strides, Michael caught up to Liz.

"Just a little bit further. There's a dead fall that will give us cover."

She nodded rather than waste her breath talking, clutched the pups tighter, and kept climbing. He wrapped his hand in the back of her shirt to give her added support and to guide her. Five minutes later, she collapsed behind the log and buried her mouth against her arm, sucking in air as soundlessly as possible. The little wolves peeked up at him from where they cowered inside her jacket. He reached over and ruffled their ears and they butted against his hand. "Easy, Liz. You'll hyperventilate. Hold your breath and let it out slow."

She nodded but didn't look up. Even so, she followed his instructions until her breathing returned to normal. "I really need to hit the treadmill." The words wheezed out in a whisper.

He bit back his grin. "You look just fine to me."

She raised her head and stared at him, blanching when she saw the wound on his head. "They said you were dead."

"They were wrong."

She shivered and he realized how deadly his voice sounded. He gently touched her chin and turned her face so he could see her bruised cheek. "They'll pay for that." He resisted the urge to kiss her as time and place were completely inappropriate and checked his weapons instead. He set up his sniper rifle in seconds and settled in to wait.

"You aren't just a forest ranger, are you?"

Her words whispered across the bare skin of his arm and his groin tightened. "No."

She remained silent for a few minutes. "Are you like...them?"

"No."

She opened her mouth for another question but snapped it shut as something crackled through the underbrush. From the corner of his eye, he watched her curl into a ball around the pups. Good girl.

Liz glanced up almost as if she'd heard his thoughts. He touched her cheek with the tip of his forefinger and offered her a smile. He was in his element now. In the distance, a wolf howled. Moments later, a second wolf answered. Nakai still hunted. With help now.

A branch snapped to his left. Michael swiveled the barrel of his rifle.

"I should have checked you closer when I took you out back at your cabin."

Michael's lips curled into a one-sided snarl, but he didn't reply, knowing the guy had only a vague idea of where they were hidden.

"Just leave the wolves where you are, take the girl, and get the hell out."

He remained silent.

"Fine. You wanna do this the hard way?"

Michael squeezed the trigger a millisecond before a muzzle flash exploded in the dark. The bullet flew over his head as the scent of warm blood filled his nostrils. Someone heavy and clumsy thrashed through the underbrush.

"Boss? Boss, where are you? Joe's dead."

"Shut the fuck up and help me!"

Michael remained quiet as a spray of bullets erupted. He could hear both men breathing in the silence that followed.

"Girlie? You still out here? I know I hit your boyfriend back in the house. C'mon out. You help me get the wolves to our employer and I'll let you go."

"Oh right!" Liz responded before he could stop her. Her eyes glinted as the sliver of moon ducked out from behind a cloud. She held her index finger to her lips. Curious, Michael waited to see what she'd do next. "I should believe you why?"

The man laughed. "I'll sweeten the pot. I'll make sure your boyfriend gets medical attention. Otherwise, I'll just come get you and leave his ass to bleed to death out here."

"Ha! I have his gun and I know how to use it."

Michael turned his head, listening. The big mercenary was on the move, despite being injured. The guy was attempting to sneak around behind them, even as his cohort tried a pincer maneuver. He wasn't worried about the subordinate. He unholstered his automatic pistol, anticipating the action. He tracked the stupid one, squeezed off two quick rounds and covered Liz's body with his own as the man squealed and fell. He whipped his arm around and fired almost blindly, emptying the clip a second time.

"Fuck!" The big man stumbled back down the mountain, followed by the sounds of the second man scrambling along behind.

Damn but he was out of practice with the short stuff. He needed to set up a firing range. He reloaded his pistol and leaned in briefly to whisper, "Let's go," in Liz's ear. He couldn't stop his lips from brushing across her temple. He paused just long enough to get his bearings and then urged her to the right, following a faint game trail.

A few minutes later, they reached the SUV. Nakai, still in wolf form, sat beside the front wheel, tail curled across his front paws, tongue lolling. Michael tossed the bundle of clothes toward him. The wolf picked them up in his teeth and trotted around the front of the vehicle and headed into the woods.

Liz stared at him. "You...own a wolf?"

He chuckled. "No man owns that wolf. Here..." He moved to the SUV and opened the back gate. He took the pups from her and put them into the cargo area. They pressed close to his hands wanting pets and reassurance. He indulged for a few moments until the crack of a dead branch had him jerking Liz to the ground as he crouched, his pistol in his hand.

"Glad to see you have not lost all your reflexes."

Liz's fingers dug into his shoulder as she gasped. He stood and helped her up, but kept his body between her and Nakai.

"Liz Graham, Jacob Nakai. We served in the Army together." He did his best to stop the growl rattling in his chest and also ignore the knowing gleam in the older man's eyes. He was not moonstruck. The whole idea was unacceptable.

"Wh-wh-where did you come from?"

"The woods."

Liz relaxed a little as she recognized the humor in Jacob's voice. "Where's the wolf?"

"What wolf?"

"The wolf that..." Her jaw snapped shut as she gulped. "What are you people?"

And there it was—the question Michael had been dreading. Wolves tended to mate within their community for this very reason. Mac McIntire mating Hannah Jackson had been an anomaly, but one that worked out, despite a very rocky start. And Liz Graham was far too astute for her own good—or his.

"We need to get out of here, in case those men have reinforcements closer than we do."

Jacob chuckled. "Best I take shotgun." He hustled Liz into the back seat and shut the door on her protests.

Michael stared at the other man for a long moment before trotting around the vehicle and climbing into the driver's seat. He put the SUV in gear and pulled back onto the fire trail but headed up instead of back to the main road. He knew this area, knew how the roads and trails intersected. He could only hope the mercenaries hadn't done their homework.

🐾🐾🐾🐾

A WOMAN SHE didn't recognize waited on the front porch of Michael's cabin and Liz was curious about her. While Michael and Mr. Nakai were both Native American, she didn't get the sense they were related beyond a deep tie from time spent in the military, which would certainly explain a lot. But not everything. She had not hallucinated that wolf taking the bundle of clothing from Michael and the appearance of the man dressed in those same clothes moments later. She didn't believe in werewolves. Or skinwalkers. Or any of that voodoo mumbo jumbo. Just the thought raised the hair on her arms. She absently smoothed her palms across her forearms.

"There's no such thing," she muttered under her breath just as the back door opened. Mr. Nakai's face crinkled and there was a smile hidden in the wrinkles.

"There are many things in this world, child, both unseen and unheard." Mr. Nakai's eyes twinkled.

Had he somehow read her mind? If not, his statement was much too cryptic for her brain to decipher. She believed in empirical knowledge, test results, and facts she could prove. Not mindreading or...disappearing wolves. And reappearing men. The old man nudged her toward the house.

The woman waiting on the porch waved as they approached. Mr. Nakai introduced them. "My wife. Tala, Dr. Liz Graham. She is Michael's...friend."

Liz caught the nuance in Nakai's tone. "No. We're not...friends." The older couple just laughed and exchanged what could only be called a knowing look. She thought she caught a word that sounded something like moonstruck but she had no clue as to what it might mean. Michael appeared at her side holding the wolf pups. Despite his strength, he handled them with great gentleness.

"Thought you might want to say goodbye."

"Goodbye?" She blinked rapidly, studying his face for some idea of what he was talking about.

"To the pups. Jacob and I are taking them back to the den."

She shook her head adamantly. "You can't!"

He arched one brow, his expression daring her to explain her denial.

"They smell like humans. The pack won't take them back. They'll...the pack will kill them or drive them out and they'll starve. They aren't even fully weaned yet." One corner of his very interesting mouth quirked. She struggled to pull her focus back to his eyes, only to get lost in his warm, caramel-brown gaze. He really was the most handsome man she'd ever seen.

"You will have to trust me. The pack will accept them. And nurture them." He offered the pups for her to pet and he leaned down to whisper in her ear. "I will teach you about Wolves, their mating, and how they take care of their families."

His breath whispered across her skin and she shivered. Swaying under the rush of emotions swirling toward her middle, she tightened her knees and clenched her thighs in order to remain standing. Oh, but that felt good. Clenching her thigh muscles sent wonderful little spasms through other muscles, buried deeper...buried exactly where she wanted Michael to be. She gasped and opened her eyes just as he stepped back from her.

"Stay safe, little doctor. I will return to you soon and start our lessons."

Oh, lord, he had a wicked grin. Every last one of her girly bits donned a cheerleader's uniform and started shaking pompoms. He winked at her and if her knees hadn't remained locked, she would have planted her butt in the dirt. Bemused, she watched Jacob kiss his wife before following Michael into the woods. The woman waved her toward the cabin.

"Come. You look like you need a bath and fresh clothes and food in your belly."

Liz nodded and followed. "Thank you, Mrs. Nakai."

"Tala. We are not formal people. Come in. I made stew and cornbread. Michael, he's not such a cook but I found enough to make a meal. After you eat, you can clean up and change clothes."

She followed the older woman blindly. The aroma emanating from the cabin made her mouth water and her stomach rumbled ominously. Tala laughed and urged her to sit at the table.

After a quick bowl of stew, a longer shower, a change of clothes, and now a lingering second bowl of stew with hot cornbread, Liz felt almost human. At the same time, she wondered if she'd fallen down Alice's rabbit hole. Tala had loaned her a skirt and after rolling it at the waist a couple of times, she could walk without tripping over the hem. Her bra and panties were draped over the shower rod in the bathroom to dry and she wore a khaki tee shirt Tala had borrowed from Michael's dresser upstairs in the loft bedroom.

Liz swallowed a bite and returned the other woman's penetrating gaze. "What?"

"I wonder if you are ready for what is to come, Doctor."

She almost choked on the next bite. "What do you mean?"

"You are a woman of science. But sometimes, a person has to see and believe with their heart, not their brain. I hope you will be able to do this when the time comes."

"When the time comes? I...Mrs. Nakai...Tala. I...forgive me. I'm totally lost here."

The woman's eyes crinkled with mirth. "As were we all. It is not my place to explain what comes. But I offer these words to consider. Believe what you cannot prove but feel in your heart to be true. Laugh. At yourself, at your mate, at life. Laughter sees you through the tears."

"Wait...what? Mate? What the heck are you talking about?"

Tala chuckled. The sound reminded Liz of brownies fresh from the oven. "Finish your food, Dr. Liz."

She helped Tala clean the kitchen and straighten up the cabin, though it was obvious the woman had already been busy cleaning up the mess made by her kidnappers. Glass no longer littered the floor, lamps had been set upright, and things were back in some semblance of order. They settled into chairs out on the front porch to relax. The wind teased the pine trees and she could almost imagine voices whispering out in the forest. Liz smoothed down the hairs on her arms and attempted to dissect her feelings. She'd never reacted so strongly to any man. She wasn't a virgin, technically speaking. Most of her encounters had been of the "Slam-bam, thank-you, ma'am" variety. She didn't think she was frigid. She liked men. Okay, she liked men with broad shoulders and muscled thighs and all those shallow things she really thought a woman of science should ignore. Men with brains were desirable as mates, too. She shivered. There was that word again. Mate. Had being out in the woods, kidnapped, rescued, shot at, and forced to live some sort of thriller plot ignited her basic instincts? The muscles deep in her middle clenched and quivered. If she didn't know better, she'd think her womb was doing the happy dance. Natural selection. Biggest, strongest, fiercest. Oh, yeah, that described Michael Lightfoot to a T.

Lost in thought, she jumped a foot out of her chair when said alpha male's low laughter startled her.

"Where the heck did you come from?" She slapped at his arm and connected, then had to shake her hand. "Ow."

She stared at his face and her middle went all squirrelly again. She'd never seen a man look so...hungry.

CHAPTER 25

THIS WAS NOT the time to be thinking about filling his hands with her lush curves. Liz was out of her element, still sported bruises that made his blood boil though not from passion, and she was currently looking at him like he'd grown a second head. He groaned as that second head throbbed in anticipation. He stuck his hand out, palm forward to halt her.

"Don't come any closer." His throat constricted and strangled his voice. The words came out mangled and she gave him an odd look.

"But you're hurt. I need to check your injuries."

"I'll be fine. Just trust me on that." He'd forgotten about the two extra gunshot wounds he'd picked up at the cottage. They were minor and he'd been so focused on Liz, on making sure she was safe, he hadn't paid any attention. Once they'd arrived back at his place, getting the pups home to the pack had been the important task. Now, though, the sun sank below the tree line and shadows gathered under their branches. Scents danced on the evening breeze but his nostrils were filled with the sweet essence that would forever define Liz. She still smelled of coconut but there was another fragrance—he sniffed again. Orange and ginger notes swirled beneath the sweet umbrella drink scent.

The amused clearing of a throat broke his concentration. He cut his eyes to the door of the cabin where Tala and Nakai waited. He arched a brow and took one step back from Liz, even as he shifted his body in a subtle stance that put him between the woman and the other Wolf. He didn't appreciate the amused glances the two exchanged.

"We have a motel room down in town."

Tala danced around him and offered a hug to Liz. "Be well, little sister, and remember what I said." As she returned to her husband's side, her hand brushed across Michael's arm. He looked down into her smiling eyes. "We will see you in the morning. But not too early." She chuckled again and winked at him.

The older couple walked to their Jeep. Nakai helped Tala into the passenger side and before he ducked into the driver's seat, he tossed a short salute toward the house. Michael returned the gesture.

Once the Jeep was out of sight, he turned to Liz. She wore one of his old Army tees. His chest swelled with…not pride. Possession. He wanted this woman with a need as old and primal as time itself. Shadows lengthened and the night swelled with sounds as little animals ventured out, as birds settled, as insects sang to the rising moon.

"We should go inside." His voice sounded like he'd swallowed a handful of gravel and he had to clench his hands at his sides to keep from touching her.

She tilted her head, a curious bird watching a predator but not sensing the danger. He shouldn't lose control like this. The full moon was over a week away yet he couldn't deal with the distraction she presented. He should hustle her out to his SUV, take her down the mountain and send her back to where she came from, but even as he considered that, his whole body tensed and quivered in anticipation. His wolf snarled and he realized he could never let her go. Not willingly. But he wouldn't force her. Too many times, too many Wolves forced the mating. That never worked out well. He inhaled, held his breath until some of the tension released, and then exhaled.

"We need to talk." She stepped toward him and he backed away. His nostrils flared as her scent teased his senses. He had to swallow—several times—before his voice worked again. "Liz. Don't."

She stopped advancing, a puzzled look on her face. "What's wrong? I may be a biologist and my area of expertise might be genetics but I'm capable of looking at your wounds and slapping a bandage on them." She tilted her head again, the curious bird overwhelming all sense of caution the woman might feel.

"No." The word came out more snarl than human speech. He reached down and stuffed his wolf deep inside his soul.

Her expression changed. Slowly. A shadow of fear appeared in her eyes and he wanted to slam his fist into a wall. He didn't want to scare her. Or hurt her. And if he didn't control the beast, he'd do both.

Liz continued to stare at him. She inhaled and her full breasts strained against her shirt. All his blood drained to his groin and what had been a painful erection engorged to excruciating proportions. He'd had blue balls before but nothing like this. Ever. He groaned and turned away from her.

Her hand fluttered against his back, as ephemeral as the wings of a moth drawn to a candle. "Michael? What's wrong? Let me help."

"You. Can't."

Her palm flattened and she pressed closer as she tried to peer around his body to see his face. Before he realized what he was doing, he whirled and backed her up against the wall, his dick pressed against her soft tummy, his mouth on hers—taking, tasting, branding her as his. She fought him, her hands balling into fists as she beat ineffectually against his chest. A small part of his brain warned him to stop but it was too late. The wolf would claim his mate and claim her now.

With supreme effort, he gentled the kiss. His tongue teased her lips then his teeth nibbled along her jaw to find the soft spot under her chin. He stilled the frantic thrusting of his hips and managed to return his breathing to some semblance of normalcy. Her hands crept around his neck and she relaxed against him. Her lips seared his skin as she kissed his cheek and he raised his head to kiss her again, gently this time. His tongue traced the seam of her lips, asking permission rather than plunging in without invitation. She opened for him and he deepened the kiss. Her acceptance helped calm the wolf and he relaxed. He broke the kiss but pressed his forehead against hers, his breath ragged like he'd just run a marathon.

"I'm sorry." His voice sighed across her skin. Unable to face her, he kept his eyes closed. He was such a coward.

"Wow." She sounded awed and breathless and not afraid at all. "Just...wow. No idea what you have to be sorry for."

He wanted to laugh as his wolf preened. Michael suppressed the wry grin threatening his mouth. What an ego his wolf had. "Yeah. My thoughts exactly." He inhaled and exhaled, then had to do it all again. "I'm sorry."

"Again, for what?" She sounded puzzled now and not quite so breathless.

He backed up a step. Retreating was the hardest thing he'd ever done. He cupped her cheek in his calloused hand and marveled at the difference in textures, unable to move for fear of abrading her skin. "For a lot of things. We still need to talk."

She shook her head. "No. Not unless you're going to let your body talk." She blinked and a crooked grin skewed her expression. "Isn't that an old song or something?" She cut off his reply by placing her finger across his lips. "I'm not a complete novice at this sex thing, but I can honestly say that I have never wanted sex with any man the way I want it with you. Like, right now want it." She sucked in a deep breath, her nostrils flaring, then blew the air out as her lips formed a little "o". "Maybe it's adrenaline. Maybe it's just rampaging hormones. I don't care. It's...it's crazy. Like romance novel crazy. My breasts...my...uhm... Well, down there..." She dropped her chin and her eyes followed but stopped when her gaze collided with his groin. Her irises dilated, her mouth dropped, and her nostrils flared again. He smiled as her skin flushed. "Did I do that?" She squeaked. Like a little mouse.

"Yes."

She opened her mouth to speak but nothing came out save for a breathy sigh.

"I want you, Liz. Like I've wanted no other woman in my life. And yeah, that's a cliche but in this case, it's also the truth. But you need to go into this with your eyes open. You need to understand what is happening."

She giggled, a sound he never expected to hear from her. Her nerves were showing. "Informed consent, right? I'm an adult, Michael. I know all about the birds and the bees, probably better than most people. We don't know each other. This is purely physical. I get that. And it's okay. I'm using protection—"

The growl escaped before he could control it but she ignored it and continued.

"Not because I'm promiscuous but... Well, just write it off as TMI, okay? Sex is—"

"This isn't about sex, Liz." He forced his fingers to relax where they gripped her biceps. "This is about so much more. Until we talk—"

Her lips plastered against his and her fingers pressed against his back. After a long moment, she broke the kiss. "Shut up, Michael. You talk too much. I want you. You want me. That's all that matters."

His resolve shattered. The wolf roared to the surface. He wrapped his arms around her and lifted. By reflex, her legs circled his waist and her ankles hooked behind his back. He groaned as his dick pressed against the damp heat at her core. He took the stairs two at a time and all but fell onto his bed, still cradling her. He wanted to rip off her clothes but controlled his fingers so they fumbled with buttons on the skirt instead of tearing the material.

"Too slow!" She slapped his hand away. "Let me."

He grinned at her husky voice and watched as she stripped. Moments later, he followed her lead and they were both naked. This time, he was the one left stunned. She might be short but her lush body looked perfect to him. "Wow…" She blushed, her skin turning rosy from her toes to the top of her head. "I'm going to eat you up."

She managed a short laugh before he spread her knees and dipped his head between her thighs. He inhaled deeply, her scent filling him with a peace he'd never known before. The wolf wanted to roll in the scent, to wear it in his fur. The man wanted to taste her, and did. He lapped at her, the tip of his tongue teasing her clit and places even more intimate. She squirmed beneath his tender assault so he gripped her hips to hold her still. He would taste her until he was full and she was screaming his name. He nipped and suckled. His tongue tasted her deep inside and his heart thundered with each of her moans.

"Yes." The word sighed from deep within her. "Oh, Michael, yes."

He grinned. Close but no cigar. He found the spot he'd been searching for and dragged the tip of his tongue across it. She stiffened. A finger replaced his tongue which then found her quivering clit. He stroked her, curling his fingertip across that spot as he nibbled her. She gasped. Closer. He added a second finger and her inner muscles clenched around him, milking him as he stroked inside her. His cock was so hard he felt like it might shatter if he didn't bury it deep within her. But not yet.

She arched her hips, despite his grip on them. Her fingers scrabbled into the patchwork quilt that covered his bed, fisting the thick material. "Please," she begged.

"Come for me, Liz. Just let go. I'll catch you."

He thrust with his fingers, hard and fast now. Her muscle contracted around him as she panted. Her areolas puckered and her nipples turned to little buds without a touch from him. She gasped, her shoulders coming off the bed. "MICHAEL!"

She shattered around him. And he "caught" her, just as he'd promised. The frenzy his fingers had built up deep inside her eased as her climax retreated to little quivers and shudders. He didn't stop. Oh, thank god, he didn't stop. His fingers continued to stroke her even as he kissed his way up her tummy, pausing to suckle both breasts, before his mouth found hers.

"That's my girl," he whispered and she smiled in spite of herself.

"Am I?" She couldn't help but ask.

"Are you what?"

"Your girl?"

She felt his smile. "Always."

One word. One word zinging straight to her heart. Something in his voice made her breath hitch in her chest again. He meant it. She was his. For always. She didn't know how or why, but she was absolutely positive of that. Warmth spread through her that had nothing to do with the rush of blood pounding in her veins. For the first time in ages, she felt like she belonged. And it felt right—felt perfect, in fact—right down to her bones. Before she could voice her next thought, Michael shifted so that he lay on top of her, his hips cushioned by her thighs. The head of his erection pressed against her entrance and while her brain insisted it was too soon for more stimulation, her body opened in welcome. He slid inside her with infinite care. This was no invasion like before. This was sweet and...she blinked. And pushed at the hard wall of his chest.

"Michael, you didn't put on a condom."

He pushed up to stare down at her. "You said you were on birth control."

"I'm on the pill but...but..."

He dipped his head to kiss her. "I'm clean, honey. And so are you."

Something in his tone convinced her. She suspected he'd been celibate for a long time. A man didn't get that huge and hard and...needy if he got regular sex. His penis throbbed inside her and she gasped as her muscles fluttered over and around him like a flock of butterflies. His hips lifted and he slid out of her. In a frantic bid to keep him buried, she clenched around him. He chuckled in her ear as he pressed back inside. Only to pull out again. Oh goodness but he filled her and felt so good as the smooth head of his erection rubbed inside her. He kept his thrusts slow and easy even though she felt his muscles tense. His teeth grated as he clamped his jaw tight. He walked on the very edge of losing control trying to make this good for her. But she wanted him out of control. She wanted him pounding into her, wanted him to take her on some primeval level that she'd have to think about later. Right now, though, she wanted to find that place he'd taken her with his mouth and fingers.

She arched her hips, rolled them to take him deeper inside. He gritted his teeth and choked back a groan. Liz felt powerful. She pushed against him again, speeding up the pace of her thrusts. He responded, his hips lifting and rising in a tempo as old as time. Yes, this felt primeval. And perfect. As she had when he picked her up to carry her to his bed, she wrapped her legs around him, tilting her hips. The change in angle made her gasp. And him growl. He sounded so...fierce when he growled. And wild. Untamed. Like the wolves. Her hands stroked along his back and she reveled in the strength of his muscles as they bunched under her caress. He panted now and throbbed, triggering an answering pulse deep inside her. Something behind her belly button twisted and she felt like there were wings in her stomach, flailing and battering at some unseen cage as her emotions tried to soar. Forget fireworks. Forget stars. She wanted to fly.

"Liz?" Her name sounded more like a snarl...or a prayer on his lips.

"Yes," she urged. "Oh, yes, Michael." Her breath caught in her lungs and she sped up the rhythm, her body open and accepting all of him as he thrust inside her. Her nails dug into the skin on his back and he hissed.

She felt him grow harder and thicker if that was even possible. She didn't know. Didn't care. The first hot jets of his climax filled her, washing against her cervix which triggered her climax. She came hard, clamping around him like a vise. She felt...free, like her soul soared above the earth, dancing among the stars. Her body went boneless. This was how a cat must feel. She wanted to rub against Michael, wallow in his maleness, and purr her contentment.

He collapsed on top of her, his breath raspy in her ear. In a few moments, he made a move to roll away but she tightened her embrace.

"I'll squash you." He rolled to his side, but stayed connected inside and out.

His heart thudded against her breast. Her heart probably felt the same to him. She'd never been loved like this. Ever. A little aftershock rocketed through her body and she shivered. His penis throbbed inside her as her muscles clenched around him. "Mmmm."

He chuckled. She loved the way the sound echoed in his chest. "Mmmm, yes."

Warm and drowsy, she was ready to forget about everything but this moment in this man's arms. She nestled against him and his arms tightened around her. This. This was how a woman should feel after being well and truly loved by her mate.

CHAPTER 26

LIZ AWOKE TO an empty bed. She sat up and groaned as muscles, bruises, and places rendered sore by some amazing loving all protested. She looked around for something to wear but all her clothes were missing. All of them, including the skirt Tala loaned her.

"I've seen you naked." Michael's voice floated up the stairwell and she blushed. "I have a hot bath running for you. Come down."

Feeling shy, she stripped the top sheet from the bed and wrapped it around her, toga-style. She cautiously descended and managed to meet Michael's amused gaze with her head up, even though she could feel the flush rushing to stain her chest and face. He met her halfway and scooped her into his arms. She protested for about five seconds and then relaxed, snuggling against his hard chest and shoulder. He was definitely an alpha male and she felt petite—a rather new and enjoyable feeling—and very...loved. She gasped a little and Michael shifted her in his arms so he could see her face.

"What's wrong?"

He looked so worried and concerned she reached up to smooth the lines knotting his forehead. "Nothing. I...everything." She inhaled to ease the constriction in her chest and offered him a shy smile. "Lots of emotions swirling around in my head and I'm not used to them. So much has happened in such a short time, Mike." She grinned as he frowned. "You don't like it when I call you Mike?" This was much safer territory.

"I like whatever you call me, but Mike is not a name I'm used to." He shrugged and she was surprised by the ease he held her and accomplished the gesture. "Most people call me Lightfoot. There aren't many who call me Michael."

She kissed the corner of his mouth. "Someday, I want to hear about you. About your childhood. About your time in the Army." A sound far too similar to a growl rumbled in his chest and she realized those might not be good memories. She kissed him again, deeper this time. "Some day. Not now, 'kay?"

Yes. Some day. He would eventually have to spill his secrets. Should have before he claimed her last night. His wolf preened and ignored the slice of guilt that flavored this morning. Michael nodded before setting her on her feet in the bathroom.

Steam rose from the water in the old-fashioned tub. The same tub that had sheltered her not so long ago. Her knees shook and Liz might have had to sit had Michael not hugged her closer.

"Shhh, sweetheart. You're safe now. I won't let anyone hurt you. Not ever again."

Her heart fluttered but she swallowed her panic. His words sank in. Calm replaced her fear because she believed what he said. She'd never felt so safe in her life. She inhaled and his scent filled her. Considering how sated and content she'd felt upon awakening, she couldn't believe her body wanted his attention now. He chuckled and the sound echoed in her ear as she pressed against his chest.

"There will be many more nights, little doctor. And mornings. A few afternoons. But for now get into the tub and let the water soothe you. I won't wear you out. Not yet, anyway."

She giggled and rubbed her cheek against his bare skin. "Mmmmm." She loved the immediate reaction she received as his penis swelled behind his gym shorts and pressed against her tummy.

"Wicked woman." His voice sounded thick and even as he moved his hips away, his arms tightened around her.

With what seemed like supreme effort on his part, he backed off. He offered his hand to steady her as she dropped the sheet to step into the tub. The temperature was perfect and she sank into the warmth with a contented sigh.

"I'll call you when breakfast is ready."

She opened one eye to discover he hadn't moved. He stood next to the tub staring at her with a hot and hungry look. Something feral flashed in his eyes and she shivered. He reminded her of the wolves in the pack as they surrounded her. She stared up at him, her heart beating wildly, but not with fear. Passion, need, love, yes, those were the feelings swamping her. She didn't believe in love at first sight. She was a scientist. But she had no other name for her feelings, not did she want to exam them very closely. He smiled and she melted. He was so devastatingly handsome she couldn't breathe. She blinked and when she opened her eyes, he was gone.

"Damn." She seldom cursed but no other word seemed able to express her feelings. She forced air into her lungs and leaned her head back against the tub rim. The tub was so huge, she could have laid down in it—and promptly drowned. Instead, she kept her head above water, closed her eyes, and floated as the heat soaked into her aching muscles. Now she understood the phrase "bone tired."

Michael left the bathroom door open a crack so he could hear Liz if she called. Jacob and Tala would arrive shortly and Tala was bringing clean clothing with her. At some point, he would take Liz to Cheyenne to pick up her clothes or at least take her shopping. In the meantime, he wanted to talk to the older man and to the others from the 69th. Something dark and dangerous was occurring and it involved wolves. The wild kind, not the shifter kind, but he couldn't help wondering if there might be a connection to before. Why were a bunch of mercenaries shepherding a couple of geeks so they could steal some wolf pups? And why kidnap Liz? He went cold at the very thought of another man putting his hands on her. He would find the big mercenary and kill him for hitting her.

Ever attuned to his surroundings, he was waiting in the shadows of the front door as the late-model Jeep pulled in and parked next to his SUV. Tala emerged and reached back in to snag some sacks. Nakai held a rifle and wore a well-used Colt .45 automatic pistol in the holster belted to his side.

"You look loaded for bear."

"I don't hunt bear."

Michael's smile didn't reach his eyes. "No. What we hunt is far more deadly." His expression softened as he glanced at Tala. "She is in the bath. I'll take her the clothes."

The older woman surrendered her bags and grinned. "Then I will cook. You look a little peaked, Brother Wolf. Both of you will need your strength."

He didn't deny her insinuations. He tapped on the bathroom door and slipped through, shutting it firmly behind him. "Tala and Jacob are here. She brought clothes. As much as I like you in my shirt, I might have to kill Jacob if he looked at you too closely." He'd meant to keep his tone teasing but the inherent threat rang loud and clear. Liz offered him a bemused stare.

"I can see jealousy will never be an issue." Her eyes twinkled even as she offered the slight dig.

"Never." This time he let the growl take over and relaxed as she laughed. A sense of humor would help her in the days to come.

"Don't take long." Tala's voice carried through the door. "Eggs don't taste good cold." The scent of ham and bacon frying permeated even through the closed door.

His stomach rumbled, echoed by Liz's. They both laughed. He offered a towel and his hand to help her stand and climb over the edge. He would have stayed to dry her off but considering the raging hard-on he sported, they'd miss breakfast. He kissed her, pulling her close so she could feel what she did to him. "This will not go away until I have you in my bed again," he promised before turning her loose and ducking out the door.

Lightfoot refused to acknowledge the look Jacob gave him. Instead, he went to the cabinet and pulled down plates. Tala and the other man already had steaming mugs near at hand and the woman deftly handled several pans on his stove. He even managed to locate enough silverware to add some semblance of order to the table. After he filled his cup with the freshly brewed coffee, he leaned against the kitchen counter and waited for Liz.

Liz opened the bathroom door. She'd dressed in jeans and an over-sized plaid shirt that did nothing to hide her curves. If he'd been a man who blushed, he'd be beet red at the look Tala and Nakai exchanged. The older man coughed and muttered something that sounded suspiciously like "moonstruck pup." He chose to ignore the gibe. Michael wouldn't add credence to the man's assertions even as his gut twisted and his free hand opened and closed with the need to reach for Liz, to touch her and hold her and take her back to bed. Dammit.

Over scrambled eggs, home fries, ham, bacon, and biscuits, they talked about the mercenaries and their interest in the wolf pack.

"We need to figure out who hired them and why." Michael bit the words out, his anger at the men's rough treatment of Liz seething deep inside.

"Is it possible the snake once again rears its head?" Jacob cut his eyes to Liz.

"Did they say anything around you, Liz? Any hint of where they planned to take the pups or who is directing the operation?"

She shook her head and her nut-brown hair glistened in the sunlight streaming through the window. Her lips drew his gaze and he longed to capture each word as they spilled from her mouth with his own.

"I only know Big Dude was adamant that the pups come from this particular pack. Which doesn't make sense..." Her voice trailed off as the others watched her with expectant expressions. "Unless...they want the pups for the same reason I came out to study them." She stared at her empty plate, ignoring everyone else as she worked through her thoughts. A few moments later, she inhaled, exhaled, and raised her eyes to look at Michael.

"Some of the wolves in this pack have a recessive gene."

"What does that mean?"

"I'm not sure. I only started my study of the blood tests and the slides I managed to dig up. Two of the wolves, a male and a female, carry a microchip so they can be traced. This study has been ongoing for...I don't know. Five, maybe six years now? It started before I went to work for the Wildlife Department. I stumbled across the file and since genetics is my area, I was intrigued. I wanted to come see the pack in person." She leaned back in her chair and breathed again. "Nobody has studied the pack since those initial reports. The Department doesn't have the kind of money to do implants and then just walk away."

Michael exchanged looks with Jacob. "I would say, yes, the snake once again rears its head. We should notify the colonel and the others."

The old man nodded his agreement then cast a thoughtful look toward Liz. "Did you copy the file?"

Startled at first, her expression changed to one of affront. She sputtered a few words about trust, co-workers, spying, and then the indignation died. "Yes. But it was only so I'd have a copy with me. I didn't want to go through the hassle of checking out the official file."

"That's my girl!" Michael grinned even as he fought the urge to take her into his arms and kiss her.

"It was in my backpack..." She glanced around the room, looking for it. When she didn't find it, she raised a stricken gaze to him. "Do you suppose they took it?"

"Where did you put it?"

She pushed back from the table and walked to the living area. Then she retreated to the front door, turned and pretended she was walking inside, as if retracing her steps. Her eyes lit up and she bounced toward the couch and dropped to her knees. "Got it!" She yanked and tugged until the pack worked free from under the couch.

After breakfast, Michael, Nakai, and Liz talked around the kitchen table while Tala washed up. Liz offered to help but the older woman waved her off. Calls, cryptic and mysterious, were made and then Michael and Nakai decided to return to the den to check on the pack.

Michael showed Tala where he kept his weapons and ammunition. Liz bristled. "Hey, I can shoot, too."

He pulled her into his arms and kissed the top of her head. "We had this conversation before. Do I need to ask again if you have ever shot at a person, little doctor? Or an animal with more than a tranq gun?"

She sighed heavily, the sound muffled by Michael's chest. Her arms circled his waist and she nuzzled against his tee shirt. "Mmmm?" He chuckled and she felt the vibrations against her cheek. He placed a gentle finger under her chin and tilted her head up.

"This is what I think, little doctor. I do not expect trouble but just in case, Tala is a good shot and we will be back if something happens. You must promise me to keep yourself safe?"

Gazing up into eyes that reminded her of hot caramel dripping over ice cream, she wet her lips with the tip of her tongue. Hard and thick, his erection pressed against her tummy and she wet her lips again. Michael looked like he wanted to eat her as he gazed down. A whimper gathered in her throat but she swallowed it away. How could she want this man so desperately? She could barely walk after last night and here she wanted to pounce him and ride him until they both exploded—over and over again. He bent his head and covered her mouth with his. Liz felt the kiss all the way to her toes. After long, breathless minutes, he released her and stepped back.

"Stay safe, little doctor. I'll return as soon as possible."

He backed away and she felt... Inhaling deeply, she assessed her feelings. Horny. Definitely. She wanted him on her, in her, all around her. She needed his kisses and his arms, his touch and his smile. But there was something more, something deeper. The scientist didn't believe in soul mates or any of that romantic nonsense. But she felt him in her heart, in her bones. She ached with the need for him. The simple task of breathing hurt as she watched him gather weapons and a small pack.

Movement flickered in the corner of her eye. Nakai was kissing Tala and Liz could almost feel the heat that sprang up between them. They were old enough to be her grandparents but the love and passion they shared was evident, even to a casual observer like her. As the men left, she and Tala followed them onto the front porch and watched them melt into the forest. She blinked. One moment the two men paused to turn and wave and the next they were gone, swallowed whole by the pines and bracken.

"How do they do that?"

Tala chuckled. "They are born to it, Liz. You will learn as you spend time with Michael. Would you like more coffee?"

Liz nodded but before she could offer to fetch it, Tala ducked back inside. Moments later, she returned with steaming mugs. The women settled into the only two deck chairs undamaged from the previous attack. They sipped coffee in companionable silence and after refills, they visited. Tala spoke of her life with Jacob, of their children and grandchildren and, much to Liz's surprise, their great grandchildren. She would have pegged the woman's age as a spry seventy, if not younger.

"You said Mike and Jacob—" Tala's laughter cut her off. "What?"

"Mike? I do not believe anyone has ever called him that. He is Michael. Or Lightfoot. You must be very brave to call him that." Her eyes twinkled with good humor and Liz snickered.

"Michael just sounds so formal. And I must admit, he looks so startled when I call him Mike that it's worth it just to get a rise out of him."

Tala nodded, her expression sage. Liz guessed the woman held a great deal of wisdom. "Why does everyone but you call your husband Nakai?"

"I think it is a military thing. Or a man thing." She lifted one shoulder in an eloquent shrug and stood. "Another cup of coffee to wet our throats and loosen our tongues, yes?" Tala stepped back into the house to refill their cups.

Liz accepted the steaming mug then leaned her head back and closed her eyes, letting the peace of the forest wash over her. Long moments passed before she spoke. "It's beautiful here."

"You are not a city girl?"

She laughed and opened her eyes to watch the older woman. "Oh, I suppose I am. I love my Starbucks as much as the next woman, but I could live in a place like this. Provided I had a cappuccino machine." She waggled her brows to show she was teasing and rewarded by Tala's chuckle.

"I do not think Michael could live in a city. He, like my Jacob, can be…uncivilized."

Liz wrinkled her forehead as she puzzled through possible meanings to that. "Should I ask?" She chuckled, though the soft bark sounded nervous even to her own ears.

Before she could reply, Tala turned to face the road. "A vehicle is coming. Get inside and gather your things. We must go."

"Go? Go where? Maybe that's the authorities."

Tala shook her head. "No. Bad men. We must go. Come, Liz. Come now. We have to get to the woods and hide until our men return."

The woman grabbed her arm and tugged. Hard. Tala was much stronger than she looked and remained insistent as she jerked Liz toward the door. Inside the cabin, Tala urged her toward the back door. She planted her feet and grabbed the back of the couch. "No. This is just insane. I—"

Whatever she'd been about to say disintegrated in her mind just like Michael's SUV. The explosion blew out the few windows left unbroken on the front of the house. Stark terror galvanized her muscles where Tala's entreaties had failed. She snagged the file and stuffed it in her backpack before sprinting out the door hard on the older woman's heels. They'd just made the cover of the tree line when the house seemed to explode. Fire erupted from the windows and dark shadows prowled through the smoke.

Liz choked back a sob. Once again, the idea she'd fallen into Wonderland was all too real, only the White Rabbit didn't carry guns and blow up things. Thankful she'd tugged her hiking boots back on her feet after dressing, she followed the very nimble Tala deeper into the woods. She worked to control her breathing and remain quiet when all she wanted to do was collapse on the ground and have the screaming meamies. As she struggled to keep up with Tala, Liz calmed enough to realize the landscape looked familiar. They were headed in the general direction of the wolf den.

Michael! Surely he and Nakai had heard the explosions and were headed back. She tried to remember how far she and Michael had traveled the other night. They had to be close now...

Tala turned to say something, but gasped as she stumbled and fell to her knees. Liz rushed to her and had to press her hands to her mouth to keep from screaming. A bright red splotch spread across the front of the light pink shirt Tala wore. Like an arrow stuck in the middle of a bull's eye, the shaft from a crossbow quivered with each labored breath the woman took. Liz dropped down beside her, unsure of what to do. If she dragged the woman to cover, she'd do more damage. But she couldn't leave her in the open.

The woman snagged her hand and squeezed. Liz gazed into Tala's pain-filled eyes. "Hide. They will think I am dead. I will slow them down so you can escape."

"No." The denial hissed out between her lips. "I can't leave you, Tala. I—" Leaves rained down on her head and shoulders as bullets zinged through the air. She gasped.

"Go. You must live. For Michael."

Choking back her tears, Liz scuttled on her hands and knees into the underbrush. She wished now that she'd borrowed another one of Michael's drab tee shirts. Her red plaid was as big a target as— She choked off that thought. She couldn't go there. She had to lead the bad guys away from Tala. If she could do that, then maybe Tala could hold on long enough they could get medical help for her. Finding a dead log to hide behind, she paused to catch her breath and peek over the top. Shadows flitted through the woods. Their pursuers wore camouflage.

She peeled off her shirt and draped it over a branch she dug out of the leaves around her. If she could put some distance between them, she could plant it as a decoy. Maybe. Hopefully. She had no other choice. She scrambled away, bent over double to make a smaller target. It didn't help. Bullets once again thudded into tree trunks around her. She screamed, the sound out of her mouth before she could stop it. She needed to work toward the west, which she thought was to her left but she was so turned around she was no longer sure. She slid down the lip of a small gully, found her balance as she hit bottom, and took off at a dead run. At a bend, she paused long enough to scramble to the bank, plant her decoy, and take off again. This time she did her best to be quiet.

Her lungs burned and each breath turned to agony. The ditch dead-ended much too soon. She popped her head over the top and had to clamp her hands over her mouth and nose. All she'd done was circle right back to the small glade where Tala lay. A man in forest camouflage stood over the prone woman, his arm extended and a wicked looking automatic pistol in his hand.

Liz wanted to scream, to distract him, but self-preservation kicked in. Even as his finger tightened on the trigger, she watched in horror as the scene unfolded in slow motion. Tala wasn't dead—wasn't unconscious. She raised the rifle she'd been carrying and pulled the trigger. The gunman grunted, spun around and dropped to his knees. He stared right at Liz, his eyes wide, his expression stunned. A dark stain blossomed on his chest. His dying finger convulsed on the trigger of his pistol and bullets sprayed as the clip emptied.

She slithered down the slope and curled into the fetal position, her arms over her head as she tried to block out sounds and sights her mind could no longer process. Shouts and the noise of heavy bodies crashing through the underbrush couldn't be ignored. Liz crept to the lip of the gully and peeked over once more. Four men stood over Tala. One had kicked the rifle away.

"Gawddammit. The old bitch killed Rolf. Make sure she's dead. Then we find the other one."

Petrified by the threat in the man's voice, Liz couldn't move. Three men raised weapons and aimed at Tala. Before they could fire, all hell broke loose. One man collapsed face first across Tala's legs. A black shadow leaped into the clearing and took down a second man. The leader dropped to a crouch, spinning to look for the next direction of attack. His subordinate wasn't as quick. Even as the boom from the gunshot that took out the first man echoed, the third man stumbled backwards as his face dissolved.

Liz retched but she couldn't look away from the carnage. The wolf savaged the man it had attacked. The same wolf she'd seen with Michael at the cottage. Or at least her stunned brain thought it was the same one. She was so intent on the scene, she didn't hear the snap of a branch behind her until a hand grabbed her. She screamed and bit the hand clamping on her mouth. Her nostrils flared. Big Dude. She'd recognize that cheap aftershave anywhere. Her stomach lurched and she retched as bile rose in her throat. He hauled her against his chest and dragged her up the slope and out into the clearing. He hefted her and her feet dangled.

"Call off your dog, ranger boy. Maybe I won't slit your whore's throat."

Liz felt the bite of cold steel against her throat but she didn't stop struggling. She kicked and squirmed, flailing with her arms and reaching back to claw at Big Dude's face. He laughed and squeezed tighter with the arm he'd clenched around her waist. Black dots swam before her eyes and she stilled. She strained to hear some sound, some retort from Michael. The wolf lifted a bloody muzzle and stared at Big Dude, the ruff on his back spiked. The animal fairly vibrated with intent but she could detect no sound. In fact, the entire forest had silenced. Even the wind seemed to hold its breath, waiting for some signal.

"Let her go."

Big Dude laughed. "I'm not that big a fool. She comes with me."

"Suit yourself."

She gasped, despite her best intentions. Maybe Michael didn't care as much as she thought. Would he really sacrifice her? He had to know that if this guy took her again, she wouldn't survive. She fought again, in real earnest, until she heard an angry wasp. Something hot whizzed over the top of her head and she stilled. Her heart pounded in her ears but not loud enough to block out the soft splat as that hornet bit Big Dude. Something wet and sticky rained down on her head. The knife at her throat dropped away. The arm around her solar plexus relaxed. As soon as her feet touched ground, she scrambled away. She managed to stumble a few steps before she collapsed to her knees, retching her guts out. Hands touched her back, pulled her hair away from her face and she batted ineffectually at them.

"Liz? Shhhh, sweetheart. You're okay. I have you."

Michael. She turned blindly and clung to him, her face buried in his chest. The fear she'd swallowed gushed out with her panting breath. He gathered her close and rocked her as her tears flowed and sobs racked her body. Moments passed. Then minutes. She forced deep breaths into her lungs and hiccuped. Warm hands smoothed across her back.

"Tala!" She pushed away from the sanctuary of Michael's body and glanced at the fallen woman. The wolf snarled and tugged at the man lying across her.

Michael stood and helped her up before turning to the wolf. The animal snarled and bared his teeth but seemed to relax as Michael grabbed a booted foot and pulled the dead man away. Struck dumb, Liz watched as the wolf whined and licked Tala's face. The older woman buried her hands in the animal's fur.

"Nakai? Come back, my friend. Your mate needs you." Michael squatted on his heels on the other side of the prone woman.

The wolf raised his head and stared at Michael. She blinked tears away as the wolf's form wavered and contorted. Liz watched transfixed as the sounds of popping joints, of ripping skin, of a body seeming to turn inside out assaulted her. She shuddered and wanted to retch again but choked down the dry heave swelling in her gut. A wolf changing into a man? It wasn't possible. This was the stuff of nightmares...of an insane mind...of novels. Wasn't it?

Naked, Nakai touched his wife with infinite care and gentleness. He lifted and cradled her, ever mindful of the crossbow shaft sticking out of her chest. He held her to him, smoothing back the hair on her forehead before kissing her.

"You are as beautiful now as you were the first day I saw you," the old man murmured.

Tala coughed and bloody foam bubbled on her lips. "I am an old woman." She lifted a hand with effort. A light touch of her fingers against his mouth stilled his words. "You have loved me well. We have many children. The children of our children will sing my name." Her hand dropped but Nakai grabbed it and held it to his chest over his heart. "Keep me locked away here. I live for so long as you do, always by your side, always in your heart."

Tears clouded Liz's vision. She felt like a voyeur intruding on this most private of moments. If they could get help, maybe Tala could be saved. She opened her mouth to say something of the sort but the other woman's body arched and then seemed to deflate as her last breath sighed out. Nakai, his face pressed to his wife's, held her and rocked back and forth as a keening cry struggled from his throat to wing across the forest.

Her cheeks slick with tears, Liz could only sit and watch. The hair on her arms prickled as she stared at the two men kneeling beside the dead woman. Nakai raised his head and a howl exploded from somewhere deep in his chest. Seconds later, Michael raised his face to the sky and his howl joined the first. In the distance, a third howl echoed, and then a fourth. In moments, an otherworldly chorus lifted myriad voices to the sky, all seeming to sing Tala's soul on its journey. Michael turned to glance at her and she caught the flash of something red and feral in his eyes. He might look like a human but a beast prowled just below the surface. How had she not seen it before?

She wiped her cheeks with the back of her hand. As soon as Michael looked away, she jumped up and ran. She heard him calling her name but she didn't stop. Terrified, she put her head down and pumped her arms and legs in a mad dash. She glanced over her shoulder. Michael loped behind her, his longer legs gaining on her easily.

"Liz! No...wait! Watch—"

CHAPTER 27

LIZ OPENED HER eyes and Michael recognized the moment she realized where she was and remembered what had happened. Panic overshadowed the fear lurking in her gaze. Before she could do much more than shrink back from him, the door whispered open and a cheerful nurse in teddy-bear scrubs padded in.

"Well, look at us all bright-eyed and bushy-tailed." Michael winced but the nurse ignored him, focused completely on her patient. "We thought you might sleep another whole day away. Let me get your temperature and blood pressure and then I'll go get you something to eat."

The nurse set about her duties with barely a glance in his direction. Liz opened her mouth to speak but got a thermometer shoved in her mouth instead. He watched, concerned for both her health and for what she might say. His kind had remained the stuff of legend for centuries. Very few people knew the whole truth about the Wolves. Keeping their existence a secret had kept them alive. Satisfied with her patient's vital signs, the nurse bustled out with nary a look back as the door whispered shut behind her.

"What are you?"

The accusation in that question arrowed straight to his heart. Despite his best efforts, he was well and truly moonstruck. After Liz knocked herself out running into that damned tree trunk, he'd carried her back to his cabin—or what was left of it. The local volunteer fire department, the sheriff, and the state police had all been on scene. It drained every ounce of his self-control to let the paramedics treat Liz and transport her to the hospital. He'd stayed for the investigation. He'd stayed for Jacob so the man could mourn his mate.

Almost eighteen hours later, he'd arrived to sit vigil at Liz's bedside. He hadn't slept. Hadn't eaten. Had done nothing but worry about what he would tell her. How he would explain what he was, what *they* were now. Michael inhaled as he sorted through the words tumbling through his mind.

"Not what you think." He reached for her hand, the need to touch her overwhelming his good intentions to give her time to adjust to what was happening.

She shifted away. "How do you know what I think, Michael?"

"You're a scientist, right?"

Liz eyed him dubiously but nodded.

"Technically, I am a *lupi versi pellis*. A lycanthrope."

"A werewolf?" Hysteria tinged her whisper.

"No. Yes." He rubbed his hand across his forehead, eyes closed for a moment. He missed her mad scramble for the call button, only looking up when the alarm sounded.

The same nurse as before rushed in. She slammed a food tray on the bedside table and flipped the switches to silence the irritating beeping. "Now what's got you so upset, honey?"

Liz could only point his direction and mouth words. He winced. This was not going well at all.

"What's that you're saying?" The nurse leaned closer and Liz, her eyes so wide the whites showed all around the irises, whispered in her ear. "Oh now, honey. You've had a terrible scare and a bad concussion to boot. We never know what head injuries will make us think. You just lay back and have some of this orange gelatin. Get some food in that tummy of yours and you'll feel better in no time at all.

Liz worked her mouth but nothing came out. With her bug-eyed look and her mouth moving, she reminded Michael of a fish in a bowl. He winced as she pointed an accusatory finger at him as words finally formed. "Get him away from me!"

The nurse glanced over at him. He read nothing but sympathy on the woman's face. "Darlin', why don't you step out in the hall for just a bit. We'll get this little lady settled. Don't worry. We'll take good care of her."

He didn't want to leave Liz. Not only did his wolf crave to be near her but the man feared for her safety. Just because he'd dispatched those mercenaries up on the mountain didn't mean others weren't nearby to swoop in and snatch her up. He would do whatever it took to keep her safe. And by his side. But antagonizing the medical staff was not a smart thing to do. He did as the nurse asked.

A few minutes later, she appeared from Liz's room. "I gave her a bit of a sedative, Ranger Lightfoot. Head trauma can do odd things to a person. I'm sure she'll be fine in no time at all. The police are still waiting to speak to her. I'll tell them what I'm going to tell you. Go away. Let her rest and recuperate."

The growl rumbled in his chest before he could swallow it. The nurse chuckled and patted his arm. "You alpha males are all alike. Nobody is going to get to her. This is a secured area of the hospital and there's a policeman at the nurse's station."

Michael had been outmaneuvered and was smart enough to admit it. If he pressed the issue too hard, the nurse would become suspicious. He needed backup and he needed them now. Nakai had elected to stay near the wolf den pending the autopsy on Tala. Then he would accompany her body to their home in Arizona. Even as he formulated plans he nodded at the nurse. "Will someone call me when she wakes up again?"

The nurse gave his shoulder a motherly pat. "Of course."

🐾🐾🐾🐾

HEART POUNDING, LIZ opened her eyes. She was still in a hospital. But which hospital? She glanced over at the blonde woman sitting in the one comfortable chair in the room and didn't recognize her. Her heart rate kicked up and the heart monitor beeped ominously.

"Deep breaths, Liz." The woman offered a smile to go with her calm voice.

"Do I know you?" Her voice sounded weak and tremulous and she hated it.

The woman chuckled. "No. I'm Hannah McIntire."

"Why are you here?"

"Suspicious little thing, aren't you? That's good. It will keep you alive and safe."

"Safe? Why do I need to worry about my safety?" Liz did her best to look guileless but the woman's eyes narrowed.

"You aren't that dumb, Liz, at least according to our mutual friend."

She gulped and before she could stop herself, the question was out of her mouth. "Are you a good witch or a bad witch?"

Hannah laughed, the sound rich and deep. "Touché. I suppose it depends upon which side you're on. My husband served with Michael and Nakai in the Army. He was their sergeant major."

"Was?"

"Their unit disbanded a few years ago."

There was more to this story, Liz was sure of it, but the woman didn't reveal what it was. "Uhm...Hannah, right?" The woman nodded. "I'm confused. A lot."

228

Hannah's smile broadened. "I'm not surprised. Getting thrown into their world and having a moonstruck Wolf to boot can be disconcerting, to say the least."

Her mouth opened and closed several times but no words came out. She swallowed around the lump clogging her throat.

The other woman leaned closer and patted her arm, the gesture seeming awkward but kind. "You have a lot of catching up to do, Liz. But this is not the place to discuss everything that's going on." Hannah stopped talking and tilted her head toward the door. Footsteps stopped on just the other side. Moments later, whoever had listened at the door moved on. "See what I mean? Until we figure out who is friendly and who isn't, we need to tread very carefully."

Hannah reached into her hip pocket and pulled out a leather case—like the ones TV detectives flipped open to prove their identities. Sure enough, the woman flicked it open with practiced ease and presented it to her. Liz grabbed the ID and read it closely. It looked real but she wasn't sure what an actual Department of Defense ID looked like. As if reading her mind, Hannah offered a knowing smile.

"It's real. I'm a special investigator with DSS. The Defense Security Service. When I was on active duty, I was attached to the Joint Chiefs at the Pentagon. That's how I met Mac, my husband. And his little ragtag band of misfit toys."

"I heard that."

Liz shrank against the pillows at her back. She hadn't heard the door open and the man who filled the entry terrified her. He was huge, with muscled arms and a chest like a stone wall. Hannah rose immediately. "Liz, my husband, Ian McIntire, though most people call him Mac. What's wrong?"

"We have to go."

He advanced on the bed, and started flipping switches. When he reached for her hand with the IV needle, Liz flinched away.

"Don't touch me!"

He glowered at her but Hannah slid between them. "Mac, back off before you scare the poor girl to death. What's going on?"

"There are a couple of suits downstairs asking about Dr. Graham. We need to get her out of here. Now."

The last word came out more like a growl and the hair prickled on Liz's arms. "Who are you people?"

They ignored her, Hannah giving orders like doing so was second nature. "I'll get a wheelchair. You can't just carry her out. Leave the IV in and attach the bag to the chair. Once you two are on your way, I'll go stall the men in black."

Bewildered, Liz put up a feeble fight but something about their urgency kept her from screaming for help. In moments, Hannah returned with the wheelchair and they settled her into it with a blanket over her legs. Mac wheeled her down the hallway toward a bank of elevators and they grabbed the first one that opened. Down in the lobby, Hannah split off for the reception station while Mac headed for the door. Two men, in suits but looking like they should be in uniforms of some sort, hovered at the exit. Mac leaned low, his head and body partially blocking her face. As he wheeled her outside, he spoke loud enough for the men to overhear.

"The kids sure have missed you, honey. They'll be so happy to see their mommy again."

She ducked her head but watched the men from the corner of her eyes. Their steely gazes glanced over the two of them. Out in the sunshine, Mac picked up his pace. A big, silver SUV slid to a stop and the back passenger door popped open. Before she could react, Mac scooped her into his arms, deposited her in the backseat, and slammed the door. Seconds later, he jumped into the front passenger seat and the vehicle sped off.

Liz snagged her seatbelt and put it on. Her heart insisted these were the good guys but her brain wanted to debate the point. Had she jumped out of the frying pan into the fire?

At the next corner, the back door opposite her opened and Hannah jumped in. The woman, her hair tousled and eyes twinkling, settled in and buckled up.

"Those are some very unhappy fuckwits back there at the hospital. We caught them flatfooted and whoever they work for is going to be damned pissed."

Mac glanced over from the front seat. "Fuck, Hannah... And no, I will not watch my language, since you aren't. I'm sure Dr. Graham has heard the word before. Stop distracting me, woman. You better not have taken any chances."

"I am perfectly capable of handling myself. And Michael was right to call us. We need to notify Harjo."

The driver adjusted the rearview mirror so he could see Hannah. Liz didn't recognize him but his eyes seemed kind. "I thought you shut down all the biological stuff at Area 51, Hannah."

"I did, but we've heard rumors for years that another private lab under government contract moved into the facility." Hannah shifted in her seat to stare at Liz. "I know you feel a bit lost, Liz, but you really need to trust us. At best, these guys want you because you're a geneticist. At worst, they want you dead so you can't testify against them."

She gulped. "D-d-dead?" Spots swam in front of her eyes and she closed them, hoping to find her equilibrium. "You're right. I don't understand a thing about this. About who you are. About Michael. About...what...he is... And Nakai. Tala." Her throat closed and tears sprang up behind her closed eyelids. "Poor Tala."

Hannah's hand patted hers where she'd fisted them in her lap. "Tala was very special. To all of us. These same men are after you, Liz."

Shaking, she opened her eyes to meet Hannah's worried gaze. "It's because of them, isn't it? Michael and Nakai. Was Tala one of them, too?" Liz didn't care that her voice sounded full of disgust. Whatever they were, it was wrong. Morally. Genetically. Scientifically. She couldn't wrap her brain around the concept.

The men in the front stiffened and Hannah's eyes glinted dangerously. "You have a great deal to learn, Dr. Graham. Since you're supposed to be a scientist, I hope you'll keep an open mind."

The strains of "Bad Moon Rising" echoed in the car. Mac turned to stare at the driver. "Really?"

The man worked to keep his expression serious as he passed his cell phone to Mac and the big man answered with a curt, "We have her."

Oh, yes. Definitely from the frying pan to the fire.

CHAPTER 28

LIZ LAY ON the bed, her back propped up by pillows and the headboard. She forced air into her lungs because the men in the room with her seemed to suck it all up. Mac was the biggest man there but the other two seemed larger than life as well. So much energy surrounded them a person would have to be dead not to notice. Michael leaned on the wall next to the bed. The other men kept their distance and Hannah sat on the foot of the second bed in the motel room. Under Michael's watchful eyes, the driver had removed her IV, checked her injuries, and made sure her pain levels were manageable. She'd learned his name was Sean and that he was a former combat medic. He'd been brusque and capable, but he'd also been gentle.

Conversation buzzed around her and she listened intently—and learned a lot, most of which she saved to process later. Werewolves? For real? Only they didn't call themselves that. And the condition was likely linked to the Y chromosome. Her inner scientist was intrigued even as the rest of her was terrified. She glanced up to find Hannah watching her intently. She stared back. The other woman offered a tight smile.

"You'll do, Liz Graham. I see the wheels turning. But don't let your brain override your heart."

That was easy for Hannah to say. She... Liz blinked. Hannah had walked into the middle of this life clueless, too. She remembered that much of the conversations in the car. She watched the looks Hannah and Mac shared, noted their exchanges with a detached perspective. As the other woman reminded her, she was a scientist. Granted, psychology wasn't her strong suit, but she could observe and postulate. She saw two people totally committed to each other. They might disagree. They might rub the other the wrong way, but when push came to shove, they presented a united front.

Liz glanced over to the long, lean body propped against the wall near the head of her bed. Michael appeared to be monitoring the conversation but his entire focus centered on her. She felt if all the way down to her bones. She might fear him but she wasn't afraid of him. How messed up was that? No, she didn't fear him, she feared what he was. It was...unnatural. But watching him, and the others, she concluded that they were comfortable in their own skins—no matter what form that skin took. She also recognized that these men were honorable and loyal. A girl could do a whole lot worse in this day and age. She tilted her head, watching Michael watch her. Her heart swelled, even though she knew it couldn't actually do so physically. Love was nothing but hormones. Just chemical reactions in the human body. She blinked and leaned forward. Wasn't that, at its core, what occurred in the men's bodies—a chemical reaction that changed them from men to wolves?

"Oh, crap. They want you to run experiments on."

Everyone in the room stared at her and Liz realized she'd said the words out loud. "Oh, holy hell, whoever is behind this wants to practice Frankenstein medicine." She shuddered and retched. Michael was beside her on the bed immediately, his arms scooping her up, poised to take her to the bathroom. She inhaled and swallowed the bile.

"No, I'm okay. You can put me down."

He did so immediately and as soon as the heat of his body moved away she felt...bereft. Tears stung her eyelids and she blinked them away. She snagged his hand before he could retreat. His long fingers wrapped around hers but he still looked wary, like a dog kicked more than once. Her chest hurt and she offered her other hand to him. Before she could take a breath, he enveloped her in a gentle bear hug. Something shifted inside her and she knew with complete certainty that all was right in her world.

"I'm sorry, baby." His words whispered through her hair.

"No. I'm the one who should be sorry."

"Ahem. Debrief is over, guys. I think Michael and Liz need some alone time." Hannah chuckled, the sound deep and seductive. "I know I could certainly use some...sleep."

"Great. You mated couples really piss me off, you know? I'll be in the bar." Sean didn't sound half as upset as his words indicated.

With her head buried against Michael's shoulder, she heard the others leave. He kissed her forehead and eased her back against the pillows.

"I need to secure the door. I'll be right back."

He was gone and back in what seemed like a heartbeat. He stripped to his jeans and stretched out beside her, offering his arms and shoulder to cuddle into. She did. Her heart shifted again. How could she have ever fought this feeling?

"We'll work through this, Liz. But you have to believe me. You are my life. You are smart and funny and brave and I never thought I'd be lucky enough to find a mate as perfect as you."

She laughed. "Flattery will get you almost everywhere."

His arms tightened and he kissed the top of her head. "Truth." With a gentle finger under her chin, he tilted her face up to look at him. "Always truth, Liz. Between us. There will be no secrets. I will never lie to you. I will never hurt you."

She leaned up and offered her lips for a kiss. He met her halfway. "Truth. Always." She breathed the words against his skin.

Her life had taken a dramatic turn and eventually, her head would catch up with her heart. In the meantime, she had a man to show how much she loved him. And a wolf pack to protect. And a mysterious syndrome that had its basis in a recessive gene on the Y chromosome. What had Michael called the Wolves? *Lupi versi pellis.* He'd told her that loosely translated, it meant something like "they turn the skin of wolves."

"I love you."

The tightness in her chest loosened further. She smiled and kissed him again, deeper this time. "I love you, too."

"We'll get through this, Liz. I promise. I won't let anything happen to you."

"I know." And she did. "I trust you."

The relief in his eyes rocked her soul as she realized love and trust didn't necessarily go hand in hand.

"We have to move the pack, Michael."

"Yes."

"We have to protect them."

"Yes." He kissed her again. "Tomorrow, Liz. We'll make things right tomorrow."

"Yes." The word came out muffled as she curled in with a yawn. She could fight exhaustion no longer. In moments, she was sound asleep.

🐾🐾🐾🐾

CHILLED, LIZ SOUGHT the warmth she'd snuggled against all night only to discover the space beside her empty. She jerked to a sitting position, her heart hammering. She might be alone in bed, but Michael was still there in the unfamiliar room with her. He stood at the window, curtains drawn back just enough to see out. The neon sign in front of the motel flashed a desultory red and blue, a lazy strobe of colors that purported to offer comfort and rest. The lights reminded her too much of the lights on the ambulance and other emergency vehicles at Michael's house. Which had burned down. The horror of Tala's death washed over her and she curled her fist to her mouth to keep from crying out. With shallow breaths, she watched Michael, recognized the stiff set of his shoulders, the jutted chin challenging the night.

Liz slipped out of bed and padded over to him. She touched his back, her fingers seeking the heat of him, the connection. His arm slid around her and tucked her against his side. He kissed the top of her head and then his gaze returned to the skyline above the motel. She stared out the window, looking for what held his attention. The moon rode low on the horizon. Half moon. One face light, the other dark. A magical yin-yang fitted more precisely than any jigsaw puzzle.

"Like us," she murmured. "The moon is like us." She glanced up, caught the barest flicker of a smile tug the corner of his mouth but it was gone in a blink. Silence stretched between them. She could almost imagine the tick of a clock measuring the seconds.

"Are you okay with this?"

She glanced up at him. She owed him honesty. "I don't know."

"I'm sorry."

Liz pulled away from him so she could see him better. One side of his face flickered red then blue while the other remained in shadow—like the moon. "For what?"

"For...this." He gestured with one hand, a sweeping motion that encompassed the room, the motel, the world beyond. "I should have given you the choice."

She didn't need to see his whole face to read the regret etched there. "I'm sorry you're saddled with me." Hurt leaked into her words despite her best efforts.

Michael stared at her, his caramel eyes flashing gold in the haphazard light from the window. "I'm not."

She inhaled and the ache in her chest eased slightly. "I know you didn't have a choice. That I don't have a choice."

"Stop." He clutched her to his chest. "I could have walked away. I would have for you, if you had said no. I thought I could do it. I was too weak. I need you too much." His lips clamped onto hers. His arms crushed her to his chest and she felt his heart thudding against his rib cage. When he finished the kiss, his forehead rested against hers. "I thought there was always a choice. I could have sent you away. But I am selfish. I want you. You, Liz. I want your laughter and your sighs. I want to see your eyes flash with anger. I want you in my bed. You already live in my heart, where you belong."

Liz sniffled and stared at him, her mouth slightly agape. Her eyelids drifted shut as he kissed her forehead again and her breath hitched in her chest.

"I love you, Liz. Not because I have to, but because I want to. You are my other half." He turned her to look out the window. "You are the light to my dark. Like the moon."

"Then it wasn't a bad moon when we met?" She hated that she sounded so tremulous.

"No moon is bad with you at my side. We will move the wolves and we will find a way for you to continue your research. Mac and Hannah believe you are on to something. There are bad men out there who mean to do bad things. It's up to us to help stop them." He let the curtains drop back, plunging the room into a deep gloom, highlighted by that red-blue-red strobe from the neon motel sign leaking in around the edges.

She smiled and rose on her tiptoes. Right before her lips brushed against his she whispered, "We will. Together we can do anything."

"Yes," he agreed. Liz giggled and when Michael arched his brow in a quizzical expression, she laughed. "You going to tell me what is so funny?"

"You." She worked to keep her face solemn but the sassy grin leaked through.

He continued to stare at her but hid his own smile as she flushed and her nipples budded beneath the tee shirt she'd slept in. His cock stirred, the movement drawing her eyes to his groin. This was the joy of mates. This need, this soul-deep wanting would always be there, growing stronger with the passage of time.

"You are a man of few words." She hesitated as she spoke but managed to get the sentence out as her eyes grew rounder.

"Yes. And a man hungry for his mate. Come to bed." He picked her up, silencing her retort with a kiss. A knock on the door interrupted him.

Michael set her down, grabbed his pistol and listened at the door before Liz could even catch her breath. He felt her worried gaze and motioned her toward the bathroom. He heard the brush of her bare feet across the worn carpet and then silence. Pressing his ear to the door, he listened. His nostrils flared. Two men. Human. He caught Liz's muffled voice. She was on the room phone. He heard the grating of a key in the lock. He'd thrown both the deadbolt latch and the security chain. One of the men cursed then bit off the words. The second man answered but the only word Michael could make out was "window."

Before he could react, he detected the sounds of a scuffle. In seconds, he had the door open only to find Sean and Mac grinning at him.

"Took you long enough, bud." The big medic bent over to check the pockets of his prisoner.

"You and Liz okay?" Mac didn't look up from his man.

"We're good." He glanced over his shoulder. "Get dressed and packed up, Liz. We need to move out ASAP." Michael turned back to Mac. "Black Root?"

"Probably. No ID on either of them."

Hannah trotted up. "Found their signature black SUV around the corner at the truck stop. No paperwork in the glovebox."

Her husband flashed a dubious look in her direction. "How would you know that?"

"Gosh, some asshole busted out the window. I figured I should check for owner info so I could notify them."

Sean guffawed. "That's right neighborly, Hannah."

Michael slipped back inside to dress. Minutes later, two vehicles pulled out onto the highway, the two captives bouncing around in the back of their purloined SUV, driven by Sean. In the other SUV, Michael drove with singular focus while Hannah and Mac worked their phones. Liz huddled in the back seat, the buzz of one-sided conversations whirring around her.

"Roger, that Colonel," from Mac.

"I don't care what it takes. I want IDs on those guys," from Hannah.

Liz covered her mouth with her hand to stifle her whimper. She was made of sterner stuff, though if anyone should be allowed a meltdown, she should get to be first on the list. She raised her gaze and caught Michael watching her from the rearview mirror. She read pride in his eyes—pride in her, and something that rocked her soul. Love. The vise clamping around her chest loosened. She inhaled deeply and offered him a smile that didn't feel quite so tentative. She could do this. What's more, she wanted this...this whatever it was between her and Michael. For the first time in her life, she belonged.

CHAPTER 29

SEAN WALKED AWAY from the black SUV without a backward glance. The men had been offered a deal—one neither of them accepted. He could live with that. Too bad they couldn't. A half mile away, he stripped out of his clothes and bundled everything up. Moments later, a big brindle wolf snatched the pack in his teeth and trotted into the desert. At a ground-eating lope, the wolf headed toward a small town on the horizon.

When the timer on Black Root's SUV triggered, Sean was behind the controls of his demolition company's helicopter after a business meeting with a mine owner who was looking to open up a new vein in an old silver mine. The bodies would have vaporized and the desert would reclaim any of the vehicle but just in case there were nosy neighbors, Sean was alibied.

Everyone had secrets. Including him. He had one stop to make before he met the rest of the team on the Navajo reservation. The deaths of innocents left a bad taste in his mouth. He didn't get back to this area very often and he had respects to pay. Besides, it wasn't like Mac had ordered him to keep those two scumfuckers alive. And he had offered a simple deal: the name of the man they worked for in exchange for a running start. Not his problem if they decided to be stupid.

He flew into the setting sun toward Sin City. Goodbyes were never easy and they took all forms. He had one to say before he joined the rest of the team in Arizona.

🐾🐾🐾🐾

MICHAEL HELD THE two tiny microchips in the palm of his hand. The alpha pair, once recovered from the tranq, had rejoined the pack with no ill effects—and much safer for having the chips removed. The pups were growing well, the pack settled into their new territory. The Montana Rockies were vast and the Wild Wolf Project provided the perfect cover. Since Liz and the Project's vet had removed the chips, no one could track the pack.

Sean had worked some sort of computer magic to corrupt files so all mention of this pack had disappeared— as if they'd never existed. Much like the Wolves themselves ten years ago. Hannah's magic had erased all mention of the Wolves, Whiskey teams, and the 69th. Only a handful of trusted people knew the truth.

Anyone trying to follow a paper trail on Michael or Liz would eventually hit a series of dead ends. They'd both been transferred. And transferred again. Every I dotted, every T crossed. Until they simply faded into the vast bureaucratic forest of paperwork. That Liz had no family to speak of and hadn't been on the job in Cheyenne long enough to make close friends made things easier—with less feelings of guilt for Michael for taking her underground. He knew how important disappearing was for her safety. They would make their own family. Their own pack. With wolves and Wolves both. For now, Liz's research was of utmost importance. For all of them. For the children he hoped to have with her someday. And for the boy, Liam, all the Wolves already considered their own.

Watching the sparkling water of the mountain stream, Michael let the peace of the place fill him. He held his hand over the water and turned it over. The two black dots glittered in the air before landing on the water. With a sound like laughing children, the stream carried the chips away.

🐾🐾🐾🐾

MAC PACED TO the window and stared out. The scenery included the motel parking lot and the traffic streaming by on the nearby highway. He didn't want to be here. Didn't want to face what they had come to do tomorrow. In the meantime, though, he had other problems. He turned and studied his wife. Her hands were jammed in her pockets and she met his gaze defiantly. She didn't want to be here either. "You'd best fill us in."

"With what I know? You won't like it." Hannah's gaze scraped across every man in the room. "None of you."

He didn't doubt that for a second. He trusted his mate but Hannah had remained secretive all afternoon. "At this point, that's pretty much a given. Just spit it out."

Hannah hunched her shoulders. "Black Root has been removed from the approved contractors list."

Mac knew her. "But?"

"*But* is right. Every thread I tug in this investigation? That name comes up at the end of it. Or some subsidiary thereof. They had government contracts—and not just security services but in R and D too." She cut a quick glance at him before her eyes skittered away.

Dammit. Hannah was his mate. They didn't have secrets between them. What did she know that she hadn't told him yet? "Babe?"

"DNA. Gene therapy and manipulation."

"Manipulation? What's that even mean?"

"Hell if I know. I'm not the scientist here." Hannah nodded toward Liz Graham. "That's the doc's field, not mine. All I know is back channel chatter keeps picking up terms like super solider, science fiction, Frankenstein gene." Her brow creased as she raised her eyes to meet his. "If I had to guess, I'd say they've figured out what makes you guys special."

Now he understood. Liam. Their son. Who carried the same DNA as Mac and the other men in the room. *Lupi versi pellis.* Not much scared his wife, but a threat to their child? All bets were off. "Then it's time to hunt."

🐾🐾🐾🐾

A FINGER OF smoke curled into the closed air of Nakai's hogan, beckoning like the hand of a lover. Here in the heart of Navajo land, family and friends gathered in his home to mourn Tala and to participate in the Blessingway ceremony. The singer's voice crooned a song to the solemn beat of the drum. The small fire crackled, the pops and crackles a sharp staccato above the sonorous chant. They'd brought Tala home to be buried and now the Navajo medicine man performed the rite to bless them all.

Liz watched with wide eyes, her chest barely rising and falling with her measured breaths. Michael relaxed. Tomorrow, he and Liz would head back to Montana. The team moved the wolf pack before coming to Arizona and they had jobs waiting with the Wild Wolf Project. They would watch over the wolves and Liz could do her research. Mac and Hannah would work the back channels to keep track of their enemies. Colonel Harjo would do what he could at the Pentagon. The wolves would split up again. That part sucked. He rubbed at the spot above his heart with his fist. These men were his pack, Mac and Hannah his Alpha pair. He missed the camaraderie—the connection with the others. Hadn't realized how much until they were all together again. He'd called and they'd come. They helped keep his mate safe and Liz was now a valued member of the pack.

His mate. He loved the sound of that. Liz. She was his life and one day, she would bring his pup into the world. Liz turned her head to gaze at him and he couldn't breathe for a moment. A smile curved her lips and he had to resist the urge to kiss her. Her attention returned to the ceremony and he glanced at Mac and Hannah and then Jacob Nakai. The old Indian had aged a century in the last few days, the grief etched on his face as deeply as the fissures on the mesas that squatted around this valley. A small child crawled into Nakai's lap—one of his great grandchildren. The toddler patted the old man's face with chubby hands and kissed him.

Birth. Life. Death. A new life started the cycle all over again, as it should. As it always would. His hand covered Liz's where her slender fingers rested on her thigh. He'd found his life with her and so the cycle would continue.

"Yes." Her whisper teased across his skin as her fingers laced with his. *I love you.* Her thoughts caressed his mind.

My mate. His heart swelled in his chest until he couldn't breathe for the love he felt.

Always.

Dear Reader:

In the course of writing the nine stories in the Moonstruck series, I discovered there were scenes that needed to be cut to fit that particular novella, even though those scenes affected the overall series arc. I also found out there were scenes I didn't write that, in retrospect, needed to be added. That's the joy of this brave, new publishing era. I can fix things. I can put those deletions back in. I can write the additional scenes. And I can tell the full story of the Wolves and their mates and families and get it into the hands of my readers.

From these realizations came the idea of presenting four full-length novels—with those added scenes, and a fuller, deeper exploration of the Moonstruck world. I hope you'll stick around for the rest of the journey.

As an author, I'm always humbled when readers love my characters as much as I do. I live with these people during the course of their stories. They are very *real* to me and to know that they *live* in readers' imaginations leaves me gobsmacked. Thank you.

I leave you with one favor to ask. People talking about a book is a priceless gift readers can give an author. When you like a book, please consider leaving a review and suggesting it to your friends. Heck, even if you didn't like it, leave a review so the writer knows why. I appreciate the "I hated this book and here's why" reviews. They help me learn and grow as a writer. Of course, I also do little squee dances (which totally freak out Cooper, Boone, and Adidas) when I get a nice review.

Again, thank you for visiting my worlds. The door is always open so don't be a stranger. Happy reading!

~Silver James

Thank you!

Thanks for reading MOONSTRUCK: SECRETS. I hope you enjoyed it. Reviews help other readers find books to read. I appreciate every review, good or bad. Please consider leaving one at Amazon or on Goodreads. If this is your first Moonstruck book, please check out the rest of the series and my other books, too.

Coming soon –
Two New Series set in the world of Moonstruck

Nightriders MC
Night Shift – Book 1

Hard Target
Double Cross – Book 1

Also Coming in 2015:

The Full-length Moonstruck Novels
Moonstruck: Secrets
Moonstruck: Lies
Moonstruck: Betrayal
Moonstruck: Retribution

Penumbra Papers
The Devil's Cut

Still Available – the original digital novellas in

MOONSTRUCK
The Award-winning Series

Blood Moon
(Moonstruck –Book 1)
Army Major Hannah Jackson knows where the

skeletons are hidden at the Pentagon and now she's been tasked with keeping the secrets of Army Special Sci Ops Unit 69—the Wolves—and their secret is a doozy. That a civilian corporation wants to exploit the Wolves is a matter of pressing concern.

Sergeant Major Ian McIntire doesn't trust Hannah as far as he can throw her—and that's quite a ways considering he's an alpha werewolf. The woman is a pain in his butt and with the Blood Moon coming, the unit needs to complete their mission and get home before tempers flare. While she might know most of their secrets, the one she doesn't know about the moonstruck Wolf might just get them all killed.

When a covert operation goes wrong, Mac must trust Hannah to save his men—and his heart. Secrets, lies, and betrayals are more personal under the full moon, but when a Wolf loves a woman, he'll do whatever it takes to keep her safe.

Warning: Pursue an alpha Wolf at your own risk. Hot sex, bad words, and action of the blood and guts kind will ensue.

WINNER 2013 INTERNATIONAL DIGITAL AWARDS SHORT PARANORMAL NOVEL

Bad Moon
(Moonstruck –Book 2)

Former Army sniper Michael Lightfoot lives a simple life as a forest ranger in Wyoming. The job fits his need to run wild when the moon is full—until two special wolf pups are kidnapped, along with Dr. Liz Graham, the wildlife biologist who makes him want to howl.

The last thing Michael expects when he meets the feisty doctor is to be moonstruck, but the alpha Wolf has more on his plate than just convincing Dr. Liz to love him for who he is. She's being stalked by mercenaries who stole two wolf pups for an unknown faction. Now, with her life in danger, he must reveal his true self to save her. Reuniting with some of his old Army Special SciOps unit, Michael takes on the corporate raiders who want more than just his hide—and Liz's expertise.

Secrets, lies, and betrayals are more personal under the full moon, but when a Wolf loves a woman, he'll risk heart and soul to keep her.

Warning: When a moonstruck Wolf meets his mate, hot sex will ensue. If his mate is threatened, bad words and violence of the blood and guts variety will definitely occur.

Hunter's Moon
(Moonstruck –Book 3)

Dr. Jacey Randolph just might be crazy. A rescued wolf is more than he seems and his ability to get into her head—literally—makes her doubt her sanity. After the death of her husband in the Gulf War, she returned to the family ranch to run an animal sanctuary. Bad enough she has to fend off advances from the local sheriff, but now she's turning into some sort of Dr. Doolittle. Except she doesn't talk to animals, dammit.

When Colonel Joshua Harjo, an old friend of her husband's, shows up on her doorstep with a wild tale that the wolf is actually Marine Captain Nathaniel Connor, Jacey must make a leap of faith—and jeopardize her heart—to get involved with the wolf and a group of former Army SciOps soldiers in full rescue operation mode.

Secrets, lies, and betrayals are more personal under the full moon but when a woman loves a Wolf, he can do no wrong. And Jacey Randolph is not about to let a little thing like a band of mercenaries keep her from the Wolf she loves.

Warning: Explosions, death, and sex go hand in hand when a group of Wolves and their women fight for their existence.

Wolf Moon
(Moonstruck Book 4)

Sean Donaldson, former combat medic and demolition expert, answers an SOS from an old Army buddy and rides smack dab into the middle of a conspiracy. Murder and kidnapping are just the tip of the iceberg. Going undercover with a biker gang seems the quickest solution but Sean's best intentions are complicated by Annie Simmons and her son, Cody.

Annie is a waitress at the Half Dollar Bar and Grill just scraping by to provide a better life for her son. She doesn't want a man in her life, especially a scary dude like "Boomer," the big biker who steals a part of her heart. What she doesn't know about the lies he's told can hurt her...and put Cody in danger.

Secrets, lies, and betrayals are more personal under the full moon but when a Wolf fights for his heart, he'll risk his life to make sure the family he loves survives.

Warning: When it's the month of the Wolf Moon, anybody who gets between a moonstruck Wolf and his mate deserves what they get. Blood, sex, and four-letter words dead ahead.

Bride's Moon
(Moonstruck Book 5)

When the remnants of Special SciOps Unit 69, the Wolves, reunited to save a group of soldiers used as lab rats in a secret experiment, Colonel Joshua Harjo never expected to command the covert government unit again. Someone near the top wants the 69th back on active duty and Harjo is tasked with making it happen, along with keeping the men the Wolves rescued top secret.

Amy Rouse is the best "cat herder" around and she's recruited for administrative duties with the new unit, a job with perks—Wolves and their commanding officer, Joshua Harjo, the man of her dreams. Amy didn't count on murder, mayhem, and a redheaded Deputy US

Marshal to complicate her life.

Secrets, lies, and betrayals are more personal under the full moon, but when a man loves a woman, nothing will stop him from tying the knot.

Warning: The road to romance is never smooth and a runaway bride might just jinx a highly sensitive operation.

Rogue Moon
(Moonstruck Book 6)

Rudek Tornjak is a Wolf without a pack. A man scarred by his past, he prefers it that way. While living in the shadows of the French Quarter, whispers of treachery and betrayal reach his ears—along with accusations implicating him in unthinkable acts. He comes out of hiding to confront his accusers only to discover he's under a death sentence. On the run, he encounters Isabelle Fontaine, a woman with a past of her own she'd rather keep hidden.

Family is everything to Izzy and she'll do whatever it takes to keep hers safe. Crossing paths with a shadowy corporation and a rogue Wolf puts the people she cares about in jeopardy—not to mention her own life and heart.

Secrets, lies, and betrayals are more personal under the full moon, but when a betrayed Wolf fights for his honor, no one is safe—not even the woman he loves.

Warning: Doubt a Wolf's honor and you'll get a serving of hot blood and guts to go.

Christmas Moon
(A Moonstruck Novella)

The Wolves have been busy since blowing up half of Louisiana. Thanks to the government, there's a bounty on their heads so they're living off the grid. But Christmas is here and the kids want to know if Santa will find them this year. Not a problem until the phone call asking them to find and rescue a pregnant girl. On December 20th. In

New Mexico. Piece of fruit cake, right?

Walking into a firefight with a drug cartel is never easy, but with Hannah's wrath and Liam's first change on the line, Mac and the Wolves face a harder choice—save the girl or save Christmas.

Secrets, lies, and betrayals are more personal under the Christmas moon, and it might just take the magic of Santa to help the Wolves save the day and make it home to their families in time. Because in the end, it's all about family.

Warning: Santa's making his list and when the Wolves go into action, they'll find out who's naughty and who's nice.

FINALIST 2014 INTERNATIONAL DIGITAL AWARDS SHORT PARANORMAL NOVEL

Blue Moon
(Moonstruck Book 8)

DJ Collier is a manhunter. As a Deputy US Marshal, she'll go after any fugitive, but the names in the secret file dumped on her desk must be ghosts considering the lack of information she can gather. Where better to hunt them than in the last place she encountered the elusive group of military Special Operators? She never expected to find death, destruction, and a sexy Wolf determined to make her his in the Louisiana bayous.

Antoine Fontaine has lived in the bayous all his life. Always standing on the outside of his close-knit Cajun family, he thinks he's one of a kind. He never expected to discover another like himself, much less a whole group of SpecOps Wolves who welcome him into their pack. He has no idea what it means to be moonstruck until he rescues a feisty Deputy US Marshal. Now, he'll fight to the death to keep her.

Once in a Blue Moon, a Wolf finds his mate and even if

he's up to his ass in alligators, he'll keep her safe. Warning: Hot sex, explosions, and mayhem of the blood and guts kind dead ahead.

Moon Shot
(Moonstruck Book 9 –
A Moonstruck/Hard Target Crossover Novel)

Scorched earth. The Wolves are damn tired of being hunted. They've licked their wounds and now it's time to take the fight to the enemy. They're moving on up—all the way to the hallowed halls of government. Intelligence reports indicate their enemies are getting closer—and more personal. Assassination of the Wolves and their families is on the menu and SEAL Team Atlantis has the kill order.

Unexpected allies, a new baby, and the healing of old wounds give the Wolves something to live—and fight—for. Every last one of them is ready for a Happy Ever After.

Retribution. There are three things a Wolf holds sacred—his mate, his pups, and his pack. Threaten any one of them and you'd better be checking your six. Threaten all three? Just remember—secrets, lies, and betrayals demand payback and the Wolves are ready to hunt.

Warning: Wolves don't hold a grudge, they get even.

Don't Forget Silver's Exciting
Urban Fantasy Series

The Penumbra Papers
Cases from the Shadow's Edge

Penumbra: Etymology: New Latin, from Latin paene almost + umbra shadow

These "Cases from the Shadow's Edge" explore the

forces of light and dark as they dance through shadows humans barely glimpsed prior to the Big Rip. Since then, all manner of preternatural magicks intermingle with humans in ways mysterious, magical and, in some cases, criminal. Much to humanity's surprise, there really are monsters under the bed and the things that go bump in the night are bigger and scarier than anyone ever imagined.

Vampires. Ghouls. Faeries. Ghosts. Werewolves. Creatures of legend and nightmares. Overnight, reality took on a whole new meaning. The world's best and brightest from every discipline—physics, theology, anthropology, chemistry, to name only a few—all tried to explain the rip in the cosmic curtain. Sade Marquis has her own theory. The monsters have been here all along, flying just under the radar of normal perception. They've been masquerading as mundanes—their term for humans. Of course, Sade knows the truth of the matter. She was raised by a master vampire and her pet "dog" shifted into a boy the night of her twelfth birthday. Sade's very good at keeping secrets. She has a lot of them.

This is where *Special Agent* Sade Marquis enters the mix. A human FBI agent with an X-Files mentality, Sade's been handpicked to fill a new slot within the Bureau—Preternatural Liaison Officer with the MAGIC Unit. The Magical Activity, Grievances, and Inhuman Crimes unit is in charge of investigations involving magicks. It's her job to deal with all the monsters, and she's very, very good at her job. That makes the magicks very, very afraid of her. As they should be...

THAT OL' BLACK MAGIC
Penumbra Papers #0.5

Along with her FBI partner—and werewolf best friend—Caleb Jones, Sade is sent to New Orleans to investigate the murders of several high-ranking magicks. The Big Easy is neutral territory so Sade must find and arrest the culprit before war breaks out between the Realms. Things look up when the gargoyle Sentinel, Roman, a permanent fixture in Sade's childhood, arrives to keep the peace. Maybe.

The investigation is hampered by Sade's faerie nemesis, Ariel—the King's Seducer. Oh, and then there's the new dragon in town, Nikolas Constantine. Sade can't decide whether to arrest his ass or admire it.

When guilt and innocence come to play in the French Quarter, it'll take Sade's brand of crazy to sort it all out.

WINNER 2014 INTERNATIONAL DIGITAL AWARDS SHORT PARANORMAL NOVEL

SEASON OF THE WITCH
Penumbra Papers #1

Sade Marquis. Her best friend turns furry. Her godfather is a master vampire. Her mother was once the mistress of Oberon, King of the Faerie Court.

When the Veil between the mortal and magical realms rips, FBI Special Agent Sade Marquis is in a unique position to head up the newly-formed MAGIC unit. She's the only human who knows exactly what goes bump in the night. When things go to hell in a handbasket and there's magic in the air, Sade is the agent FBI Director George Bailey wants in the trenches. She's savvy, snarky, and sexy but she may have met her match when she's sent to Chicago to investigate the murder of a congressional aide.

Is the vampire, Kristian St. John, guilty as sin? Once a Templar knight, Sinjen now teaches history at the University of Chicago. He must rely on Sade to clear his name and track the real culprit.

Together, they unravel the clues to a mystery that began a thousand years before. If they don't solve the murders of six young women, the whole world—human *and* magick—will suffer the evil consequences.

FINALIST 2014 INTERNATIONAL DIGITAL AWARDS
LONG PARANORMAL NOVEL

From Harlequin Desire:
Red Dirt Royalty

Cowgirl's Don't Cry
The wealthiest of enemies may seduce the ranch right out from under her!

Cassidy Morgan wasn't raised a crybaby. So when her father dies and leaves the family ranch vulnerable to takeover by an Okie gazillionaire with a grudge, she doesn't shed a tear—she fights back.

But Chance Barron, the son of said gazillionaire, is a too-sexy adversary. In fact, it isn't until Cassidy falls head over heels for the sexy cowboy-hat-wearing attorney that she even finds out he's the enemy. Now she needs a plucky plan to save her birthright. But Chance has another trick up his sleeve, putting family loyalties—and passion—to the ultimate test.

The Cowgirl's Little Secret
She's back at his ranch...with baby in tow.

When nurse Jolie Davis comes home, she knows it's only a matter of time before she runs into Cord Barron— the Barrons own this town. In fact, it was their oil business rivalry with her father that caused her break up with Cord in the first place. But no amount of family meddling can deny the fact that she had his secret son. Now, four years later, as her ex is wheeled into the ER— while she's on duty!—it's time to come clean. Because it quickly becomes clear that Cord is determined to reclaim her...

BOOK LIST BY SERIES

Moonstruck:
Blood Moon – Book 1
Bad Moon – Book 2
Hunter's Moon – Book 3
Wolf Moon – Book 4
Bride's Moon – Book 5
Rogue Moon – Book 6
Christmas Moon – A Moonstruck Novella (#7)
Blue Moon – Book 8
Moon Shot – Book 9
A Moonstruck/Hard Target Crossover Novel
Moonstruck: Secrets – Book 10

Penumbra Papers:
That Ol' Black Magic
Season of the Witch

Mystery Novella:
Café Midnight

From Harlequin Desire
Red Dirt Royalty
Cowgirls Don't Cry
The Cowgirl's Little Secret

From the Wild Rose Press:
Faerie Fate
Faerie Fire
Faerie Fool
Faerie Reign
(Digital boxed set of first three books at a special price)
*Faerie Faith (Twelve Brides of Christmas)

Class of '85 Reunion Series:
*Fairy Tales Can Come True
*Promises, Promises

Dearly Beloved Series:
*Best Laid Plans

*Digital Only

ABOUT THE AUTHOR

Silver likes walking on the wild side and coffee. Okay. She loves coffee. LOTS of coffee. Warning: Her Muse, Iffy, runs with scissors and can be quite dangerous. An award-winning author, she's been a military officer's wife, mother, state appellate court marshal, airport rescue firefighter and forensic fire photographer, crime analyst, technical crime scene investigator, and writer of magic and mystery. Now retired from the "real world," she lives in Oklahoma and spends her days at the computer with two Newfoundland dogs, the cat who rules them all, and myriad characters all clamoring for attention. She writes dark urban fantasy thrillers, time travel romance, and sexy contemporary romance.

To find out more about Silver and her books, visit her website: www.silverjames.com. She loves to connect with readers on Facebook (Silver James, Author) and Twitter (@SilverJames_).

www.ingramcontent.com/pod-product-compliance
Lightning Source LLC
Chambersburg PA
CBHW070906180626
46817CB00003B/942